THE YID

THE YID

Paul Goldberg

PICADOR

New York

This is a work of fiction. All of the characters, organizations, and events portrayed in this novel are either products of the author's imagination or are used fictitiously.

picadorusa.com • picadorbookroom.tumblr.com
twitter.com/picadorusa • facebook.com/picadorusa

Picador® is a U.S. registered trademark and is used by St. Martin's Press under license from Pan Books Limited.

For book club information, please visit facebook.com/picadorbookclub or e-mail marketing@picadorusa.com.

Grateful acknowledgment is made for permission to reproduce from the following:

Anna Akhmatova, excerpts from "Anno Domini" from *Complete Poems of Anna Akhmatova*, translated by Judith Hemschemeyer, edited and introduced by Roberta Reeder. Copyright © 1989, 1992, 1997 by Judith Hemschemeyer. Reprinted with the permission of The Permissions Company, Inc., on behalf of Zephyr Press, www.zephyrpress.org.

Designed by Steven Seighman

Library of Congress Cataloging-in-Publication Data

Goldberg, Paul, 1959–
   The Yid : a novel / Paul Goldberg.—First edition.
      pages ; cm
   ISBN 978-1-250-07903-9 (hardcover)
   ISBN 978-1-250-07904-6 (e-book)
  1. Jews—Soviet Union—History—20th century—Fiction.   2. Soviet Union—History—20th century—Fiction.   I. Title.
   PS3607.O4434Y53 2016
   813'.6—dc23
                         2015029503

Our books may be purchased in bulk for promotional, educational, or business use. Please contact your local bookseller or the Macmillan Corporate and Premium Sales Department at 1-800-221-7945, extension 5442, or by e-mail at MacmillanSpecialMarkets@macmillan.com.

First Edition: February 2016

10 9 8 7 6 5 4 3 2 1

For my parents, whose names were in the lists:

Goldberg, Boris Finiasovich—born 1932
Rabinovich, Sofia Aronovna—born 1937

באר-קאָכבא: א קנעכט, ווי נאָר ער נעמט די
שווערד אין האנט, ער ווערט אויס קנעכט.

שמועל האלקין, באר-קאָכבא
מאָסקווער מעלוכישער ייִדישער טעאטער, 1938

БАР-КОХБА (взмахивая мечом):
Раб, взявшийся за меч,—не раб!

Самуил Галкин, *Бар*-Кохба
Государственный Еврейский Театр, 1938

BAR-KOKHBA (raising a dagger):
A slave who wields a dagger is not a slave!

Shmuel Halkin, *Bar-Kokhba*
Moscow State Jewish Theater, 1938

THE YID

In the early morning of March 1, 1953, when Iosif Stalin collapsed at his dacha, he was preparing to solve Russia's Jewish Question definitively.

Military units and enthusiastic civilians stood poised to begin a pogrom, and thousands of cattle cars were brought to the major cities to deport the survivors of the purportedly spontaneous outbursts of murder, rape, and looting.

Stalin intended his holocaust to coincide with the biggest purge Russia had seen.

The West would have to choose between standing by and watching these monstrous events or taking the risk of triggering a world war fought with atom and hydrogen bombs.

Stalin's death was announced on March 5, the day his pogrom was scheduled to begin.

Act

I

1

At 2:37 a.m. on Tuesday, February 24, 1953, Narsultan Sadykov's Black Maria enters the courtyard of 1/4 Chkalov Street.

A Black Maria is a distinctive piece of urban transport, *chernyy voron*, a vehicle that collects its passengers for reasons not necessarily political. The Russian people gave this ominous carriage a diminutive name: *voronok*, a little raven, a fledgling.

At night, Moscow is the czardom of black cats and Black Marias. The former dart between snowbanks in search of mice and companionship. The latter emerge from the improbably tall, castle-like gates of Lubyanka, to return laden with enemies of the people.

The arrest of Solomon Shimonovich Levinson, an actor from the defunct State Jewish Theater, is routine. An old, likely decrepit Yid, Levinson lives alone in a communal flat at 1/4 Chkalov Street. Apartment 40. No hand-wringing wife. No hysterical children. No farewells. No one to hand the old man a toothbrush through the bars of a departing Black Maria.

In the parlance of state security, arrests are "operations." This operation is easier than most: collect some incriminating rubbish, put a seal on the door, help the old man into the truck, and a little before dawn, the Black Maria drives back through Lubyanka's armored gates.

Lieutenant of State Security Sadykov is slight and pale. His hair is straight and dark red. He is a Tatar, a dweller of the steppes, a descendant of the armies of Genghis Khan, an alumnus of an orphanage in Karaganda. With him are two soldiers, naïve nineteen-year-old boys from the villages of Ukraine, dressed in anemia-green coats, each armed with a sidearm. One of the boys carries a pair of American handcuffs.

Another night, another knock-and-pick. The function of the green, covered light trucks that fan through Moscow at night is clear to everyone. There is no reason to hide their purpose or to flaunt it. It's best to approach through the courtyard, turn off the engine and the lights, and coast gently to a halt.

The driver, one of the nineteen-year-olds, skillfully pilots the vehicle through the dark, narrow cavern of an archway built for a horse cart. With the engine off, he surrenders to inertia.

Bracing for a burst of frost, Sadykov and the boys step out of the Black Maria. A thin coat of crisp, pristine snow crunches loudly underfoot. Sadykov looks up at the darkness of the five-story buildings framing the sky above the courtyard. The night is majestic: dry frigid air, bright stars, the moon hanging over the railroad station, pointing toward mysterious destinations.

Whenever possible, Sadykov avoids going through front doors, favoring tradesmen's entrances. The back door of 1/4 Chkalov Street is made of heavy oak, devilishly resilient wood that has defied a century of sharp kicks and hard slams. Protected by an uncounted number of coats of dark brown paint, it stands impervious to weather and immune to rot. Opening the door, Sadykov and his entourage plunge into darkness.

Since 1/4 Chkalov Street is close to the Kursk Railroad Station, travelers use the building's stairwell as a nighttime shelter. As they await morning trains, these vagabonds curl up like stray dogs beneath the staircase, their bodies encircling suitcases and burlap sacks. If it's your lot to sleep beneath those stairs, you have to be cold or drunk enough to tolerate the overpowering smell of urine.

Ignoring the odor and the sound of a man snoring under the stairs, the three soldiers feel their way to the second floor. Sadykov lights a match. A blue number on a white enameled sign identifies apartment forty.

With the match still lit, Sadykov motions to the boys. When duty takes Sadykov and his comrades to large communal flats, the arresting crew has to wake up someone, anyone, to open the door and, only after gaining entry, knock on the door of the person or persons they've come to collect for the journey through Lubyanka's heavy gates. More often than not, the proverbial "knock on the door" is a light kick of a military boot.

Three men standing in cold, stinking darkness, waiting for someone to hear the kick on the door is not an inspiring sight. They might as well be scraping at the door, like cats, except cats returning after a night of carnage and amour are creatures of passion, while nineteen-year-old boys with sidearms are creatures of indifference, especially at 2:55 a.m. on a February night.

On the tenth kick, or perhaps later, the door opens. Sadykov discerns a frail face, an old woman. Blue eyes set deeply behind high cheekbones stare at the three men. These old crones are a curse, especially for those who arrest people for a living.

Whenever a Black Maria or its crew is in sight, a Moscow crone is certain to start mumbling prayers. Sadykov regards prayers as futile, yet he secretly fears them. He has an easier time with hand-wringing middle-aged wives; their hysterics affect him no more than a distant cannonade. (As a product of an orphanage, Sadykov has had no exposure to familial hysterics.) For reasons Sadykov cannot fathom, a prayer threatens, even wounds.

"Does Levinson live here?"

Making the sign of the cross, the old woman disappears into darkness of the hallway. The three men walk in. It's a long hallway of a five-room apartment, with three doors on the right facing Chkalov Street, and two on the left, facing the courtyard.

Sadykov lights another match.

He hears a door creak. It has to be the old woman. She is watching. Her kind always watches. No, righteous she can't be. She may be the resident snitch, and now she lurks behind the door, pretending to drag God into this purely earthbound affair while in fact savoring the results of her anonymous letter to the authorities.

Sadykov doesn't know which door is hers, yet hers is the door he wants to avoid.

According to instructions, Levinson's room overlooks the courtyard. That leaves a choice of two doors.

During operations, neighbors sit behind closed doors, like trapped rodents. And in the morning, they feign surprise and indignation. Just to think of it, Levinson, an enemy! A loner. Always grumbling. Had no use for children. Hated cats. Fought in the partisan bands along the Trans-Siberian Railroad during the Civil War. Would have thought he was one of us, a simple Soviet man, but with Yids nothing is simple. Treachery is their currency of choice. And if he really is a traitor, fuck him, let him be shot!

Have you seen old Yids creaking down the street, going wherever it is they go, carrying mesh bags and, in their pockets, rolled-up newspapers? With the pigmentation of youth wiped off their faces, they still look dark, bird-like, bleached angels ready to fly to God, or the Evil One.

Such is Sadykov's mental image of Levinson.

Lighting his third match of the night, Sadykov steps up to another door. This time, he doesn't order the boys to kick.

He knocks three times with the knuckles of his clenched fist.

There is movement behind the door, no more than what you'd expect.

"Dos bist du?" asks a raspy voice in a language that isn't Russian.

"Poshel v pizdu," answers one of the nineteen-year-olds in Russian.

Sadykov and the boys don't know the meaning of the question *Dos bist du?* Why would they know that these words mean, "Is this you?" But, of course, the Russian words *"poshel v pizdu,"* translated literally as "go in the cunt" or "fuck off," rhyme with this enigmatic question.

It's a dialogue of sorts:

"Dos bist du?"

"Poshel v pizdu."

It's more than a rhyme. It's a question and an answer.

When you are nineteen, you play with your kill. On your first operation, you get a sense of newness that you think will never go away.

You get the power to choke off another man's freedom, even end his life. Sadykov's first operation took him to a big four-room apartment on the Frunze Embankment; it was a colonel, a war hero.

The man was silent at first, placid, but in the middle of the search, he grabbed a Walther he had hidden in the desk drawer, placed the muzzle against his lower lip, shouted "Long live Stalin!" and pulled the trigger. He did this in front of his wife and daughter. Another crew had to be called for cleanup.

You never forget your first operation or the second, but after you get to the fifth, you realize that one man's suffering is like another's, and your memories start to change shape around the edges.

Sadykov is beyond the exhilaration of the job. He is almost twenty-five, and he has been doing this for over six years. He wants every operation to end before it begins. Perhaps one day he will get a transfer, perhaps to investigations.

"Otkroyte!" Sadykov knocks again. Open the door!

"Ikh farshtey. Nit dos bist du."

The meaning of this exchange escapes Sadykov, but it merits unpacking.

2

Had there been a Yiddish-speaking audience present, it would have surely rolled with laughter.

Try to imagine the situation described above as a vaudeville skit:

They come to arrest an old Yid. They knock on the door.

"Is that you?" the old man asks in Yiddish.

The goons answer in juicy Russian. (The rhyme: *"Dos bist du?"* / *"Poshel v pizdu."*)

"I see," responds the old man. "It's not you."

In this scene, the audience never learns whom the old man refers to as "you," but it's a safe guess that he is not anticipating the arrival of Lieutenant Narsultan Sadykov and his boys.

You can imagine what the audience would do. They would emit tears and saliva. They would slap their knees. They would turn beet red from elevation of blood pressure and constriction of air supply. Alas, at 2:59 a.m. February 24, 1953, a Yiddish-speaking audience is not in attendance at 1/4 Chkalov Street, apartment forty.

The time has come for Solomon Shimonovich Levinson, a man known to friends as *der komandir*, to take a journey in a Black Maria.

Yet, surely you will agree that the absence of spectators makes his final, decisive performance more pure. It merges comedy, tragedy, absurdity, fantasy, reality, and—*voilà*—the material becomes endowed with a divine spark.

"Please wait, comrade, I will pull on my pants," says Levinson in Russian.

Standing at that door, Sadykov realizes suddenly that Levinson is the first man who shows no trepidation upon the arrival of a Black Maria. His voice is calm.

More surprised than angered, Sadykov knocks again.

He hasn't arrested an actor before. His past hauls include one violinist, an opera singer, two writers, three geneticists, one architect, several military officers, many engineers, and many more Party workers.

"*Otkroyte,*" Sadykov repeats. Open the door.

"*Otkroyte-shmot-kroyte* . . ." Levinson's voice responds in broken Russian. "What, are you? Robber?"

"*Prokuratura,*" says Sadykov.

Sometimes Sadykov is instructed to say "state security," shorthand for the Ministry of State Security, or the MGB.

Other times he says "*prokuratura,*" the procurator's office. Though these entities are technically different, when Sadykov knocks on your door, it makes no practical difference which arm of the government he claims to represent.

"*Prokuratura-shmok-uratura,*" says the old man, and the door swings open.

Yes, in this career-crowning performance, Levinson deserves a Yiddish-speaking audience, for he has combined the word "*shmok*" (a limp, at best modestly sized, penis) with the word "procurator."

Through its unforgivable failure to exist, the audience is missing a tour de force by Solomon Levinson, formerly an actor of one of the most respected theater companies in the world, the Moscow State Jewish Theater, known to Yiddish speakers under the Russian acronym GOSET.

Was Solomon Levinson a GOSET star?

No, another Solomon—Solomon *Mikhoels*—was the star, the face of the theater, an actor who could move from a village idiot to a Shakespearean king to a conniving, villainous contrabandist, an actor who could direct, a writer who could act, a laureate of the Stalin Prize, the Soviet Union's unofficial ambassador of goodwill, a leader of the Jewish Antifascist Committee, a star in Moscow, and a celebrity on Second Avenue, the Yiddish Broadway.

His fans in America understood that under capitalism, every Jewish theater had to pay for itself or even produce a profit. Under Socialism, Mikhoels and his GOSET received a state subsidy. Indeed, GOSET was the only state-subsidized Yiddish theater on Earth and, presumably, in the universe.

In 1943, when Mikhoels was sent to America to raise money for the Red Army, New York Jews and leftists of various shades stumbled over each other for a place in line. Tens of thousands came to hear him speak. He returned with millions of dollars and a big, new fur coat for Comrade Stalin, its lining emblazoned with greetings from New York Jews. He met with Albert Einstein, who, at the height of 176 centimeters, towered over him like a giant. He debated the place of politics in art with Charlie Chaplin, the courageous American comedian who had dared to lampoon Hitler in the film *The Great Dictator*. A committee of the U.S. Senate was preparing to investigate that comedian's effort to get America into the war. "I was saved by Pearl Harbor," Chaplin told Mikhoels.

In New York, Mikhoels met with Chaim Weizmann, the man who would become the first president of Israel. He caught up with his old friend, the German theater director Max Reinhardt, shared the podium with the New York mayor Fiorello La Guardia, and bowed his head at the grave of Sholem Aleichem.

Alas, for Solomon *Levinson*, Mikhoels was a mighty nemesis and GOSET not a happy place. If you regarded yourself as a talented actor like Levinson and if you were unfortunate enough to spend your entire career at GOSET, you couldn't even rise to Number Two.

The Number Two slot belonged to another actor, Venyamin Zuskin. It was beyond mere favoritism. In GOSET's established order, Zuskin had to be Number Two.

When Mikhoels played Benjamin in *The Travels of Benjamin III*, the Jewish Don Quixote, Zuskin played Senderl, his male companion in a dress, Sancho Panza in calico. When Mikhoels was Kinig Lir, his most famous role, Zuskin was his Nar. They played it like two sides of the coin, der Kinig and his Nar.

If you worked at GOSET, you worked in the shadow of Mikhoels and in the shadow of Zuskin.

What opportunity was there for Solomon Levinson to demonstrate his talent?

None. Which explains why you may not have heard of Solomon Levinson.

At the time a boy kicks the door of apartment forty, Mikhoels has been dead for five years. Killed in an "auto accident."

Where is the truck that killed him? Find it, please. Zuskin is dead, too. No phantom truck. A bullet in the head. An execution in a Lubyanka cellar.

No Mikhoels. No Zuskin. No Kinig. No Nar. No GOSET. No audience. No stage. No subsidy. No truck. *Gornisht.* Nothing.

———

After opening what sounds like a heavy latch, the occupant of the room, presumably Solomon Shimonovich Levinson, noiselessly retreats into deep darkness.

Something about the setting—the night, the snow, the long hallway, the dark room—prompts one of the Ukrainian boys to cross himself. Not much can be made of that. He is a village boy in a big city, where many things seem menacing, evil—and where many things are. Lieutenant Sadykov walks in first, the boys behind him. He fumbles for the light switch, but it's not next to the door, where he would expect to find it.

Sadykov lights another match. Ideally, the circumstances of every death reflect the life that precedes it. Death should be life in miniature, a microcosm. Arrest also. Sadykov hasn't paused to verbalize this maxim, but he feels it within the depth of his being.

As flickering, living light fills the room, the silhouette of a tall, thin man appears before the heavily draped window. The man's nose is elongated, yet proportional to his dark, deeply wrinkled face. Slowly, with considerable arthritic stiffness and with the pomp one would expect from an actor of a provincial theater, the old man bows deeply, his left hand resting on a cane, his right making a slow, ceremonious spiral on the way to the floor.

Sadykov reaches the only conclusion available to him: this man exhibits no fear, no trepidation, because he is mad.

Occasionally, when he allows himself to succumb to compassion, Sadykov believes that his passengers are better off being mad, or deathly ill, because death would spare them what lies ahead: weeks or months of interrogations, then weeks in the prison train, and, finally, felling trees or mining for gold or uranium ore somewhere in the taiga or the permafrost.

"Dear friends, welcome!" says Levinson, shooting a grin from the nadir of the bow.

Encountering unpredictable behavior is part of the job. Sadykov has seen men collapse, women tear their robes (literally tear their robes), children barricade the doors until they have to be kicked out of the way. But he has never seen a deep bow.

A clinician usually makes the diagnosis within seconds of laying his eyes on a patient. Perhaps a lieutenant of state security should be required to have similar diagnostic skills. He should be able to predict that an old man like Levinson will inevitably proceed from strange performance to muttering and singing softly in his dungeon cell.

There would be no point in subjecting him to rough interrogation, because what can a madman tell you? What art is there in beating confessions out of the demented and the frail? They will sign any protocol you place before them. They will acknowledge any political crime—plotting to vandalize the Dnepr hydroelectric power station, blowing up the smelters of Magnitogorsk, intending to change fundamental laws of physics, spying for the Grand Rabbinate of Israel and its American masters.

Sometimes, very rarely, you encounter resistance from arrestees. Suicides, too.

Sadykov has heard many a man sing "The Internationale" in the back of the Black Maria.

Arise, ye prisoners of starvation
Arise, ye wretched of the earth . . .

Lacking the depth of intellect required to realize that the words of the great anthem of the World Revolution beautifully describe the dignified, defiant spirit of the men and women crated in the back of his truck, Sadykov is unable to feel the mockery.

If there is one thing this job has taught him, it is to take nothing personally.

"Allow me to introduce myself: Solomon Shimonovich Levinson," says the old man, straightening to the formidable extent of his frame. *"Artist pogorelogo teatra."* Actor of a burned-down theater.

"We have an order for a search," says Sadykov. "Turn on the light, Levinson."

Sadykov will handle this in his usual restrained manner. If liquidation of enemies is your objective, why not accept disease, both mental and physical, as your allies? Is it not much easier to let the madmen rave until they wear themselves out?

The single bulb under a fringed silk lampshade that hangs from a wire on the ceiling in Levinson's room is decidedly unmanly. You would expect to find it in the room of an operetta singer. Its bulb is no brighter than Sadykov's match.

Of course, Sadykov believes in the absolute necessity of his job.

He believes in Comrade Stalin, and he believes in purging his country of internal enemies. However, he also realizes that, inevitably, mistakes are made, and some of the arrestees are probably harmless. It is unavoidable that when you need to arrest so many people, some of them will be innocent. Even with no training in statistics, not even knowing that there is such a thing as statistics, Sadykov grasps the concept of the margin of error, something you have to recognize and accept like any other fact of life.

With experience, Sadykov has developed a plethora of his own approaches to conducting an operation.

Doctors often speak of patients who taught them something about life, or helped them sharpen their methodology. People whose job it is to arrest their brethren similarly learn on the job. In one prior operation, Sadykov heard an old Bolshevik—a man who knew Lenin and Stalin and had photographs on the wall to prove it—demand a private audience with Stalin.

The old Bolshevik said something about the Party having taken a wrong turn and refused to budge when the time came. Fortunately, he lived alone, like Levinson. The old Bolshevik had been deathly pale, and Sadykov couldn't see a way to lead him out without breaking his limbs.

To avoid unpleasantness in that situation, Sadykov had assured the old Bolshevik that an audience with Stalin was exactly what was being planned. He was being taken to the Kremlin, not to Lubyanka.

The old Bolshevik brightened up, and all the way to Lubyanka he sang in a language that he said was Georgian. By the time the Black Maria passed through the heavy iron gates, the man was in a subdued state. He muttered passively, locked in an intense conversation with an imaginary interlocutor. Sadykov heard something about London and the Fifth Congress of the Russian Socialist Democratic Party.

"Soso, didn't I warn you about Trotsky?" he said to Sadykov when the lieutenant opened the door.

Levinson is wearing baggy, sky blue long underpants, a dark brown undershirt, a deep purple robe, and a matching ascot. (Actors of burned-down theaters have an affinity for ascots.)

He has to be in his late fifties, old enough to start to soften, yet clearly he has not. He looks muscular, angular; his movements are powerful but choppy. His imposing physique notwithstanding, Levinson looks like a clown.

"What is your name, young man?" asks Levinson, turning to Sadykov.

Usually, MGB officers do not reveal their real names, but in this case, bowing to the sound of authority in Levinson's voice, . Sadykov can't avoid making an exception.

"Lieutenant Narsultan Sadykov."

"Sadykov . . . there was a Sadykov in my detachment in the Ural. A brave man," says Levinson, pointing at one of the framed photographs on the wall.

It's a small photo of a dozen men dressed in leather and sheepskin coats and a mad assortment of uniforms: the White Guard, British, American.

A tall man in a pointed Red Cavalry hat stands in the front row, his riding boot positioned on the barrel of a Maxim machine gun, his hand brandishing a curved cavalry sword. The boys behind him have the unmistakable devil-may-care look of brigands, their commander exhibiting the Byronesque spirit of a soldier-poet.

No formal education would be required to recognize that the photo was taken in 1918, when Bolsheviks had lost control of Siberia and the surviving Red Army detachments disappeared into the forest. The fact that young Levinson was fighting for the World Revolution so far from his native Odessa, in the Siberian woods, was part of the spirit of the times and didn't need to be explained any more than one needed to explain the landing of American Marines and British troops in Vladivostok. The world's most powerful nations joined to strangle Bolshevism in its cradle, and Levinson et al. came to defend it.

It's not difficult to see how a man as imposing as Levinson would be elected the detachment commander. It's more of a challenge to grasp how he could have survived the clashes alongside the Trans-Siberian Railroad. If images are to be believed, he displayed no signs of a capacity to avoid unnecessary risks. Such is the nature of Byronism.

In 1953, would it matter to anyone—least of all Sadykov—that thirty-five years earlier, in 1918, at a time when Bolsheviks lost control of Siberia, Levinson and his band fought in total isolation, moving through the taiga between Lake Baikal and the Ural Mountains?

"Can you see the round face next to the Maxim?" asks Levinson. Then, without receiving an acknowledgment, he adds, "That's my Sadykov. Stayed in the Red Army, fought in Manchuria, Spain, rose to colonel. A carriage like yours took him to oblivion in 1938. A cousin, perhaps? Perhaps you've seen him caged someplace?"

It seems that someone forgot to instruct Lieutenant Narsultan Sadykov that a man whose job falls on the continuum between arrest and execution must not acknowledge the humanity of individuals upon whom he discharges his duties. If a person of any intelligence had written the manual for operations, it would read: *Do not—under any circumstances—engage in polemics with the arrestees and the executees.*

Of course, Narsultan Sadykov is not in any way connected with Levinson's Sadykov. Many Tatars are named Sadykov, just as many Russians are named Ivanov, Ukrainians Shevchenko, and Jews Rabinovich. How would anyone, least of all Lieutenant Narsultan Sadykov (an orphan whose father's name was unknown to anyone, likely including his mother), know whether he is related to Levinson's Sadykov?

"Young man, are you, perchance, familiar with commedia dell'arte?" asks Levinson, turning abruptly to one of the nineteen-year-olds.

Though it's impossible to verify such things, it's unlikely in the extreme that any previous victim of Stalinism had ever mentioned commedia dell'arte at the time of arrest.

"Pidaras tochno," responds one boy, addressing the other. (Definitely a pederast would be the exact translation, but the expression really means definitely a fag.) The boy utters this nonsense as though Levinson doesn't exist. Onstage this would be called an aside.

Had Sadykov understood the situation, he would have rewarded this soldier's perfect execution of denial of humanity.

"No," replies Levinson casually. "Not a *pidaras.* Why would you think that? I said commedia dell'arte. Commedia dell'arte is a theatrical movement, which began in Italy in the sixteenth century. It spread, and it never fully went away. Molière's characters are based on commedia character types. Our Gogol was influenced by commedia."

"Pedrilo," mutters one of the boys, summoning another variation on the theme of buggery.

"You are being dismissive out of ignorance. You will see in a minute that you *do* know something about commedia," says Levinson, making eye contact with the boys, then casting a glance at Sadykov.

"Madness," Sadykov concludes, but says nothing. He rifles through the old man's desk, as per instructions. No Walther there, just an empty holster from a Soviet pistol, a basic Makarov.

The irrational should be handled indirectly, if at all. Though Levinson seems to be failing in his effort to engage the audience, his story is as accurate as he can make it.

After returning to Moscow in 1920, on a lark, Levinson auditioned for a theater troupe started by a young man named Alexander Granovsky.

This was an experimental theater company inspired in part by commedia dell'arte, badly in need of clowns and acrobats.

Commedia was making a return as art for the people, and Granovsky recognized Levinson's ability to play a sad, angry clown, akin to a recurring commedia character named Pulcinella. In Russian, Pulcinella was renamed Petrushka.

"I played variations on Petrushka for a long, long time. Of course, you've heard of Petrushka." Levinson stops, as though he has just told a joke. "That would be within your intellectual grasp."

Of course, there is no childish laughter of delight, no sign of recognition, no *aha* moment.

An argument can be made that the joke is on Levinson. His revolutionary past and obvious ability to inflict great bodily harm were the source of comedy.

Granovsky's goal was to build a great European progressive theater company. What could be edgier than a menacing Petrushka? *Komandir* Petrushka, a sad, angry clown battling the forces of history. Levinson was an anachronism from the beginning. He was perfectly static, an actor who would not get any training, who would get neither better nor worse.

Levinson liked being a clown. After two years of being the agent of death, is there anything wrong with wanting to make audiences laugh, just like his father had made him laugh what seemed like centuries earlier? How is that different from becoming, say, a doctor? From his first performance to, now, his last, Levinson's default has always been to go for laughs. A critic might call this pandering.

Levinson has learned that he loves being a part of an ensemble even more than he loves the sound of laughter. It reminds him of being in the forest, surrounded by his band. Onstage, as in the woods, the river of adrenaline runs wide and missteps are fatal.

Onstage, Levinson realizes that the line between reality and imagination is perilously porous.

Giving Sadykov no chance to say a word, Levinson places his hand on the young lieutenant's shoulder and points at a photo of an acrobat, standing on his head, wearing tefillin. The object's leather belt wraps around his right leg, from the knee to the ankle, like a black serpent or a weird garter.

"That's me, in 1921," says Levinson. "Twice wounded, demobilized, but, overall, no worse for wear. Standing on my head, with tefillin. Do you know about tefillin, what that was?"

"Khuy sobachiy," says one of the boys. A dog's penis.

"Not quite a *khuy sobachiy,*" says Levinson, treating the idiotic insult as an argument in a learned discussion. "Jewish prayer rituals required every man to strap on two small black boxes, containing sacred texts: one on the forehead, another on the left arm. The ways of the shtetl had to go away. We were there to kick them down the stairs of history. With tefillin, we were slaves. Without it, we were free. Naturally, with tefillin, I stand on my head. Without it, I'd be right-side up."

Surely, the young man has no way to put this knowledge to use in his everyday life, but awaiting the lieutenant's orders, he is in no position to get on with the well-choreographed business of search and arrest. The boys know nothing about Sadykov's strategy of stepping back to let the maniacs rave till they weaken.

"Here I am, in 1935 . . ."

Levinson's cane now points at a photograph of another group: actors on a large stage. It is difficult to find Levinson in that photo, and knowing that Sadykov will make no effort to do so, he points at a man in a harlequin's leotard sitting atop a throne.

"Yours truly as Nar. Pardon me, Shut. The English name of this character is Fool.

"*Kinig Lir,* the opening scene. I sit atop the throne. Lir's throne, until they chase me away. The Nar is on the throne.

"Zuskin was in one of his dark moods. He stared at the back of the couch and couldn't say a word. I was his understudy. Nar Number Two."

That performance marked the only time Levinson and Mikhoels, the two Solomons, played in the same scene. They were a poor match. What sense did it make for the Nar to stand twenty-two centimeters taller than Lir? Levinson would not have objected to reversing the roles. Indeed, he would have been a splendid King Lear. He would have played Lear as a wreck of the great, fierce monarch. He would have been a larger-than-life Lear.

Alas, at GOSET, this wasn't in the cards.

Sadykov should not be judged harshly for failure to understand. Records show that in 1935, when this photograph was taken, he was trying to stay alive in an orphanage. GOSET's celebrated production of *Kinig Lir* was outside his life experience.

The reason for denying the humanity of your arrestees and your executees is simple in the extreme: you block them out, because as humans we have little control over our ability to listen. And when we listen—sometimes—we hear what is said. And sometimes this leads to a dangerous bond between the arrester-executioner and arrestee-executee. Nothing good comes of such bonds.

Not trained to deal with floods of complicated memories, Sadykov and the boys simply stare.

More important, let it be a cautionary tale that something in the photos sparks Sadykov's curiosity, and, perhaps unbeknownst to himself, he stands by the pictures, studying the strangely shaped ladders of the stage sets, the large crowds of actors frozen in mid-pose.

There is real Levinson brandishing a Japanese sword in the Civil War; Levinson, his foot resting atop a Maxim; Levinson wielding a dagger in the GOSET production of *Bar-Kokhba*, a thinly veiled Zionist extravaganza about strong Jews. With great displays of swordplay, this story of a rebellion against Rome gave Levinson something Mikhoels was hell-bent on denying him: a chance to shine.

"Next, we were going with *Richard II* or *Richard III*; I confuse them," says Levinson in a barely audible whisper aimed at no one. "Imagine that . . . But then that war . . . Are you familiar with *Richard II* or *Richard III*?"

Silently, Sadykov congratulates himself for allowing another old man to rave harmlessly on the way to Lubyanka.

Sadykov notices the photo of a dozen actors using the back of a Red Army truck as a stage. The truck is American, a battered Ford that ended up in the USSR by way of Lend-Lease. (Americans took too long getting into the war in Europe, but, thankfully, they did finance it, shipping arms and supplies to their allies.) Sadykov drove a truck like that once, years earlier, in training. Similarly to the Black Maria, the Ford was given a diminutive name: *Fordik*.

Oddly, recognition that they have a truck in common makes Sadykov almost sorry that Levinson slips into a rant before he reaches that photo.

Sadykov fails to recognize that in any house tour—as in any museum—it is crucial to notice what is left out.

When World War II came, Levinson experienced a fundamental physical urge to fight. Whatever it was, it emanated from his very essence, and was an expression of who he was and why he lived. You can get in touch with such feelings onstage if you are very, very good.

Under normal circumstances, Levinson would have returned to service in the rank of major. He would have preferred to enlist as a private, or perhaps as a commando, a leader of a small detachment that crosses enemy lines, operating under cover of darkness. In the previous war, this was Levinson's biggest strength. In that war he sometimes felt the pangs of remorse for slitting the throats of fellow Russians, mowing down clueless Czech legionnaires, and running one raid into the camp of U.S. Marines. Sensitivity, even a little compassion, started to creep into his soul, and the saber wound (a slash across the back by a White Army officer just as Levinson's sword entered his chest) came almost as a relief. He thought he was done with killing.

In the fateful summer of 1941, with Panzers roaring through the former Pale of Settlement, the urge to kill had returned.

In his late forties, Levinson was no longer prone to Byronism. Now, the urge was to kill and survive, and kill again, as directly as possible, preferably silently, in darkness. Levinson understood both who he was and who he wasn't. He was a lone fighter, at his best in a detachment of fighters he knew, fighters he had learned to trust. No, a soldier he was not. He required autonomy. Taking orders was not his forte.

Yet, on June 27, 1941, five days after German troops poured across the Soviet borders, a commission of doctors found Levinson unfit for service. This finding came with no explanation. It was utterly absurd. He felt no less battle-worthy than he had been in his early twenties.

Within a week, Levinson was on a truck full of actors, heading toward the retreating Red Army. Yes, while the Red Army was abandoning positions, moving eastward, toward Moscow,

Levinson and his players were heading westward, toward the Panzers.

He wanted to find the front even as it moved back toward Moscow, toward catastrophe. Whatever history dragged in, Levinson would be on its cutting edge. He fired few shots in that war, but he was there, always as close as he could get to the front. There were a dozen of them: musicians, singers, actors. For four years, *der komandir* brought the Bard to the trenches, mostly in Russian, sometimes in Ukrainian, and sometimes in Yiddish.

Since Mikhoels was nowhere near that truck, Levinson could choose any part he wanted. Mostly, he played Lir.

These performances invariably concluded with the stunt that made Levinson famous.

After the bow, Levinson came out of character and said, "I fought with swords in the Civil War, but I developed this leap on-stage, to slay Romans. I think it will work just as well against the soldiers of the Third Reich."

Levinson then picked up a pair of smallswords and, with no visible preparation, suddenly allowed his body to unfold into a dazzling leap, a pirouette with a sword in each hand.

With repetition, the leap became higher, faster. You might dismiss this as a vaudevillian display not grounded in character, but if you are inclined to be charitable, you might see that *Komandir* Levinson was leading Red Army soldiers on an airborne journey across the chasm that separates the stage from life.

The doctors who found Levinson unfit for service in the Great Patriotic War could have been right.

As Lieutenant Sadykov and the boys continue to search Levinson's room, the actor's demeanor swings suddenly from animated to deflated. Just as Sadykov expected, Levinson starts to settle down. He is wearing himself out; psychopaths always do.

A physician might have begun to suspect a presentation of cardiac symptoms or a sudden seizure.

Levinson eases his frame onto the floor, letting the cane drop in front of him.

This is of no concern to Lieutenant Sadykov and the boys.

They look into desk drawers and rifle lazily through Levinson's belongings. Sadykov opens the mirrored glass door of an armoire, bracing for a strong scent of stale wool and naphthalene.

They aren't looking for anything in particular, for surely they've realized from the outset that if this man has any material of a conspiratorial nature, it would be outside their intellectual grasp. It would likely be in a foreign language, or in some sort of code.

Squatting, Levinson sways lightly, his hands clutching his chest beneath the loose cloth of the robe. This is a position that suggests a combination of prayer; chest or gastrointestinal pain; and, perhaps, a stiff, arthritic spine.

With eyes wide open and focused on Sadykov and the boys, Levinson starts humming a tune, swaying with its simple rhythm. A student of Yiddish culture would recognize it as a *nign*, a singsong that starts softly, slowly:

Ay-ba-da-bamm-ba, addadabam,
Ay-biri-bombom biribibom
Biri-bi-bomba, biri-bi-bam . . .

Since an ordinary *nign* is intended to express feelings, not to impart verbal messages, this *nign* cannot be described as ordinary, for Levinson molds its sound, dropping in fragments of familiar words, gradually shaping partial phrases. *Tatatatambadi, yambadi yam . . .*

Several of the sounds that creep into that rubbish pile make the boys chuckle, and when the Russian phrase *"Gruzinsky khuy sosyot tatarin-kurva"* (a Tatar traitor sucks a Georgian cock) emerges as a leitmotif, Sadykov realizes that Levinson's behavior can be ignored no longer.

"Stop the noise, Citizen Levinson," orders Sadykov.

Levinson drops his response into the flow of his *nign*: *"Ne mogu."* I can't.

They stare at each other.

Sadykov is, by function, a predator, but an exploration of his eyes reveals that he doesn't live to hunt.

Untouched by the passion of pursuit, he is going through the motions of playing a role, an actor badly cast. Why would any arresting officer allow his arrestees to rave? Why would a hunter establish contact with his prey? These are fundamental errors that could have been prevented through better training.

Levinson's stare reveals something completely different. This dying scene is his alone: the set, the cast, the costumes, even the orchestra is his.

The boys look away. They have nothing at stake. Deployed, they are lethal. Undeployed, they drift into passivity. They await orders. They feel no urgency to slit throats. They are the opposite of citizens. They are your basic cogs, and can anyone imagine anything more soulless than a cog? Would anyone be surprised that Levinson's biggest fear involved leading men of their ilk on a nighttime raid?

Levinson has no particular dislike for Tatars, Georgians, or, for that matter, men who pleasure each other orally.

On the night of February 24, 1953, his goal is to use the so-called problem of nationalities and what will later be known as homophobia to his tactical advantage. The formula is remarkably simple: the nineteen-year-olds are Slavs (Ukrainians), their lieutenant a Tatar, and their ultimate commanders—Beria and Stalin—Georgians.

To defend the honor of his uniform, to defend his manhood, Sadykov now has to beat this old madman into submission.

Sadykov takes a step toward Levinson.

Levinson is not an inviting target. There can be no assurance that he will not stiffen or even fight back. His exaggerated courtesy and deranged singing notwithstanding, something in his eyes says plainly, "Don't come near."

The instant he bends over the actor, Sadykov surely understands that he has made a mistake, for Levinson's arms are no longer clutching his chest.

As they swing open, suddenly, forcefully, spring-like, Sadykov feels a cold intrusion beneath his chin. It's far short of pain. Sadykov wants to emit a scream, but cannot. His legs no longer support his body. They buckle, and black arterial blood gushes onto the front of his tunic.

Levinson continues the trajectory of his twirl toward a Ukrainian boy whose hand grasps the handle of a sidearm. He is spring-loaded, graceful.

This movement is not rooted in Levinson's bloody adventures in the taiga along the Trans-Siberian. There, he was unburdened by technique. This is all stage.

In 1937, the pirouette with smallswords, which Levinson first performed in a shepherd's getup as the curtain fell at the end of the second act of *Bar-Kokhba*, made Levinson famous among Yiddish-speaking audiences in Moscow and in the provinces. Indeed, in the touring company, Levinson was promoted to the part of Bar-Kokhba.

And now, in 1953, Levinson is airborne once again, a one-man Judean Air Force: a single pirouette, two Finnish daggers, two throats severed, a *nign* stopped. An acrobat would have bowed, but an acrobat Levinson is not.

The third boy is spared in the leap.

He is becoming cognizant of the fact that his tunic is smeared with the blood of his comrades. This is only his third operation. He started the night with a sense of power. Now, in a flash of smallswords, the sense of power has vanished, replaced by what can best be described as a porridge of questions: Why? How? Who is this man?

The boy raises his hands, an absurd gesture that bespeaks his inability to think strategically.

What is the meaning of surrender to a resister of arrest? How would you expect Solomon Shimonovich Levinson to take you prisoner in the center of Moscow? How would he feed you? How would he house you, especially if you happen to be a soldier of the MGB? Most important, do the Geneva Conventions apply to individuals who find themselves in situations of this sort?

These largely theoretical problems resolve themselves as this would-be prisoner takes a panicked step toward the door. Levinson is all adrenaline now. Movement of the adversary is all it takes to make him pounce. A moment later, the boy lies on the floor, the handles of two Finnish daggers protruding from his back.

It's anything but an accident that *der komandir* aims at the throats of his would-be captors.

This choice of targets is consistent with his frustration with what is known as the Jewish Question. The Jewish Question is the subject of many conversations in the winter of 1953. In the streets, people say that Jews have always used Christian blood in their rituals, and that they continue to do so.

They say that Christian blood is used in matzos—dry,

cracker-like bread they eat on their Easter. They say that if you look at it, you see the scabs. Also, they say blood is added to sweet *pirozhki* called hamantaschen. The victims are usually children, who are bled painfully, slowly. But if the Jews can't find a child to bleed, they use an adult, and if they are afraid of being discovered, they slit their victim's throat instead of waiting for the blood to drain out of the pinpricks.

They say that when Jews pray, they strap little black boxes with magic writings onto their heads and arms. They hide diamonds in those boxes, too.

They say that the Jews who had become doctors since the Revolution are now secretly killing Russians under the guise of medicine. They do this out of pure hatred, not as part of religious observance, so no bleeding is involved. The newspapers say that a group of them, who worked at Kremlyovka, brought on the death of Comrade Zhdanov and conspired to kill Comrade Stalin. They were caught and imprisoned. Murderers in white coats.

They say that a Jewish doctor was draining pus from the swellings of cancer sufferers and injecting it into healthy Russians. He was caught on a bus, and it couldn't be determined how many people he had injected. They say he used a special thin needle of his own invention. You wouldn't feel it, but if he stuck you, you were dead.

They say he was a professor named Yakov Rapoport. They say he was arrested and kept in a Lubyanka cellar.

Levinson surveys the carnage. A smile creeps onto his elongated face. A line pops out of the mass of all the lines he'd ever committed to memory. It flashes before him, a spark from a play never staged, a text never translated:

Ikh for bald opvashn, inem Heylikn Land,
Dos merderishe blut
Fun mayn zindiker hant.

It's wordier than the English original, and the meter is off, but Levinson is not a poet. This is the best he can do to relay the words spoken by Henry Bolingbroke in the final scene of *Richard II*, as the coffin of the murdered monarch is brought onstage:

(I'll make a voyage to the Holy Land,
To wash this blood off from my guilty hand . . .)

On February 24, 1953, at 3:34 a.m., exactly four hours before sunrise, as a consequence of Levinson's brilliant pirouette with Finnish daggers, Bolingbroke's parting line is awash in fresh blood, and comedy, tragedy, and history abruptly join into one mighty stream.

3

On February 24, 1953, at 3:57 a.m., Friederich Robertovich Lewis gets out of a taxi at 1/4 Chkalov Street.

After more than two decades of shuttling between Moscow and the industrial cities of the Ural—Magnitogorsk, Chelyabinsk, Sverdlovsk—Lewis considers himself primarily a *sibiryak*, a Siberian.

As an outsider, he understands that Moscow is best appreciated before dawn, with moonlight and a fresh, thin sprinkling of snow. Its streets turned white, the big, grimy city acquires a purity of form, even the delicacy of a Japanese print. White powder, of course, is a promise of something better.

His destination, the residence of Solomon Shimonovich Levinson, an actor known to friends and family as *der komandir*, is on the second floor of a prerevolutionary building overlooking a small park strewn with the ruins of plank-and-wrought-iron benches.

Lewis has a key to *der komandir*'s communal flat. He takes off his shoes, hangs up his sheepskin coat, and, stepping softly, walks through the long dark hallway of the *komunalka*. He knocks on the door, trying to wake up Levinson and no one else. This is a formality. Levinson's door usually stays unlocked.

Related by marriage, Levinson and Lewis are survivors of what had been a large extended family. Loyalty to the dead is an element of their bond. There is a practical element as well. Lewis needs a cot in Moscow, sometimes for weeks at a time, and Levinson isn't inconvenienced by the presence of a guest.

Over the years, they developed a greeting ritual. Every time Lewis knocks on the door of his room, Levinson responds in Yiddish: *"Dos bist du?"* Is that you?

"Neyn, nit ikh bin dos. S'iz Elye-Hanovi!" Lewis answers. No, it's not me. It's Elijah the Prophet!

There are variations on this theme. Lewis can announce himself as *der Royte Kavaleriye* (Red Cavalry), *klezmorim mit muzike* (an orchestra with music), Yoske Pendrik (a mocking Yiddish name for Jesus Christ) or Molotov *mit* von Ribbentrop.

He looks forward to the customary torrent of insults delivered in Levinson's raspy voice.

Lewis no longer objects to the nickname Levinson gave him sometime in the thirties: *der Komintern-shvartser.*

This is grossly inaccurate. Lewis had nothing to do with the Comintern, the organization formed to stoke the flames of World Revolution. It was a job with the Arthur G. McKee Company of Cleveland that brought him to Russia two decades and two years ago. The other part of the nickname—*shvartser*—is accurate and therefore not offensive in the least. His pigmentation, which is unusually dark for an American Negro, gives him the appearance of an African sovereign.

This time Levinson doesn't answer.

Lewis opens the door, and before his eyes adjust to darkness, his toes come in contact with a large, dark shape, and a warm, sticky liquid starts to seep into his thick woolen socks. After his initial shock, Lewis comes to the realization that he is standing in a pool of blood and that his toes are wedged beneath the fingers of a dead man.

"You crazy old motherfucker," he whispers in English. "Now you done it."

"Red yidish," says Levinson, who speaks no English.

Three corpses lie on the floor, each in its own dark puddle.

"A meshugene kop," says Lewis, shaking his head in disbelief.

A madman.

Lewis has seen many a bloodied corpse. His encounters with violent death began when he was a child, during race riots in Omaha. In 1931, Lewis arrived in Magnitogorsk to become a welder in Stalin's frozen City of Steel. Safety was a bourgeois luxury, casualties not a problem. Welders worked on rickety scaffolds or walked the girders thirty to fifty meters in the air, struggling not to lose their footing on the ice, praying to stay upright in the brutal Siberian wind. Those who fell out of the sky were christened *krasnyye lepyoshki* (red flatbreads).

The presence of three corpses per se doesn't shock Lewis. The uniforms do. In addition to accepting that this is not a hallucination, he has to assess the implications of having become an accessory to a crime against the state.

First, he whispers nervously in Yiddish. (In his private papers, the Afro-American poet Langston Hughes wrote that during his extensive stay in the USSR he spent an evening with a Negro welder and engineering student who expounded on his interest in Yiddish. Hughes's interlocutor explained that speaking Yiddish allowed him to express solidarity with the Jewish working masses. Saying *fuck you* to both Jim Crow and the Black Hundreds, he felt like a "double nigger." This was, of course, Lewis.)

In a dull rant, Lewis calls Levinson an *alter nar* (old fool); an *alter payats* (old jester); and, of course, a mad, wild *alter kaker* (old

shitter). He wishes Levinson a case of cholera in his side, the draining of his blood by leeches, an abundance of painful boils, an
uncontrollable lice infestation, and a variety of other illnesses,
plagues, and medical conditions.

With each curse, he blows off more steam, bringing closer the
moment when he will be able to begin the deliberate process of
integrating this fantastic event into the world of real things.

Upon arrival in the USSR, Lewis noted that his new comrades almost uniformly exhibited a shocking indifference toward death.
In Magnitogorsk, a human life was regarded as an input, an
attachment to a welding torch or a mason's trowel. He shuddered to
think of what happened when his new countrymen went to war.

Covering his eyes with a shaking hand, Lewis presses his brows
until they cover his eyelashes, creating something of an inner shelter. Then, in the darkness of his skull, he counts, starting at ten
and descending slowly to one.

"When did this happen?" he asks, regaining a semblance of
control.

"About thirty minutes ago," says Levinson. He seems unaf-
fected by what he has done.

"And you've been sitting in the dark since?"

Levinson nods.

"Why did you do it?"

The old man has to think before he answers. "Because I knew
how."

If you have weapons and combat skills, and if you don't fear
violent death, why not fight back? This is at least somewhat
logical.

"Did you expect that I would go peacefully?"

"*Neyn*," says Lewis in Yiddish. Upon reflection, he adds in English, "You mother. What the fuck do you think this is? The fucking Civil War?"

In theory, the hopelessness of struggle shouldn't preclude resistance. There is no shortage of people like Levinson, whose combat skills exceed those of soldiers of the MGB. Yet, these veterans invariably choose to surrender and hope that by some miracle they might survive. For whatever reason, in Moscow of 1953, people don't take arms.

"*Red yidish,*" requests Levinson.

"*Der Royter komandir!*" Lewis whispers, calling Levinson a Red commander. This is, of course, accurate.

"*A shmutsiker Komintern-shvartser!*" retorts Levinson, calling Lewis a Comintern Negro and questioning his hygiene.

This is both unfair and inaccurate. Lewis looks remarkably fresh for a man who had spent two shifts at an auto plant.

In Moscow, a city that is wearing out the clothing leftovers of the war that ended eight years ago, Lewis stands out. A top-ranking Soviet engineer, he looks the part.

His roomy, gray-blue gabardine suit maintains the uniform-like sharpness it had in the morning. Even his starched white shirt looks crisp after a sixteen-hour double shift at the plant.

His suits—he owns four identical suits—were tailored by a GOSET costume designer out of a bolt of trophy German gabardine woven for the officers of the SS. Lewis bought the fabric on the black market, then took the bolt and a photo to the tailor. There were two men in that photo: Comrade Stalin and the American Negro actor, singer, and political activist Paul Robeson.

Lewis wanted his suits to be cut like Robeson's, but the costume designer took an unauthorized extra step, exaggerating the jacket's houlders to endow his lean, narrow-shouldered client with Robeson's famously imposing stature. If you observed Lewis from a distance, you would not suspect that he is only five and a half feet tall.

Lewis's shirt is manufactured by Brooks Brothers out of American cotton, a fabric no less pregnant with symbolism than the gabardine in Lewis's suits.

As they stand over the corpses, Levinson and Lewis are unable to stop calling each other names.

"In d'rerd!" declares Lewis, pointing at the ground, suggesting that God smite Levinson on the spot.

"Afn yam!" counters Levinson, challenging his interlocutor to defecate in the ocean.

"Fuck you."

"Fok yu! Fok yu!" mimicks Levinson, adding a third *"Fok yu!"* for good measure, for Solomon Shimonovich Levinson is an actor, and actors know when to pause and when to keep a joke rolling. This skill serves them especially well in situations where they do not understand their lines.

What difference does it make that Lewis killed no one?

The authorities will classify the entire affair as a conspiracy and liquidate everyone they can get their hands on. Failure to report a state crime—especially a state crime of this magnitude—constitutes a capital crime.

Lewis has never renounced his American citizenship. The instant he opened the door of Levinson's room, the murder of Lieutenant of State Security Narsultan Sadykov and his boys became an act of an *international* conspiracy.

"What do we do?" asks Lewis.

"I don't know. I didn't expect to survive."

"You have no plan?"

"I didn't want to go peacefully. I didn't. I made no plans beyond that."

"I guess that makes sense."

"How about this for a plan, Lewis: You will leave, as though you've never been here, and I will sit and wait."

"For what?"

"For them. Maybe I'll kill three more."

"You are a crazy, stubborn old Yid."

"Rikhtik," says Levinson. Correct.

"You really want me to leave?"

"Rikhtik. What else is there to do?"

"I don't know. I guess we could throw the bodies somewhere."

For reasons that escape him, Lewis is in no rush to get out of that room. In fact, he feels something akin to pride. This feeling surprises him. Indeed, he hasn't experienced anything like it since the months of celebration of the victory over the Nazis. Is he drunk with the kills that are not even his?

"Where do you suggest we dump them?" asks Levinson.

"In the river, I guess."

"Do we drag them one by one for three kilometers to the embankment?"

"That wouldn't be practical."

"Also, the river is iced up. And what do we do with the Black Maria?"

"I don't know."

"And you call me a meshuggener?"

"Yes," says Lewis.

"Fine, let's try something, but before we do, let's wipe the traces of Africa off your face, Mr. Paul Robeson. This is real life, not Othello."

Levinson opens the door into the darkened corridor.

"Ol'ga Fyodorovna, Moisey Semyonovich," he calls out loudly.

Two doors open slowly, each with its own time-honored creak, releasing its own dim glow at opposite ends of the corridor.

"May I have your attention for a moment?"

"Razumeyetsya," says the old woman in crisp, correct Russian. Of course.

"Avade," says Moisey Semyonovich in Yiddish. Of course.

Closing the doors of their rooms, they set out toward Levinson's.

The late Lieutenant Sadykov was mistaken in identifying Ol'ga Fyodorovna Zabranskaya as a pious Moscow crone.

Her thick, black woolen robe is open low enough to expose a golden Russian Orthodox cross as well as a coquettish white silk negligee. Her hair is dyed pitch black, and her bangs, which cover the wrinkles on her forehead, are cut with such precision that drafting tools might have been used. Her svelte frame and graceful movements complete the story.

While Ol'ga Fyodorovna appears not to be through with love, Moisey Semyonovich Rabinovich appears not to be through with combat. He wears an officer's black riding breeches held up with massive suspenders. His striped sailor's shirt shows off his impressive musculature, which he hones with twenty-kilogram weights for at least an hour every day. His massive chin is arguably his most threatening feature.

Levinson stands in the doorway. The door shields all but a small portion of his room.

"I had a little disturbance during the night," he says.

"I heard it," says Moisey Semyonovich. "How many?"

"Three," says Levinson.

The idea that an old man who was judged unfit for service in 1941 could rapidly and silently liquidate the entire crew of a Black

Maria without sustaining as much as a scratch is beyond belief. Yet Moisey Semyonovich says nothing.

Ol'ga Fyodorovna is silent, too.

She closes her eyes for an instant of what must be a meditation on the subject of death.

"We did our best to cover them," Levinson says apologetically, opening the door.

He and Lewis had made a small pyramid of the bodies, placing Sadykov and one of the boys facedown to form the bottom layer, and dropping the second boy on top. Though the bodies are partially covered with a sheet and a bedspread, Sadykov's bare left foot protrudes from beneath the covers.

Ol'ga Fyodorovna crosses herself. This is a private matter between her and God.

"This is Mr. Lewis, of course," says Levinson, pointing at the white-faced man. "I have altered his appearance."

Lewis stands at the writing desk by the window, leaning against a bookcase.

The pigmentation of his face is neutralized with a mixture of white tooth powder and TeZhe Cream, a fatty foundation of Soviet theater makeup. Excess chalk makes him look almost as white as the exposed left foot of the late Lieutenant Sadykov.

Polite nods are exchanged. What do they think this is? A tea party?

The self-preservation instinct commands Lewis to head for the border, any border, or, better, to hide for now and head for the border later.

Were it not for his training in engineering, his obsession with understanding systems, and—yes—love, Lewis would have left Russia sometime in the late thirties, certainly before the war.

Over the years—rarely—he has had thoughts of returning to America, but that would mean abandoning his profession and leaving his new life. All this to become what? A middle-aged welder? A graying railroad porter? A club car waiter? A commie-nigger on J. Edgar Hoover's watch list? A lynching waiting to happen?

Now, he is facing similar prospects in the land of victorious revolution. Where would he run? Swim across the frigid waters of the Baltic? Head for Turkey, China, Iran, Afghanistan, Mongolia? He has heard from an uncle, a veteran of the Great War, that France is a fine place for a Negro, but how would he get there?

"As you can see, I need your help," says Levinson.

"Yes, *khaver komandir*," says Moisey Semyonovich.

"My pale-faced friend suggests that we use the Black Maria to dump the bodies," says Levinson with no apparent emotional investment, waiting for a comment from Moisey Semyonovich. He pauses. "What do you think?"

Moisey Semyonovich is a man of pathological bravery. Anyone who saw him at a time of duress would detect no trace of fear. It vanishes, along with an entire tangle of human emotions.

An extraordinary, indeed mystical, combination of luck and skill was required to sustain his life through late February 1953.

His occupation—manager of Drugstore Number Twelve, at 3/1 Chkalov Street, a location true Muscovites call the Earth Berm, Zemlyanoy Val—isn't prominent enough to attract attention or engender suspicion.

Yet he is a man with a secret of such horrendously lethal potential that even he refers to himself as *nedobityy* (one who hasn't been killed), a man inexplicably overlooked, left behind, to live for the time being.

"We could wrap the bodies in canvas, throw them out the window, and hope that no one is looking," suggests Moisey Semyonovich.

"Where do we get the canvas?" asks Lewis.

"I have a trench coat," says Levinson.

"I have two," says Moisey Semyonovich.

"Why two?" asks Lewis.

"One's mine, the other—German."

"Would you consider it an imposition if I asked you to clean up the blood?" asks Levinson.

"I would consider it an honor," says Moisey Semyonovich. "Unless you want me to come with you."

"No, friend," says Levinson, embracing Moisey Semyonovich and nodding to Ol'ga Fyodorovna, who has the most fundamental of reasons to protect her personal space from his incursion.

"The officer you killed surely has a seal and a strip of paper in his pocket," says Moisey Semyonovich. "We'll clean up the blood and seal the room."

"Making it look like I have been arrested?"

"We'll tell them you were carted off."

"And leave it to them to find me in their own cellar?" Levinson pauses to consider the scenario. "This will not make them proud." Another pause. "And the officer in charge will want to conceal my disappearance, and the disappearance of these three men."

"As their *komandir*, he'll be held personally responsible," adds Moisey Semyonovich, moving his hand horizontally across his throat. "Their *komandir* is your unwitting accomplice. He'll need to conceal this to save his neck."

Ol'ga Fyodorovna sits on a backless stool, her gaze focused on the stream of blood trickling from the partially covered pile of bodies.

She turns to Lewis next, addressing him in the same whisper she uses to address God. "You were a Christian once, *gospodin* Lewis?"

Lewis nods. "There was a time, briefly . . ."

"I am sorry," she says, wiping away a solitary, glistening tear. "I am sorry if our country has hardened your heart."

"My heart was quite hard before I arrived. Your country had nothing to do with my loss of faith."

"This saddens me all the more."

"Please, Ol'ga Fyodorovna," says Levinson. "Let's not be diverted to sentimentality when we have urgent matters before us."

"These are not *matters*, Solomon Shimonovich," gasps Ol'ga Fyodorovna. Her blue eyes continue to drill through white-faced Lewis's. "These were men entitled to dignity and respect. Two Christians, and perhaps one Muslim.

"It's futile to speak about such things with the Jews," she continues, addressing Lewis. "But we are the ones to blame. We made them into who they are, a coldhearted people who see no virtue beyond survival. Solomon, it's hard to imagine that you had a mother. Did you?"

"Funny you've never asked before. Yes, Ol'ga Fyodorovna, my dearest. I did have a mother."

"Did you know her?"

"No."

"Did she die when you were young?"

"No. She ran a brothel."

"And your father?"

"He was a thief. Him I knew."

"A murderer also?"

"Sometimes."

With a dull triple thump, the bodies land in the snow behind the Black Maria. The street sweeper Vasya Zuyev, who lives beneath Levinson, sleeps like a drunk and sees nothing.

Lewis's suitcase is the fourth item to drop out of Levinson's second-story window. Zuyev sleeps through that as well.

In a matter of minutes, the bodies lie stiffening in the cage of the Black Maria.

Wearing bloodstained MGB uniforms, Lewis and Levinson climb into the truck. Since it's a given that no one would dare steal a vehicle of this sort, the former crew had left the key in the ignition.

"Blazhennaya ona, nasha polu-monashka," says Levinson as Lewis turns the key. *"Yurodivaya."* Literal translation: Our half-nun is crazy.

But let's not be fooled by the literal. It's a testament to the spiritual paucity of the Anglophone culture that the words *blazhennaya* and *yurodivaya* translate simply as mad, for they connote a completely different view of madness, an ability to tap into the spiritual realm and communicate insights the rest of us are not given the power to obtain by conventional means.

Few foreigners would emerge intact from an excursion through this linguistic minefield, but Lewis knows enough Russian to grasp the complexity of Levinson's words. The old woman is disengaged from reality while pretending to channel a supernatural insight.

Ol'ga Fyodorovna's nickname, *polu-monashka* (half-nun), is curious on many levels.

The expression comes from an official attack on Ol'ga Fyodorovna's acquaintance, the poet Anna Akhmatova.

"Half-nun, half-what?" one might ask. The Politburo member Andrei Zhdanov, before his untimely demise, called Akhmatova a "half-nun, half-harlot" for her ability to combine the spiritual with the romantic. (In a historical twist, Zhdanov's death from heart disease led to allegations of medical murder, becoming Crime Number One in the Doctors' Plot.)

"Haven't driven since 1930," says Lewis as the Black Maria

sputters backward at a rapidly increasing speed toward the court-yard's archway.

"*Shvartsers* have cars in America?"

"*Yidn oykh,*" says Lewis in Yiddish. So do Jews.

Moving rapidly, the Black Maria backs onto the deserted Garden Ring.

"Woo-wee!" Lewis lets out the great Afro-American cry of joy, which he mistakenly believes will strike Levinson as primal to the point of vulgarity, but what the fuck difference does that make? "Woo-wee!" is blurted out with gusto, viscerally, with no hint of restraint, the sound you may have heard in the stands of the Negro Leagues when Satchel Paige pitched and Josh Gibson hit homers.

You would have heard something similar beneath the canopy of a Tuskegee Airman's plane as fire engulfed the opposing Messer. It was possible to hear a proper "Woo-wee!" on Red Ball Express, from the colored guys whose unheralded truck driving made it possible for white General Patton to press gloriously through the Reich. "Woo-wee!" An unrestrained sound of triumph. "Woo-wee!" indeed. Before the reverberations of his voice die down in the cab of the Black Maria, Friederich Robertovich Lewis comes to the startling realization that he hasn't let loose a proper "Woo-wee!" in at least a quarter century.

If ever a man grasped the meaning of cries of freedom, *Komandir* Levinson is that man.

Consider one wild charge against the White Army in 1918.

His is a wild *"Ura!"* with an *a-a-a* that never ends. *"Za mnoy, rebyata!"* Follow me, lads.

This being a civil war, the same cries come from both sides of that suicidal charge. Sword drawn, Levinson gallops toward death, his boys behind him. They square off, *Komandir* Levinson against a White Army major, a man twice his age. They look each other in the eye, aristocrat vs. Yid, count vs. yeshiva reject, *komandir* vs. *komandir*.

The major is amused to see dark features in an elongated face, topped off with a great big Jewish beak. Had someone taught him that such things happen, the major might have lived.

But it's too late to learn. Pierced through the heart, the major falls, and Levinson returns, with a gash across his back, but breathing, the memory of that cry imprinted on his soul.

Lewis throws the truck into neutral and shifts rapidly to first gear. As the truck lunges forward, the corpses shift in their cage.

At an intersection, the Black Maria rips through a red light.

"Where are we going?" asks Lewis.

"We are going right on the Garden Ring, then straight until I tell you to turn left."

They are silent for a few minutes.

"That thing you said about your parents; is it true?"

Levinson nods.

"You belong in films, Lewis," says Levinson as the Black Maria turns right on the Garden Ring. "In films, they have car chases."

For over twenty years, Levinson has never missed an opportunity to put Lewis's name and the word "film" in the same sentence. This is not entirely gratuitous, just a tad toxic.

Lewis's hands clench the wheel a little harder. Not even with three corpses tossing about in the Black Maria will he be provoked into the reminiscences Levinson is so relentlessly trying to trigger.

"Mikhoels is dead," he says to Levinson. "Can't you people let go of a grudge?"

After running another red light, the Black Maria passes one of the just-completed skyscrapers. Just then, an identical light truck pulls out of the building's tall brown granite archway, blowing its horn and heading toward them.

"What do we do?"

"We stop," says Levinson.

Two Black Marias come to a stop in the middle of the street, facing in opposite directions.

"Open the window," says Levinson through his teeth.

"Ey, rebyata, zakurit' yest'?" asks a young soldier at the wheel. He wants a smoke.

Not having seen Sadykov alive, Lewis doesn't know whether the man whose blood-soaked uniform he is wearing was a smoker, but as he reaches into the trench coat's breast pocket, his fingers find a thin cardboard pack.

It's not a surprise that Sadykov smoked Belomorkanal, a brand named after the Stalin White Sea–Baltic Sea Canal, built by prison labor in the 1930s.

Lewis extends the opened pack to the young man.

"Talk to them," whispers Levinson in Yiddish, and the command reinforces Lewis's flagging confidence.

"Kogo vezyote, rebyata?" asks Lewis. Whom do you have there, boys? This happens to be the first question that comes to his mind. He knows that, like a disease, the conversation he has started will have a predictable middle and end.

"Professor *khuyev*," answers the young man. A fucking professor.

The driver takes the pack out of Lewis's hand and counts out three cigarettes for the crew.

"A Yid?" Levinson prompts in a whisper.

"Zhid?" Lewis translates, taking back the pack of Belomor and slowly sticking it back in his pocket. The play will carry him through. There is no thinking to be done.

"A secret Yid. Wouldn't know it if you looked at him."

"The worst kind. Can take you by surprise," prompts Levinson.

"Maybe he is a half-blood," suggests Lewis, disregarding Levinson's cue. He can navigate through such conversations without help. He knows the phrase that will come next:

"Gitler ikh ne dobil," says the driver. Hitler didn't finish them off.

This phrase comes up frequently in casual conversations in February 1953, and one can easily learn to anticipate its recurrence.

"A my dobyom!" says Lewis. We'll finish them off!

"Zeyer gut," Levinson whispers in Yiddish. Very good.

"A u vas-to kto?" asks the driver. Whom do you have?

"Toyte yidn," prompts Levinson through his teeth.

"Dead Yids," Lewis translates into Russian.

"Has it begun?" asks the driver. A broad, joyful smile appears on his face. *"Rebyata, nachalos!"* he announces to the rest of his crew. It has begun!

In late February 1953, everyone knows that "it" is an antecedent of the final pogrom, one that will forever rid the motherland of the vermin.

"Day khot' vzglyanut', nasladitsya," says the driver. Let me at least take a look and enjoy it.

Lewis jumps out of the cab. He opens the back door, offering a view of three white, unclad corpses.

"Oy zdorovo!" says the driver, his hand involuntarily covering his mouth. This is a delight.

"Did you beat them to death?" asks one of the crew, a young man scarcely older than Sadykov's Ukrainians.

"Slit the throats," says Lewis.

As Lewis shuts the back door, the driver pauses for a moment, then bashfully asks the question that, Lewis surmises, must have been on his mind all along: *"A sam-to ty kto?"* And what are you?

"I am a man," replies Lewis, getting back into his Black Maria, and for a moment he forgets about his blood-soaked tunic and his cadaverous white face.

"What kind of man?"

"Nastoyashchiy chelovek." Lewis throws his new friend the entire pack of Belomor. *"Sovetskiy!"* A real man. A Soviet man.

The soldier catches the pack with his left hand and, after Lewis's words sink in, slowly raises his right hand in a salute.

Lewis returns the salute, raising his chocolate-colored right hand to his bleached temple.

4

At 4:39 a.m., Aleksandr Sergeyevich Kogan is sufficiently awake to be surprised when he hears the knock on the door.

Surprised because he was given reason to believe that he had a week to get his affairs in order. Could this be a mistake? Wrong door, perhaps?

Most people don't get warnings, grace periods. Kogan thought he did. Perhaps their plans have changed. The fact that Kogan is still at large is a surprise to everyone—starting with Kogan.

Exactly one year, three months, and one week ago, Kogan was stripped of his administrative and academic titles—chief of surgery at Pervaya Gradskaya Bol'nitsa, Municipal Hospital Number One, and professor of surgery at First Medical Institute. He continues to practice as an ordinary surgeon, often at the emergency room. Sometimes he makes house calls at the regional clinic. Sometimes he rides with an ambulance, mostly because he wants to, and because no one cares enough to stop him.

After dismissal, Kogan allowed his wardrobe to drift toward simpler things, which hang sack-like on his short, broad frame. A heavy cotton shirt that buttons off-center—*tolstovka*—replaces his officious coat and tie. The fedora loses its purpose and is replaced by an old military hat. Not his karakul *papakha* of a colonel (his rank when the war ended), but a basic *ushanka*, the sort a private might wear.

Being in the streets, easing pain, maybe even saving lives on occasion agrees with Kogan. While taking care of a drunk in the ER, he made a promise to himself that when this political madness ends and his posts are offered back to him with apologies, he will simply reject them and return to the life of a simple doctor. Of course, there are advantages to being a colonel, but sometimes being a private feels cleaner.

"Cosmopolitism," the reason for Kogan's dismissal, is, of course, preposterous. By birth, he is a Jew, but he is Russian to the core, a hero of two wars, a partisan in the Civil War, a military surgeon in World War II. Yet he is also proudly cosmopolitan. Having trained in Berlin and Paris, he has the skills that would enable him to practice in any hospital anywhere in the world. He can easily lecture in German and French. Alas, over the preceding two decades, he has had no opportunities to do so. And he has family members in New York and Copenhagen.

The word "cosmopolite" has become another way of saying Yid. Before the Party's hard line on cosmopolitism, a drunk in the street would call you *"zhid porkhatyy,"* a rootless Yid. Now, in the newspapers, the epithet of choice is *"kosmopolit bezrodnyy,"* a rootless Cosmopolite. It's a simple word substitution, a way of saying the exact same thing without saying "Yid," a way of making it official, acceptable. This nonsense is getting firmly implanted in the psyche of the people. Kogan feels it as a doctor. On house calls, patients call him bloodsucker, and accuse him of efforts to kill them. As a professional, Kogan doesn't take this personally, but as a patriot he wonders: Does madness ever recede? Can it get better on its own, without therapeutic intervention?

Some events in life deepen the dimension of time, as though the brackets that define ordinary instants are spread apart.

The instant of the knock, like the instant of death, can be eternal, and here it is, at exactly 4:39 a.m.

What do we do when the knock comes? Is the final instant of freedom shaped by our past lives? How do we balance the practical considerations against the symbolic? Kogan's thoughts rush in at once: "Should I remain in my pajamas? Should I put on street clothes? Is there time to change? Has my valise been packed?"

He is not torn by doubts about correctness of the Party line. He is past that. Consider the books that shaped him intellectually and spiritually: he is reading Akhmatova and Tsvetaeva, two poetesses described in the propaganda as "idealess" or worse. Akhmatova is cursed by the official ignoramuses as a "half-nun, half-harlot," a hybrid heretofore unknown to mankind. "Reading" Akhmatova and Tsvetaeva means continuously, the way a believer reads a sacred text.

Kogan is in possession of *Der Process, The Trial,* by Franz Kafka, published in Berlin in 1925 by Verlag Die Schmiede, a full decade before the Moscow Trials. (Its original owner was a German medic shot near Stalingrad.) The opening lines were scarily applicable to Moscow of 1953, despite being written nearly four decades earlier: *Someone must have been telling lies about Josef K., he knew he had done nothing wrong, but, one morning, he was arrested.*

The ending—the execution of Josef K.—seemed even more shocking because it was so amateurish, so homespun: *But the hands of one of the gentlemen were laid on K.'s throat, while the other pushed the knife deep into his heart and twisted it there, twice. As his eyesight failed, K. saw the two gentlemen cheek by cheek, close in front of his face, watching the result. "Like a dog!" he said, it was as if the shame of it should outlive him.*

Most dangerous, Kogan has developed an obsession with clinical applications of psychoanalysis: interpretation of dreams. That's about as far as you can depart from medicine based on "scientific Marxism-Leninism." Rooted in class structure, it rejects the very idea of the significance of troubles of an individual. Mental health is achieved through belonging to a collective. Self-indulgent navel-gazing is harm. A man's dream is just that. It's not rooted in class, has nothing to do with his relationship to ownership of the means of production. And obsession with sex is, of course, a capitalist vice.

Something about the spirit of the times makes Kogan read every epidemiology book he can get his hands on at the library of the First Medical Institute. Indeed, he is starting to think of purges as epidemics that start out with a small, concentrated population, then expand their reach nationally, even globally. Once he picked up a blank piece of paper and started to jot down the fundamentals of a discipline he would call politico-historical epidemiology.

One of the models he gleaned from epidemiology is that epidemics of infectious diseases can reach the peak, but then inevitably start to recede. How is Fascism not an infectious disease? How is Stalinism not a plague?

Events outside the window and in his own life convince Kogan that the climax is still far away. Things can get much worse. But what are we dealing with? Is this outburst of ignorance and hatred akin to systemic disease? Alternatively, this disease could have a single source that sends pathogens throughout the system. What if you find a way to intervene and neutralize it?

Is a therapeutic intervention possible? Of course, Kogan knows what this means. Murder. He took lives in his pre-medical past, and he has no apologies, no regrets for having done so. Perversely, he hopes that his old friends, now under arrest, were plotting to kill that old brigand Stalin. Alas, they probably were not.

Is violence an option?

Kogan knows that after three decades of saving lives as a physician he lacks the fortitude required to return to taking lives. He will be dignified, polite, professorial. Perhaps he will even use the arrest as a way to ennoble his oppressors. They are the enemy, nominally, but they are still Red Army soldiers, the grandsons of the men who served alongside Kogan during the Civil War, the sons of the men he operated on in field hospitals during World War II.

Rumor has it that the old brigand isn't in the best of health. What happens when the devil finally takes him? Will this disease start to recede?

Kogan went through these constructs a week ago, after a hellish day at the ER.

After jotting down the fundamentals of what he jokingly called "politico-historical epidemiology," he went into the bathroom, struck a match, burned the piece of paper containing the fundamentals of this new discipline, and, with a flush, sent the ashes to the Moskva River, Volga River, and—ultimately—the Caspian Sea.

And now, at 4:39 a.m., the knock.

He thought he had a week. Are they playing with their kill? Has someone turned him in? Is anyone aware of Kogan's ideological deviations? Has his turn come? How could it not? It's a simple progression: cosmopolitism, expulsion from the Party, loss of administrative and teaching positions, followed by what? Trumped-up charge of negligence in patient care? Accusations of medical murder? (The so-called Kaplan case seems to be just that.) Has time come to an eternal standstill? Will it always be 4:39 a.m.? Will 4:40 a.m. ever come?

Usually, it's the wife's lot to pack the husband's briefcase for the journey "over there." A classically packed briefcase contains a toothbrush, an extra pair of glasses, a pair of socks, underwear, a small sewing kit, and medications. He never got around to packing that bag, warranted though this action was, and now, in eternal mid-knock, it is too late. Is this his last contorted vestige of loyalty to Dusya, an intestinal torsion of loyalty?

In an odd way, he looks forward to being shipped over there, to the Siberian woods. This wish doesn't mirror a cancer patient's desire to die. Death happens only once. Hence its mystery. For Kogan, Siberia is a place altogether devoid of mystery. For a full year, he lived a partisan's life along the Trans-Siberian Railroad. Before he took the oath to do no harm, before he became *Dr.* Kogan, he was Sasha *pulemetchik*, Sasha the machine gunner.

Of course, Kogan's focus on felling trees in the forests that once gave him shelter is a mild form of denial. A public trial, a beaten-out confession, and execution in a Lubyanka cellar are a more likely outcome.

The time has budged. Kogan feels the second hand move haltingly toward 4:40. Another knock.

He gets out of bed, slips a robe over his striped pajamas, and puts on his slippers, realizing that this is the last time he will be allowed such luxuries. He walks up to the window first. Looking down, he sees the top of a Black Maria beneath a dim streetlight seven stories below.

"Should I jump? Does *primum non nocere* apply to my beloved self?"

No, jumps are melodramatic.

Kogan needs no spectators.

He opens the doctor's bag, which he keeps on the bookcase, right in the middle, next to the anatomy volumes and the *Dahl Explanatory Dictionary of the Living Great Russian Language.*

Another knock, as time moves forth and as oblivion nears.

Kogan quickly opens the small stainless-steel case used to

sterilize the syringe. He assembles the syringe, connecting the sixteen-gauge needle and inserting the plunger. Quickly, as he breaks the ampule, he looks around the apartment, pushes the plunger to squeeze out the extra air, finds the vein in his left forearm, and inserts the needle.

What are Dr. Kogan's thoughts? Is he thinking of the revolution, his comrades in the guerrilla band, the enemy boys he mowed down beneath the Ural hills? And what about the war where his mission was to heal? Is Kogan visualizing the mountain of mangled limbs he had to amputate to save the soldiers' lives? Is Kafka on his mind? Are poetry's verbal pirouettes of any comfort?

His thoughts are in a massive vat, a very real vat, filled with formaldehyde. Inside are severed parts of unclaimed bodies taken from the morgues to train his students to dissect. He first encountered those floating limbs and torsos in the twenties, when his excitement about acquiring lifesaving skills and fear of professors didn't let him take a pause and think of dignity in death.

He saw enough of that, and life which he desired he'd build anew. These severed parts didn't torment him when he taught. You need cadavers if you are to learn to heal. This changed in June of 1952. With weeks to go before the loss of everything he worked for, Aleksandr Sergeyevich Kogan thought he saw his own face on a severed head that stared at him from inside the vat.

The eyes weren't vacant. Kogan thought he saw them blink.

Another knock, then another. It's their play, they get to write it.

"I will withhold participation in the only way open to me. No, I will not give them the satisfaction of participation in public spectacles. I will not betray innocent colleagues at Pervaya Gradskaya.

"Do I say something? Do I look around for the last time? No, no time, no thoughts, a quick exit. I give the plunger a quick push. If the pain is intense, it's really potassium. The burning sensation is indeed intense. They will be breaking the door about now.

"Of course, it's potassium. What else can it be? Next, a quick, hard push on the plunger will stop the heart."

"Otkroy zhe nakonetz, yob tvoyu mat'." Kogan hears a familiar voice, pleading in Russian. Open the door at last, fuck your mother.

"Potz," says Kogan in Yiddish, pulling the needle out of the vein. Prick.

Kogan opens the door and, instead of the Angel of Death, *Komandir* Levinson walks in in all his tall, stooped, gangly splendor.

He is wearing an ill-fitting, bloodstained uniform of an MVD lieutenant. With him none other than Friederich Robertovich Lewis, in the uniform of a private—except, of course, his face is now painted white. The poor devil looks like a cadaver.

No scenario Kogan can imagine includes seeing Levinson's stooped frame in the blood-soaked tunic of an MVD lieutenant.

Squinting at the hallway lights, Kogan says in Yiddish: *"Dos bist du."* So it's you.

Suddenly, a wave of laughter erupts deep within his gut.

"We need your dacha," whispers Levinson as he and Lewis step into the apartment.

"Akh ty yob tvoyu mat'," says Kogan, through spasms of dull, deep, nearly silent laughter. Fuck your mother.

"You'd better button your overcoat, Comrade *Komandir*," he adds. "Have you slit someone's throat again?"

Levinson nods. "They came for me."

So he did it, fought back. One should never underestimate the power of a stubborn son of a bitch.

"How many?"

"Three."

"And the corpses, where are they?"

Levinson points downstairs, toward the courtyard.

"Is Dusya here?"

"I convinced her to leave me. What do you intend to do with the bodies?"

"Dacha," says Levinson, extending his hand for the keys.

"I think I might as well come with you," says Kogan. "I have a week. Fresh air will do me good."

At 5:07 a.m., Levinson opens the back door of the Black Maria. "You will be traveling in the cage."

After Kogan climbs into the cage, Lewis gets behind the wheel and Levinson in the passenger's seat.

"I hope you don't mind the company, Professor Kogan," says Levinson, looking back through the bars as Kogan eases into the seat above the corpses.

"I do, to be honest. But it's good practice."

"Comrade Lewis!" Levinson calls out as the Black Maria passes by the Kazan Railroad Station.

"Present, *komandir*," says Lewis, not looking up. The familiarity in his response verges on mockery.

LEVINSON: Comrade Lewis, what have you learned about our country over these past twenty-two years?

LEWIS: You are drunkards, brutes, barbarians. You have an exaggerated sense of duty and honor, which makes you reliable, and you are prone to messianic delusions, which makes you insufferable. Most of you cannot be counted among inhabitants of the world of real things. Am I missing anything?

LEVINSON: Where do I fit into this?

LEWIS: Not a drunkard, but the other things—yes.

KOGAN: I second that, Solomon. These comrades, whom you have offed, would concur also. Half of me wishes I saw that, the other half is glad I didn't.

LEVINSON: I was speaking with Lewis. What have you learned specifically about our peculiar traditions of law enforcement, Comrade Lewis?

LEWIS: Law enforcement? Do you have that? Do you even have a genuine police function?

LEVINSON: Continue, Comrade Lewis, you are making a valuable point. What do we have instead of the police?

LEWIS: Do you have anything but terror?

LEVINSON: Excellent! Look at what we've done so far. I killed three MGB operatives. That's three *armed* men. It was so easy. I am surprised it's not done more often. We threw the corpses in the back of their Black Maria and drove through the center of Moscow, running every red light. We showed the MGB the corpses of their colleagues. And you, Comrade Lewis, were in whiteface through much of the operation. A badly done whiteface, at that.

LEWIS: Your point, *komandir*?

LEVINSON: I am not as far as the point, Comrade Lewis. Patience, please. Only questions for now. Here is another: In our country, what will happen if someone decides to break every law in the most flagrant ways imaginable? Comrade Kogan, would you like to answer this?

KOGAN: He will get far.

LEVINSON: I am still doing questions. Here is one more: What if, instead of resting on our laurels or crawling into a hole, we take this as far as we can?

LEWIS: Am I starting to hear a plan?

LEVINSON: I have been looking at our situation this way and that, and I see no way we can survive for more than a couple of weeks if things are left as they are. Even as stupid as they are, they will find us.

KOGAN: I concur, with obvious reluctance. Of course, this situation isn't particularly significant in my case.

LEWIS: How can that be?

KOGAN: A competing life-limiting factor. Unrelated unpleasantness at the hospital. It's complete idiocy. The Special Department wants me to make a preposterous public confession, name names, that sort of thing.

LEVINSON: Comrade Lewis, there is some chance that they will not learn about our connection. So this would be a good time for you to get back to your Siberia, dive under your desk, and pretend that nothing happened.

LEWIS: I thought of that, and I don't believe it. It's well known that I stay with you when I am in Moscow. Never thought I'd need to make it secret, so I didn't.

LEVINSON: So you truly believe that you have nothing to lose? This is important.

LEWIS: Yes.

LEVINSON: I was hoping you would see it this way, because we could use you. You have a good strategic mind.

LEWIS: Use me for what?

LEVINSON: Patience! Not there yet! First, Kogan, am I to assume that you are up to trying something ambitious, something that may be our only hope?

KOGAN: Yes, you know my limitations. I don't kill. Not anymore.

LEVINSON: Squeamish you've grown in your old age. Your hands will remain clean. What I do is my business.

Lewis, Kogan is a perfectionist in all of life's endeavors. Since he has been a doctor much longer than he was a machine gunner, he may have indeed saved more lives than he has taken.

KOGAN: I hope so, Solomon. Do you believe you have reached the point where you can conclude your strategic onanism and tell us directly what your plan is?

LEVINSON: We are at that point, old goat. The plan is to escalate the process I have begun to its absolute furthest extreme. There is no point in halfway measures. They will not help us in the least. We must go for the top. The very top. Nothing less than a beheading will do.

KOGAN: Levinson, are you suggesting what I think you are suggesting?

LEVINSON: I think you understand correctly. Beheading . . . the top . . . *eto odnoznachno*. There is no way to misunderstand. You have to eliminate the root cause. How can I be more clear?

LEWIS: Beheading a specific *individual* or beheading the *system*?

LEVINSON: In our country, comrade, aren't they one and the same?

KOGAN: Whom or what do you want us to *behead*, Solomon?

LEVINSON: Is something wrong with my diction?

KOGAN: Is something wrong with my hearing?

LEVINSON: Does it have to be one or the other?

KOGAN: Are you saying you want us to behead our beloved Iosif Vissarionovich?

LEVINSON: What other choice do we have?

KOGAN: You want us to behead the Great Stalin? The Genius of all Times and Nations?

LEVINSON: Was I so vague that you have to pester me with questions?

KOGAN: You are insane, but did we not know that?

This can't be serious, Lewis concludes. Yet, Levinson's demeanor suggests that it is, in fact, completely serious. He appears to be resolute, *komandir*-like. Unless, of course, he is acting.

"You scare me, gentlemen," he says.

As a Soviet engineer, Lewis is trained to identify objective difficulties. These are daunting. How do you slip past thousands of soldiers of the MGB? How do you evade tanks, cannons, guard dogs, missiles, bombs? How do you get through the layers of defenses? How can you suggest such nonsense?

"How do we scare you, Mr. Lewis?" says Kogan. "Do you fear becoming an accessory to regicide?"

Is Kogan really getting involved in this insanity? Or is this the weirdest practical joke ever staged?

"No. Not that. Why would I give a shit about regicide? You know me better than that. I am just unable to tell whether you are genuine plotters or just two idiots."

5

The purpose of art is to ennoble. The purpose of shtick is to stuff you with the rich diet of self-parody and self-hatred for no purpose beyond making you open the wallet and burp.

The timing of these heroic events—1953—coincides with the integration of Jewish humor into the American mainstream.

The Yiddish language is still heard in America's streets. Yiddish theaters are still drawing crowds, and off-color humor fueled by vaudeville, jazz, and burlesque is flourishing in the Jewish Riviera resorts of the Catskills.

Jewish humor is completing its life cycle: blossoming, rotting, becoming shtick, transitioning into English. You can talk about Rodney Dangerfield and Henny Youngman, even include the young Lenny Bruce before he got real.

The purveyors of shtick may have been literally the American cousins of Levinson and Mikhoels. They would have been cousins who speak the same language and who are somewhat (not uniformly) aware of each other's existence. Yet, they are cousins who exist oceans apart. And, more important, they have few reasons to like each other.

In an article about his wartime visit to the United States, Mikhoels expresses deep contempt for the state of American theater.

Vulgarity is the currency of the New World that unveiled

before him. Rockettes kick up their heels in shows that get neither better nor worse. The words of Shakespeare aren't heard on Broadway. And as America's sons are sent across the seas to die and as Europe and Asia burn, New York feasts. Mikhoels seems infected with the dark mood of his old friends, German intellectuals, as they contemplate ending their lives in rat-infested hotels in Midtown.

Forget shtick. Mikhoels expresses contempt for Broadway. "Broadway brings together everything that's not serious about America," he writes. "It's the place where you find a high concentration of cafes, cabarets, and all the theaters. From the point of view of the God of Business, it's the Boulevard of Sin. It's where the entrepreneurs conduct their business."

Mikhoels understood the business schema of Broadway theater: a producer, basically a businessman, leases the premises and proceeds to seek out a director who has a play. "But if that director is someone like Max Reinhardt, who doesn't happen to have a play, he remains unemployed."

Reinhardt, a German and Austrian director and theater educator who had been a friend of Mikhoels's for decades, is in New York, bemoaning the need to please what was then the shorthand designation for Broadway's target audience: "a tired businessman," abbreviated as TBM, someone who has no use for culture or, for that matter, politics.

Reinhardt has just escaped from Fascism, yet he doesn't want to talk about Fascism. Instead, he wants to talk about theater in America, that is, the tyranny of TBM. "American theater isn't just a zero, it's negative one," Reinhardt says.

In another essay, Mikhoels describes his argument with Charlie Chaplin, who tries to convince him that his work is apolitical.

Mikhoels disagrees. The character of the Little Tramp, his travails, his efforts to survive as the machine age deals him one setback after another, is as political as it gets, he argues. And what does he make of Chaplin's film about the rise of Adolf Hitler, *The Great Dictator*?

If *The Great Dictator* isn't politics, what is?

Is it surprising that Mikhoels returns to Moscow, to GOSET, the theater born to integrate its audience into the societal mainstream, to make them strive for something better, a task that often involved using humor to evoke self-awareness, often through ridicule and shame?

Whether you are a Communist, a Zionist, or both, GOSET existed to enlighten and inspire. Please note that in the early morning of February 24, 1953, with Mikhoels gone and the GOSET lights dark, Levinson turns to the Bard to illuminate the magnitude of his defiant pirouette with Finnish daggers. Ask yourself: Would the soft-bellied comics of American wealth have either the athleticism or the sense of purpose to execute such a maneuver?

Shtick is for the TBM. Art is for the soldier.

Malakhovka is a dacha settlement forty kilometers from Moscow, a quick train ride.

At the turn of the century, Moscow's Jewish illuminati established a summer colony amid its gentle, wooded countryside. After the Revolution, the Jewish culture in Malakhovka revolved around the Orphanage of the Third International. There, the children could hear the writer Peretz Markish teach the works of Sholem Aleichem; they could learn drama from Mikhoels or Zuskin and art from Marc Chagall, a set designer who had just arrived in Moscow from Vitebsk.

In those days, Chagall's interests included erasing the boundary between the players and the audience and using costume to create moving sculpture.

Now, the great names are gone. Mikhoels run over by a phantom truck, vilified upon death. Chagall, in Paris, makes poetry out of movement, building a fabulist past. Markish shot dead in the Lubyanka cellar. Zuskin dances foolishly on the clouds, an executioner's bullet in his head, his calico dress in shreds.

In February, Malakhovka's graceful dachas stand dark and empty behind tall fences.

Gusts of chilling wind whistle through the rotting latticework of the summer theater. Rowboats by the lake lie buried in snowdrifts. The gazebos—those shaded temples of tea-drinking rituals of the summer—stand deserted beneath the wrap of bare vines, and white marble lions of Judah survey the cloud-like expanse from the tombstones at the Jewish cemetery.

At dawn, the Black Maria approaches Kogan's dacha, located on the edge of the Malakhovka Jewish cemetery.

The dacha used to be part of the grounds of a large, prerevolutionary estate. The original dacha, which belonged to a Moscow banker, burned down in the late 1920s. The plot was split into four pieces. Kogan has exactly a quarter of the original plot.

It is a simple peasant log hut, two rooms separated by a wood-burning stove and an open veranda. The stove is of typical Russian construction, large, white, with a heated surface to cook on in the area that serves as the kitchen. On the other side of the wall, there is a shelf Kogan can sleep on. This stone sleeping shelf makes the place usable even on the coldest winter days, which means Kogan can use it for his favorite pastimes: picking mushrooms in the summer and skiing in the winter.

Since paint was perpetually in short supply in the late twenties, when the place was built, the dacha was left unpainted. Kogan has done nothing to keep up or renovate the place.

The prerevolutionary owner of the dacha took great pains to shield his estate from the cemetery. This delineation of the romantic from the inevitable was accomplished with a hedge of pine trees, which now shade Kogan's little world.

The Black Maria fits snugly between the line of trees, the house, and a shed. Like three blocks of lard, the corpses lie in their cage.

Lewis doesn't get much sleep on February 24, just a couple of hours beneath a sheepskin, on a folding bed.

Anyone who has had the experience of coming awake on a jailhouse cot after a night of unbridled revelry would recognize the cluster of feelings Lewis experiences that morning.

On the bright side, there is the exhilaration of unknown origin, something that is a likely outcome of casting away the taboos, something fundamental, something liberating, something that, upon reflection, makes you wonder: "Did I actually do that?"

This sense of freedom is weighed down by dim memories of vows taken, deities acknowledged, deities cursed. "What did I do last night? Hmmm, let's see, Comrade Lewis, you became an accessory to a triple murder of uniformed agents of state security, you took part in an effort to dispose of their bodies, you had a chance to run, but chose not to, and instead you joined a plot to murder the most powerful czar Russia has known. Now you find yourself on this cot, beneath this sheepskin, at this dacha. What the fuck are you going to do about that? Ideas? Regrets?"

Even after twenty-two years in the USSR, on some mornings, he wakes up thinking that he is in Chicago. That's the magic of half-slumber: overshadowing reality, it leaves you not knowing where you are.

In Chicago, Lewis had a room on the South Side, near the university. He worked the night shift at the smelter between Chicago and Gary, and during the day he donned his Sunday best and attended classes.

He was the academic equivalent of a stowaway. Yet, in a class on Hegel, when other students meandered blindly between thesis, antithesis, and synthesis, the professor called on Lewis, the young man in the back of the room. He had the look of a student who understood, really understood the material. Even if he had been a bona fide student at the University of Chicago, Lewis wouldn't have raised his hand. His primary purpose was to learn, not to demonstrate.

Soon after he poached the class on Hegel, Lewis was moved to day shift at the smelter and he continued on his course of acquiring knowledge, this time in solitude. His knowledge of Marxism-Leninism was impressive. Once Lewis was asked to teach a night class to other enlightened workers, only to learn that their enlightenment didn't reach deep enough to enable them to take instruction in the philosophy of Marxism-Leninism from a black man. "What do you know about Hegel?" an Estonian comrade challenged Lewis on the first day. "You should be swinging from tree limbs." The Estonian completed this criticism with what he surely thought was a cacophony of piercing sounds of baboons in the jungle. Far from ejecting the racist from the class, other workers laughed. No one attended Lewis's second class. Even Lewis stayed home.

Marxism was Lewis's escape route from the construct of race. Theoretically, a man is defined based on his class, which in turn is defined by the relationship to the ownership of the means of production. National origins and race are negated, voided. That is how it should be, yet race remained un-negated, menacing

Lewis as he crossed the oceans, the steppes, and the frozen wilderness.

Had he escaped from the land of Jim Crow to become a trained baboon of World Revolution?

For a moment, he thinks that he is waking up in his room on the South Side, but that illusion vanishes as he takes a silent inventory of events of the previous night: "Siberia . . . Moscow . . . Levinson . . . corpses . . . whiteface . . . Black Maria . . . Kogan . . . dacha . . . escape . . . France . . . How the fuck did I get here?"

As soon as he asks the question, the answer comes: Solomon Mikhoels. Solomon fucking Mikhoels, the man Levinson called a *gonif*, a crook.

Were it not for Mikhoels, Lewis wouldn't have come in contact with either Levinson or Kogan, wouldn't have learned Yiddish, and—most important—wouldn't be at this dacha, praying to God that no one would notice that a Black Maria and its crew have gone missing.

In 1932, Mikhoels was shooting a talking picture, his first and only. And it is true that the film required one happy, good-natured Negro to play an American Communist, a bricklayer who joins a Jewish comrade to build Socialism in the USSR.

The story was set in Magnitogorsk, a city located on the southern tip of the Ural Mountains, on the boundary between Europe and Asia. The city was named after a mountain of pure iron, a geological oddity. The name means the city of the Magnet Mountain.

The USSR built up massive capital by dumping gold and artwork onto the world market. The funds would finance rapid industrialization. To plan the project, in 1928, the USSR hired the Arthur G. McKee Company of Cleveland, giving it the task to replicate the city of Gary, Indiana, upon the Magnet Mountain.

The city and the steel mill went up rapidly, with only a loose plan.

The place was a construction camp, where workers—mostly displaced peasants and unskilled laborers—had to survive Siberian winters in canvas tents. Workers' barracks went up; they were filled beyond capacity.

Though some visitors described Gary as the gates of hell, by comparison with Magnitogorsk, it was a garden spot.

The latter metropolis was a forest of half-completed smokestacks tied together with a tangle of pipes and railroad tracks. American earth-digging machines sat abandoned to rust in the open pits where they became incapacitated. In the residential areas, you could see the beginning of incongruously wide boulevards that became rivers of mud in the spring. There were also people's palaces, with massive columns that grotesquely mimicked Russia's imperial past. All of it was unfinished, probably impossible to complete, yet amid the chaos of construction, completed smokestacks were starting to spew out clouds of dark smoke, melting ore, making steel.

Workers' barracks, tent cities, and the zones of prison camps were woven into this mad landscape.

German architects were brought in to make an attempt at urban planning. The Germans wanted to separate residential zones from industrial, creating a kind of balance between work and life. Alas, this vision was just that—a hallucination. Construction of industrial and residential zones was well under way before planning began.

Large numbers of skilled foreign workers were brought in to exercise some control over the situation, and Lewis, an expert welder, was among them.

Dark skin was a rarity in the Soviet Union's workers' barracks. There were two Negroes in Magnitogorsk in January 1932. By February, their ranks declined by fifty percent when the African welder, who spoke French and mostly kept to himself, slipped off a scaffold and fell forty-five meters, landing on a pile of steel bars.

This left only Friederich Robertovich Lewis.

Born to descendants of freed slaves, named after Frederick Douglass, and raised in Memphis, Omaha, Chicago, and Cleveland, Lewis was what used to be known as "an enlightened worker," an autodidact drawn to revolutionary ideologies. He worked as a porter, then a waiter, and ultimately apprenticed as a welder at McKee, a company whose projects included building blast furnaces in the USSR.

One could say that Lewis's disgust with Jim Crow's America drove him to a new life in Joe Stalin's Russia. That would be a bit simplistic, but mostly true. In the late twenties, Lewis tried to join a Chicago cell of the Communist Party, hoping to be sent to the land of victorious revolution, where the color of a man's skin had been negated. But the wheels of Party machinery turned slowly, and in the spring of 1931 he asked the capitalists at McKee to send him to Magnitogorsk.

On entry to Russia, his name became Friederich—Germanized, presumably, in honor of Engels. The clerk who issued Lewis's visa knew nothing of Douglass. A Russian-style patronymic Robertovich, son of Robert, was inserted into his name in accordance with rules and traditions.

In his search for a race-free society, Lewis found himself in a place where he felt like a revolutionary from the planet Mars. There was racism in Stalin's Russia, too, a naïve kind of racism. While a foreman at McKee wouldn't hesitate to call him a nigger, a drunk on a Moscow streetcar could innocently refer to him as a primate. Along the same lines, his appearance was known to move street urchins to jump like baboons and shout good-naturedly about "djazz."

On a particularly cold February morning in Magnitogorsk, Lewis climbed to the top of a scaffold only to be summoned to the office of the *kombinat* construction director. It was unclear why the matter was so important that even the American engineer Charles Bunyan descended from Olympus, but there he was, in the meeting room, kindly offering his services as a translator.

Bunyan was one of humanity's secret heroes.

Short, bearded, bespectacled, he was as old as Lewis, yet had the gravitas of a European professor. Armed with a cold Lutheran stare (he was presumed to have been at some point a Lutheran), conspicuously grammatical Russian, and considerable ingenuity, he fought off the ideological hacks and ignorant central planners, preventing complete bungling of the project.

Lewis regarded Marxism as a powerful tool for generating mathematical insights into history and all aspects of the world around him. It was the fundamental science, the science of science. During his enlightened worker, pre-Communist phase, he became attuned to what he called "paternalism" among white comrades. His analysis of the phenomenon yielded the following insight: Paternalism = Racism Repressed. Lewis trusted his ability to see through a man, to gauge his innermost feelings about race. Turned on Bunyan, Lewis's finely calibrated gauge registered the most extraordinary reading he had ever observed: zero. No paternalism. No racism. A perfect zilch.

The difference in their social status notwithstanding, the welder and the construction director met often and spoke openly, without fear.

"You've made the right choice to come here," Bunyan once observed over dinner in his bungalow. "This is the ultimate land of opportunity. Extraordinary wealth is perpetually up for grabs. Billions of dollars in gold, soon to be dwarfed by immense wealth of oil, coal, ore, steel. All of it changed hands in 1917, and it may again."

"I didn't come here for wealth," said Lewis.

In those days, he still found it difficult to accept the idea that a white man of Bunyan's stature would find him a worthy interlocutor.

"Nor I," said Bunyan. "I came here to help them make something of it. To give them focus."

"You seem to be succeeding," said Lewis. "The blast furnaces are going up."

"By hook or crook. Do you know what makes this country run?" This was, of course, a rhetorical question. Bunyan leaned back in his chair to offer the answer: "The mandates."

A mandate was no more than a piece of paper: a letter, preferably handwritten, from a high-level bureaucrat, stating that the bearer should be given whatever it was he seeks. Some used the mandates for their personal benefit. Others, like Bunyan, to break through bureaucratic logjams.

At that time, Bunyan operated with a supply of mandates from Sergo Ordzhonikidze, the people's commissar of heavy industry.

"These are simple pieces of paper, not always on letterhead, not always stamped," Bunyan continued. "Just imagine having a mandate from Stalin himself. There would be no stamp, no letterhead, no date of expiration. Who'd ever dare to check whether it's real? And how would you check?"

"I wouldn't want to be caught with one of those," said Lewis.

"Neither would I."

Bunyan's ability to procure freight trains, copper wire, pipe, lumber, and welding torches was legendary in Magnitogorsk. Indeed, were it not for Bunyan, the construction of the *kombinat* would have turned into an exercise in marching in place, and without Magnitogorsk, Russia would have had less pig iron, less steel—and fewer tanks, planes, and Katyushas—when it needed them.

Were it not for Charles Bunyan, the war could have been lost.

As he had come down from the scaffold, Lewis showed up wearing a singed sheepskin coat, an *ushanka* with ear flaps down, and black *valenki*, felt boots that had all the traction of bedroom slippers and left his ankles wobbling. Large gloves protruded from his pocket.

"This is our brigadier of welders, Comrade Friederich Lewis," Bunyan said, introducing him to a diminutive, middle-aged, pale-skinned man and a young woman.

Lewis had never heard Bunyan call him comrade before. After all, neither of them was Soviet or, technically, a Communist. Bunyan worked for McKee and drew a hard currency paycheck. Lewis had overstayed his McKee assignment, and though he was being paid in rubles, he was still an American.

"This is Comrade Solomon Mikhoels and his assistant, Tatyana Goldshtein," Bunyan said in English. "They are from the Jewish theater in Moscow, here making preparations for filming."

Mikhoels sat beneath a large portrait of Iosif Vissarionovich Stalin. It was an oil, in a heavy gold-leaf frame, a big portrait probably done by a big artist. In accordance with long-standing tradition, the portraits of Soviet leaders weren't hung flat against the wall, but were angled slightly, to create the impression that the leader is looking down at the viewer.

Lewis nodded politely. What did any of this have to do with him?

The man looked like a Party worker, a new aristocrat traveling with his mistress. He wore a blue European suit and black leather shoes that were so small and delicate that they surely precluded any attempt at mobility in the frost and mud of Magnitogorsk.

"Kak vam nravyatsya nashi zhenshchiny?" Mikhoels asked, looking over the unusually pigmented builder of Socialism. How do you like our women?

This was not an effective icebreaker.

"Our women . . ." Lewis knew that even people who swore to have negated race could not be trusted on the subject of what was once known as corruption of blood. Did he catch Lewis staring at that girl's charcoal eyes, her thick braid, her small upturned breasts?

Did this man, who surely lived in a heated apartment, understand what it was like to live in the Magnitogorsk workers' barracks, where every square centimeter was shared with others, and where fucking was, in effect, a spectator sport?

Did he want to know about peasant girls who raised their skirts—actually, untied the drawstrings of their trousers—without waiting to be asked? Or did he want to know how Lewis's adolescence shaped his attitude toward white women? If so, he would want to hear that after the murderous Omaha race riots of 1919, Lewis's mother took to smacking him upside the head every time he looked at a white girl. Would this Comrade Mikhoels care to know that punitive measures intensify one's interest in the forbidden?

Cringing, Bunyan translated Mikhoels's artless question. He knew that Lewis's Russian was good and getting better, and he sensed correctly that with or without a translation, the question would remain unanswered.

The intense stare of Mikhoels's dark eyes glaring beneath a soaring forehead added to Lewis's discomfort.

After a long, tense pause, Mikhoels posed another question: *"Vy Kommunist?"* Another icebreaker.

"Tell him I have no *part-bilet*," Lewis replied in a mixture of Russian and English.

Indeed, Lewis was not a card-carrying Communist, and the reasons for his decision not to join the Party were inseparable from his reasons for declining to discuss "our" women.

"How can I help you?" Lewis asked in English.

"We'd like you to consider appearing in a film," said Mikhoels in Russian.

"That's not what I do," Lewis answered in English.

This wasn't a conversation. These were chunks of ice slamming into each other randomly, with great force.

"Vy budete igrat' vashego soplemennika," Mikhoels continued. You will be playing one of your tribesmen. That was an odd choice of words: tribesmen. What did he think Lewis was? A Zulu?

Surely Mikhoels understood that the audience had gone home, yet, speaking slowly, enunciating, he proceeded to lay out his film's storyline: a Jewish Communist, a bricklayer, returns to his native shtetl after twenty-eight years of laying brick in America. He is accompanied by his wife and a Negro comrade . . .

"Why?" Lewis interrupted in Russian. "Why not just have him travel with his wife and *no* Negro comrade?"

"Your Russian is very good," noted Mikhoels with a faint smile.

"And that surprises you . . ."

"It does, I confess."

The smile was still there, infuriating, frozen. What was its cause? Did this man think he had solved some quintessential mystery? Was he pondering something Lewis didn't want him to ponder? Lewis wanted out of that room, out of that idiotic conversation, away from that clueless film that shouldn't be made.

"Then maybe you'll answer my question: Why not leave that Negro at home?"

Mikhoels turned to the young woman: "Tanechka, please go down to the cafeteria and bring me a glass of tea."

The young woman got up with hesitation and slowly headed for the door. Lewis refrained from watching her leave. This was what they wanted, of course, to catch him casting a glance at her buttocks.

"Let me guess, your Negro comrade is incidental to the story," said Lewis as the door closed.

"He is . . ."

"And your main characters are Jews, all of them, no doubt, exquisitely portrayed?"

Mikhoels nodded. "It's a good script."

"And the Negro has bulging eyes, a radiant smile, broad shoulders, massive ivory teeth, bubbly enthusiasm."

Another nod.

"Zachem vam eto?" asked Lewis in Russian. Why do you need this?

"To make the whole thing passable, Comrade Lewis, to tell a deeper story. Comintern wants the Negro angle. The Negro Question is America's Achilles' heel, as they say. Personally, I don't know whether it is or isn't. Is it?"

"It can be," said Lewis. He smiled, realizing that surely Mikhoels would be pleased to see that the Negro before him had big, white, healthy teeth.

"Like you, I am not a Communist," said Mikhoels. "You are a simple welder, and I am a simple storyteller. And without you, I can't tell my story."

"Po ulitsam slona vodili/Kak vidno napokaz . . . " said Lewis, quoting a fable he had learned soon after arriving in Russia. An elephant was led through the streets, evidently for display . . .

With considerable satisfaction, Lewis noted that Mikhoels started to look tense, uncomfortable. His point seemed to be getting across.

"You need an elephant, Comrade Mikhoels, and I am not an elephant. I am a welder."

"The question of nationalities is complicated and fraught with inconsistency, Mr. Lewis."

"The Party's policy toward American Negroes should be guided by the same principles of internationalism as its policy toward Soviet Jews."

"That would be correct . . ."

"So why do you need a character who is so devoid of substance that even a clowning welder can portray him? You know what this character would be called where I come from? Repeat after me: 'a happy nigger.'"

"A happy nigger." Mikhoels mouthed the English words he had obviously not heard in the past. "Sounds Fascist," he added in Russian.

"Let me guess: his name is Jim. Nigger Jim, or Comrade Jim. Find yourself someone else, Comrade Mikhoels."

"There is no one else here."

"And in Moscow?"

"In Moscow, they are busy."

"I am not jolly enough for you."

"You are obviously a person of substance. Is there anything at all I can do to convince you?"

Was he offering money? A heated room? A door? A transfer to Moscow? Admission to an engineering institute? A trip to Crimea? A complimentary season pass to his theater? His girlfriend's ass?

The girl returned just in time to hear Lewis's reply:

"Take my advice, Comrade Mikhoels. You go get yourself a bug-eyed, toothy Jew and paint him black."

6

Where is it written that a man is entitled to a history?

Levinson has little more than a few shards of facts about his parents, but he has one feeling, the feeling of joy he felt when his father, Shimon Levinson, came to see him to play their game. Even years later, he can hear the bursts of his own laughter.

The game was simple: Shimon lifted his son to his shoulders, then said with a straight face: "So, remember me?" Solomon felt his father's big palms on his sides, then the hands parted and the child dropped down, almost to the ground, only to be caught and lifted again.

"Can you climb to my shoulders all by yourself?" his father asked, and Solomon made an honest but futile effort at jumping and climbing. Then, always unexpectedly, his father grabbed him again, usually by the hand and foot, and started a spin.

The best part was the bag. Theirs was a massive bag made out of a fishing net. Shimon must have made it himself, for such devices have no known purpose in fishing. Levinson climbed into that bag to be spun wildly. Soon after Levinson turned seven, his father stopped coming.

The boy never asked why he had lived with his aunt and uncle for as long as he could remember. And where did his mother go?

He had only the dimmest memory of her: her long hair, not much else. Even her voice was a mystery.

Facts found him slowly. His father was killed while collecting money for the protection racket he ran. His mother was back in the street, entertaining sailors. The "establishment" she had kept while she was still with his father had collapsed soon after Solomon was born.

Now other men, friends of Levinson's father, came to visit him. There were two of them, and they took turns showing up, almost always one at a time. It was part of the promise they made to his father: take care of the boy.

They threw him in the air. They spun him in the fishing net. They brought him adventure and detective books, mostly Russian translations of Walter Scott, Jules Verne, Alexander Dumas, James Fenimore Cooper, and Arthur Conan Doyle. When Levinson turned twelve, his father's best friend, an ominous-looking Russian named Nikolai, pulled out a pistol and took him to the woods to learn to shoot. Abramovich, a tough little Jew whose first name was never used, taught him to throw knives.

They showed up together when the time came to take Levinson on his first trip to a brothel. They drank vodka downstairs as two girls not much older than Levinson instructed him in the art of love. When Levinson gingerly stepped down the stairs, his father's friends applauded, then handed him a glass of vodka.

These men became his real family. They replaced his father in reminding him who he was and teaching him the tricks of survival. The uncle and aunt were mere caretakers. He formed no bond with them. When they left for America, expecting that the young man would come along, Levinson got as far as the seaport. At the gate, he turned around and ran. He thought he would be able to join his father's gang, but the gang kept him out, and he moved from one family of gang members to another, toting the books in the bag his father had made for the purpose of making him airborne.

He doesn't need to wonder where these people are now. Nikolai died somewhere in Kolyma, the gold mines, most likely. Abramovich, by then a cripple, was hanged by the Nazis when they occupied Odessa. His mother he knows nothing about, and wouldn't care to inquire, even if anyone knows.

As he awakens at Kogan's dacha, Levinson thinks of that bag. It was in his satchel when he joined the Red Army in 1918. It was lost somewhere, of course, probably at the hospital. That morning, Levinson thinks of his father's gang. He thinks of his band of partisans, of his ensemble of actors in that shrapnel-battered *Fordik*. And he thinks of the leap that made him famous.

His fate is to rely on others. His fate is to lead. His fate is to prevail.

Warmth and the smell of burning oak radiate from the stove in the center of Kogan's dacha.

Lewis's pillow is up against the stove, his eyes fixed on the light. Bookshelves occupy every square centimeter of wall space. Lewis has never seen so many books in anyone's house before. Many are thin tomes of poetry, published in small runs, four thousand or less, treasures that lesser men than Kogan used to heat their houses during the war.

That morning, as he dozes off on his cot, Lewis doesn't have a chance to appreciate the cot's construction. Made from old wooden beams and clamped with heavy bolts, it flaunts its seams and its simple, honest joints.

Pulling on the sheepskin overcoat that served as his blanket during the night, he follows the sound of agitated voices.

Outside, two coatless old men are trying to hit each other with saber-sized sticks.

"*Paskudnyak!*" shouts Kogan. A low-life!

A short, thin, balding man, he is twirling a stick, like a horseless Cossack on a death-defying charge.

"*An alte tsig bist du,*" says Levinson calmly. You are an old goat. With a deft blow, he sends Kogan's weapon flying into the snow.

"*An alte tsig?*" repeats Kogan, looking for his weapon. "I am a respected fifty-eight-year-old physician, and he says *an alte tsig?*"

"You fight like a *tsig.* Zuskin in a dress could fight better than that."

"Zuskin didn't *fight* in a dress. He *danced* in a dress," says Kogan. "And it's been thirty-five years since your Red Army."

"You fought like a young goat then, you fight like an old goat now. Once a goat, always a goat."

"Tell that to the dead Cossacks!" shouts Kogan, pulling the stick out of the snow.

Holding the stick with both hands, he charges Levinson in a desperate attempt to pierce him like a kebab.

"*Feh!*" says Levinson, deflecting the charge.

"*Vos? Dray Moshketiren shpiln?*" asks Lewis in Yiddish. What? Playing Three Musketeers?

"And what are you playing, mister? *Uncle Tom's Cabin?*" responds Levinson.

"Fuck you," says Lewis in English, setting off reverberations of "*fok yu*" from Levinson and Kogan.

It would be tempting to surmise that Kogan's wartime spree of murder was the consequence of a childhood rife with violence, ignorance, and deprivation. This would be wrong. Kogan's father was an exporter of Russian wheat and lumber. His given name was

Samuil. He changed it to the Russian-sounding Sergei, but the last name—Kogan—remained.

His holdings included freighters that docked in Odessa. The family lived in a seaside mansion. The Kogans were among founders of a Reform temple, but even as president of that temple, Sergei showed up only on High Holidays. Violin was the only instrument Aleksandr Sergeyevich played before he learned to operate a machine gun. He was, likely, one of the few men in history to move on from Stradivarius to Maxim.

Sergei Kogan didn't have a beard. He remembered Yiddish reasonably well, despite his efforts not to. His dream was to enlighten his brethren, to make them equivalent to other ethnic and religious groups. When his daughter declared her intention to marry a Dane, Sergei didn't go into mourning. He blessed the union.

Russian, German, and French were the languages spoken at the Kogan house. Sasha's Yiddish was somewhere between poor and nonexistent, but the amalgamation of German and Russian, brought to life by shreds of conversation he heard in the Odessa streets, allowed him to stumble through.

On occasion, pogroms flared up in Odessa, but the Kogan house was safe. The gendarmes were posted at its gates at the first sign of disturbance. The governor general was a friend, as was the entire bureaucracy that ran the seaport.

Sergei didn't try to dissuade Aleksandr as he gravitated toward radical groups at the gymnasium. Enlightenment is a journey, and Sergei didn't believe he had any authority to interfere.

Aleksandr read Marx tome by tome, saw the progression of his thought, but was mostly touched by early Marx, specifically *The Economic and Philosophic Manuscripts of 1844*, a work that describes the theory of man's alienation in capitalist society. This construct was harmonious with the ideas Aleksandr had gleaned from the classics of Russian literature, his other, bigger obsession.

Historical change was outside the window, and no man had the right to stay indoors. Aleksandr's progression from one circle to another seemed random at times. Briefly, he thought he was a Bundist. He flirted with terrorism on a purely theoretical level. Some of his ideological shifts hinged on personalities, the friends and enemies in the constantly changing stream of political movements.

In 1918, the Kogans were at a crossroads.

The country was going in the direction that would make it impossible for the family to remain in Odessa. With the daughter raising a Christian family in Copenhagen and the eldest son determined to join the Red Army, the Kogans took their remaining son, Vladimir, and went to New York.

With the capital they sheltered in Switzerland, they would start anew.

Levinson and Kogan led very different lives after the Civil War. Kogan enrolled in medical school, first in Moscow, then in Berlin, then in Paris, pursuing his goal to become his country's finest surgeon.

He started a family with a fellow physician, Dusya Shevchenko, a broad-faced Ukrainian woman, an internist at a regional clinic.

Kogan attended Levinson's performances at GOSET, and, being a good friend, heard every one of Levinson's complaints. The problem was, GOSET offered little training to its regular troupe, and if you were taken on as a clown and an acrobat, you would die a clown and an acrobat.

Kogan recognizes Levinson's shortcomings, but whenever his friend requires a sidekick for his antics, Kogan cheerfully plays along. Women do something similar when they waltz with partners who, left unchecked, would step on their feet and lead them into walls.

They are both unlucky in love, albeit in very different ways. Since GOSET was the kind of creative collective that worked and slept together, a succession of mistresses prevented Levinson from starting a family. Chronic immaturity that often affects actors had to be an obstacle as well. Besides, what does a stable relationship get you? Where is it written that it should be the universal goal? Consider Kogan's tortured marriage. How was it superior to Levinson's mistress juggling? Sometimes, during the war, at the army hospital, after a day of amputations, Kogan would pour himself a two-hundred-milliliter glass of freshly distilled alcohol and pronounce: "Here is how we prevent the next war: no sex for a generation."

Had he been drinking with Levinson, a pronouncement of that sort would have required a pause and an explanation.

They were almost family, or at least the closest thing to family that remained for either man. They spoke freely with each other, noting the Party's deviations from the correct course and its unstoppable, heroic march toward criminality. Now Levinson is one of the few people Kogan has told about the travesty that was going to engulf him: the so-called Kaplan case.

As clouds darken and pogroms seem inevitable, *Komandir* Levinson is determined to not be finished off quietly in a cellar. Levinson has a wild, much-rehearsed scenario, which seems to have worked. He greeted them with bizarre reminiscences and, in conclusion, a surprise. Levinson is still good with his sword and downright dazzling with smallswords. But he has become dependent upon an audience that doesn't exist.

Worse, Levinson longs for the old Maxim, the gun in the photograph on his wall. He talks about it as though it were an old battle comrade, like Colonel Sadykov, of blessed memory. Maxim on wheels, with a shrapnel shield. Made in Tula in 1905. Captured from the White Army beneath a Ural hill. Kogan personally separated it from the corpse of his counterpart.

Kogan remembers that machine well, having fired it in many a battle in 1918. If you've ever fired a Maxim in battle, you know what to do. Let them come as close as you or they dare. If they run for it, they are dead. If they crawl and get close enough to throw a grenade, you are dead. If the gun jams, you are dead.

But Kogan is no longer a machine gunner, no longer Sasha *pulemetchik*, no longer a scholar who has taken a sabbatical in the service of the proletariat.

Two benches are pulled up to the sides of a reddish marble-top table.

Levinson doesn't seem ready to sit down. He seems absolutely calm, intent on towering over the table.

LEWIS: Can we please discuss the bodies?
KOGAN: What's there to say?
LEWIS: Where do we put them?
KOGAN: You'd like to bury them, I presume, Comrade Lewis?

In Magnitogorsk, Lewis developed a clinician's capacity to remain calm in the proximity of a grave injury. Whenever a welder fell from a scaffold, Lewis could exhibit compassion, call for help, and remain with the fallen comrade to the end.

This was all the tolerance he needed, because red flatbreads, being bad for the morale of the surviving workers, were carted off to the hospital or the morgue before they turned stiff and glassy, like Sadykov and the boys. Living in proximity to three corpses bothers Lewis immensely.

KOGAN: Where do you suggest we bury them?

LEWIS: Here. Are we not near the cemetery?

KOGAN (*places a cube of rock sugar under a knife and slams it against the table*): I don't know about your Chicago or your Cleveland, but here in Malakhovka, in February, the ground is frozen.

LEWIS: So what do we do?

KOGAN: What's your rush? Put them anywhere. They will not spoil until the thaw.

LEVINSON: I agree with Lewis. It's better to dump them. Any ideas?

LEWIS: I suppose we could dress them again, put them in the Black Maria, and leave it on a railroad crossing.

LEVINSON: No, let's do the simplest thing.

KOGAN: The simplest thing I can think of is to tie them with chains and lower them into a well.

LEVINSON: Where?

KOGAN: Anywhere. Here in Malakhovka we have many wells.

LEVINSON: And then what?

KOGAN: And when what?

LEVINSON: After the thaw, you idiot.

KOGAN: Raise them after the thaw, if we need them.

LEVINSON: Now, Kogan, since you are such a clever Yid, what do you suggest we do with the Black Maria?

KOGAN: Trucks are not my specialty. Lewis, you are an engineer.

LEWIS: It's too big to hide. We shouldn't even try.

KOGAN: I like this. You have a solution, Lewis?

LEWIS: I think so. We leave it by the railroad station, in front of the *kolkhoz* market, with one wheel on the sidewalk, in the way of pedestrians and automobile traffic. Make sure everyone in Malakhovka rubs up against it at least once.

LEVINSON: Locked?

LEWIS: Absolutely not.

LEVINSON: I like this even more. And the key?

LEWIS: In the ignition.

LEVINSON: Brilliant!

KOGAN *(raising his hands to the heavens)*: Ah! Who could possibly want to steal a Black Maria?

LEWIS: And who would want to report that there is one missing? Who would want to call the place you'd have to call to report that a Black Maria has turned up with one wheel on the sidewalk in front of the railroad station?

LEVINSON: *A kluger, a yidishn kop.*

Being called an intelligent man with a Jewish mind can be considered a compliment among the tribe. However, in the special case of Friederich Robertovich Lewis, this compliment carries a load of racial connotations, which invariably fail to strike him as amusing.

"I need to go to the post office and call in sick," Lewis says to Levinson. "Would you paint my face again? But not solid white."

"Should I give you thinner lips?" asks Levinson.

"First, do the rosy cheeks. Then we talk lips."

Rosy cheeks are accomplished with a thin application of rouge on top of the screen of white.

"Lips?" asks Levinson.

"Get away from my lips."

"Then we are done," says Levinson, handing Lewis a mirror.

This time, Levinson's work is almost subtle. To avoid the cadaverous look, he made a thinner mixture of grease cream and toothpowder. Instead of forming a solid layer of white, this produces a screen that shows variations of Lewis's natural pigmentation. The rouge, however, is a little much, and on the background of light skin, Lewis's lips look cherry red.

"You look like a harlot, Lewis," says Kogan, considering his new appearance.

"Actually, I believe that now I look Jewish."

"You look like Pushkin," says Levinson.

Indeed, with his skin tone lightened, Lewis bears an uncanny resemblance to Russia's greatest poet, Aleksandr Sergeyevich Pushkin. This is not accidental, since Pushkin was the great-grandson of a Negro named Abram Hannibal by his master, Peter the Great.

At the post office, coughing into the telephone, Lewis makes a convincing impression of sickness. First, he speaks with a secretary at the Stalin Auto Plant in Moscow. Were it not for a problem with the assembly line at Stalin, Lewis would have been safely at home in Novosibirsk. After calling in sick, Lewis orders a long-distance call to Novosibirsk, to let his secretary know that he will stay in Moscow a little longer. He is free.

On a sunny afternoon, when snow squeaks underfoot, everyone is a survivor. The odds notwithstanding, Lewis feels that he is going to live. How will he get out of this? That is a matter of logistics, and engineers are good with logistics.

Emerging from the underpass at the railroad station, Lewis realizes that two young men are walking behind him.

He needs to turn left, toward the cemetery. Instead, he turns right. The young men stay close. He takes a left turn, this time heading toward the summer theater. The young men follow. Lewis quickens his pace. The young men do the same.

Langston Hughes, Paul Robeson, and many others noted that being a Negro in Stalin's Russia means not worrying about getting beaten up in the street. Lewis has nearly forgotten his old fear of venturing into the wrong neighborhood, asking for a beer in the wrong bar, looking at the wrong woman, or saying the wrong thing.

Now, in whiteface, he needs to draw on the instincts that kept him alive long enough to get to Magnitogorsk.

"Gloves . . . am I wearing gloves?" he asks himself. He is.

With gloves on, he can throw a punch without revealing the pigmentation of his fists.

Growing up on America's streets, Lewis knows how to savor the violence of a brawl. He never looks for fights, and the fights that have found him haven't been too bad (he still has his teeth), but the fantasy of busting a nasty-ass racist Irish cop in the balls still lurks within his soul.

Lewis is uniquely positioned to understand that racist mythology of Old Europe is about blood. Their niggers—the Jews—are said to suck the blood of Christians. The New World is beyond blood libel. Even America's lone anti-Semitic court case—Leo Frank of Atlanta—is about a Jew fucking and killing a white girl. Poor Leo was in a minority of one, the only American Jew to learn what Negroes like Lewis knew from birth: America is about semen.

Yes, Lewis savors the prospect of leading the two bastards into a deserted street and relegating them to a life of impotence and incontinence. And if they carry knives, that matters little. Lewis has a pistol.

"Should I prevail?" he asks himself and, his impulses notwithstanding, realizes that triumph is not an option.

Lewis's peril that day is unrelated to nasty-ass Irish cops and pigmentation. Leo Frank, too, is irrelevant.

One of the young men who spots Lewis is named Anatoly Germanovich Krutyakov. In the streets he is known by the unlikely name Kent. Born on July 31, 1935, he is on the nineteenth year of life.

Seven months earlier, Kent was freed from the Matrosov Colony for Underaged Criminals, outside the city of Ufa, in Bashkiria, where he served a four-year term for an attempt to pick pockets.

It's difficult to determine conclusively how the name Kent entered the Soviet underworld. Was it through one of many Dukes of Kent in Shakespeare, perhaps even Lear's faithful friend? Retelling of plays, novels, and films was a common way for prisoners to while away the hours, and good storytellers often found themselves under the protection of thugs craving adaptations of *The Count of Monte Cristo, Anna Karenina, Hamlet,* or *King Lear.*

Adaptations spun by Moscow University students of literature, glum lieutenants from Warsaw, and elderly intellectuals of all sorts gave these classic stories a new life. As they passed through thugs, the stories were born yet again. Thus, in a surreal cultural-linguistic leap, Kent became a verb, *skentovatsya,* to "bekent," to form a friendship, which in this setting describes forming a criminal association. On second thought, the word "conkent," had it existed, would convey the meaning with greater precision.

At the colony, Kent met Tarzan (Vladimir Andreyevich Rozhnov, born October 29, 1936).

Tarzan was freed two months before Kent and awaited him outside the zone. Though neither of the young men would have characterized himself as a homosexual, they did make rooster, wherein the stronger, more massive Tarzan invariably assumed the superior position.

Both youths lost their parents early in life. Kent's father, a tankist, was killed in the Battle of Kursk, and his mother died of typhus during evacuation. Tarzan's father, an infantry lieutenant, was killed during the first weeks of the war, and his mother went from one set of hands to another.

Officially classified as individuals without a fixed address, Kent and Tarzan risk being picked up at any moment and taken back to the camps, this time as adults, for violation of residency requirements. Malakhovka has given them something of a refuge, thanks to a fortuitous meeting with another former young convict, whose mother had married a militia lieutenant. Bekenting the militia is the best bekenting of all.

The young men broke into a dacha that, judging by a large painting and a multitude of photographs on the walls, belonged to a violinist, and for the first time in their lives, they enjoyed something that could be described as domestic bliss.

Neither Kent nor Tarzan read newspapers, but they know enough to fear that an individual with an exaggerated nose (the term is *nosatyy*, the nosed one) might use a syringe of his own design to deliver a malignant injection. They know that Jews sit on sacks of money and use diamonds in secret prayer rituals. More than anything, they sense the fear of the nosed ones, and after years in camps and colonies for young criminals, they know that fear begets weakness and weakness opportunity.

If the nosed ones aren't yet outside the law, they soon will be.

Lewis realizes that their encounter is imminent.

The first punch to his face will smudge the makeup and reveal the color of his skin. Gunfire—an uncommon event on

Russia's streets—will ultimately bring attention to Levinson and Kogan.

He will have to take one punch and fall facedown, letting the thugs kick his prostrate body. Lewis's objective is a decisive, spectacular, humiliating defeat. He will play a coward, and maybe that will give the thugs enough satisfaction that they will go easier on his back.

"*Ey, ty, bratishka, postoy,*" shouts Tarzan. Hey, you, brother, wait. Lewis turns around, flashing the men a buttery smile.

"*A kto mene zovyot?*" he asks with an exaggerated Yiddish accent. And who calls?

He will play Yid. He'll give them uvular *r*'s, with *e*'s replacing *ya*'s, with questions that answer questions (and why not?), with phrases that begin with prepositions, and with inflections that soar. He'll give them a *nar*. A fool. He'll give them Tevye, Menakhem-Mendel, Benjamin III. He'll give them a caricature of caricatures.

He would do Senderl, too, but he doesn't have a dress. A critic might object that all the rogues listed above have their endearing qualities. Endearing to some audiences, Lewis would respond. To him, these characters are only slightly more appealing than Comrade Jim.

"*Zakurit' est'?*" asks one of the thugs. Do you have a smoke?

"*Prostite mene, ya ne kuryu,*" says Lewis with a solicitous smile, in butchered Russian. Forgive me, but I don't smoke.

"Kent, look, a Yid!"

"*Ya takoy zhe Sovetsky grazhdanin kak vy,*" says Lewis proudly. I am a Soviet citizen, just like you.

"*Khuy ty. A nu goni den'gu!*" says Kent. Hand over the money, dickhead.

"Take it! Take it, comrade. Just don't beat me!" whines Lewis.

With a shaking hand, Lewis hands Kent the money—ninety rubles and some change.

"A nu Tarzanchik, vrezh yemu," says Kent, who in some situations couldn't help sounding effeminate. Slam him.

Lewis is wide open. When it comes, the slam of Tarzan's fist is as halfhearted as the MGB soldier's knock on Levinson's door.

"Govno! Maratsya ne khochetsya," says Tarzan, spitting through his teeth and kicking Lewis in the ribs. Shit! Don't want to step in it.

"Same here, asshole," whispers Lewis as his hand fondles the handle of Lieutenant Sadykov's pistol.

7

Lewis doesn't look his best when he walks through the door of Kogan's dacha. The fist has smudged the white makeup on his face, and a chunk of ice Lewis used to minimize the swelling returned half of his face to its original color.

As he walks in, Lewis notices a small *spetsovka* overcoat and a small military hat on the bentwood Thonet coatrack.

The tone of conversation he hears is different from what he has come to expect from Levinson and Kogan: it's clear, with just a bit more projection. Lewis steps back outside and, with a handful of snow, removes what's left of his white face.

There is a young lady at the dacha.

"Kima Yefimovna, this is my friend Friederich Robertovich Lewis," says Kogan.

For an instant, Lewis gets the impression that Kima looks at him with a volatile combination of bashfulness and interest. Lewis believes that while all women instantly pass judgment on men they meet, Russian women are more likely to act on their initial impulses.

Of course, men of forty and older are known to misread the looks they get from younger women. Lewis reminds himself that the girl is probably not longing for old men like himself (he is forty-two).

This has to be doubly true for even older men like Levinson and Kogan.

Something about Kima seems to conjure images of a Young Communist from wartime propaganda, a selfless heroine who spits in the faces of the Nazis. He can imagine her saying something like "You can kill me now, but others will come to avenge me," or perhaps "Long live Stalin!" She seems constricted, cold, irresistible.

Lewis bows like a Chekhovian fool.

"Pleasure to meet you . . ."

Kima's eyes—emerald, hardened with a drop of cobalt—reduce him to babbling idiocy. Colors this intense should be used lightly, and, mercifully, the shape of Kima's eyes is more Asian than Slavic. Her patronymic—Yefimovna—is likely Jewish, though.

Clearly, the bow and the officious greeting make the girl uncomfortable. That is just fine, Lewis reminds himself. She is too young. Besides, his own life changed irrevocably the moment he stepped into the blood of Lieutenant Sadykov.

"Kima Yefimovna is the finest source of local news," Kogan continues obliviously. "She lives in the railroad barracks and works in bottle redemption. All the news reaches her first."

The bottle redemption station is an odd place for Kogan to find friends.

These are dungeons where drunks bring their glassware. That crowd is motivated by simple incentives: redeem the bottle you bought the night before and get enough change for the first beer of the morning. Decent people show up in such places every now and then, usually days before payday, when money runs short, carrying milk bottles and wide-mouthed jars, determined to avoid conversations with fellow customers and to emerge with a pocketful of change.

How did this seemingly intelligent girl end up in the dungeon? Lewis smells a tragedy.

"They are putting together lists," says Kima. Cautiously, Lewis lets his gaze slip down her jacket. He sees little evidence of breasts.

"A chto znachitsya v etikh spiskakh?" asks Levinson. And what figures in these lists?

He stands by the table, his tall, distinguished torso clad in a smoking jacket that has the look of something taken off a White Army officer, perhaps in 1918. Alternatively, it came from a costume shop. And, yes, he wears an ascot. As previously established, actors of burned-down theaters have a special affinity for ascots.

"Jews," answers Kima. "And half-Jews."

"Whatever for?" asks Lewis.

Having spent two days traveling by railroad from Siberia, he should have been aware of all the widely circulated rumors.

"The rumor is, for deportation," says Kima. "The depots are filled with cattle cars."

"Which depots?"

"They say in Bykovo, Ramenskoye, Lyubertsy. And there are trains on spare railroad spurs."

"That could be anything," says Kogan. "They could be having . . ."

"Military maneuvers," offers Levinson.

"Yes, military maneuvers."

"I hear people talk," says the girl. "People you don't know, in the railroad barracks. They say the trains are here for the Jews."

"This could be just a fantasy of certain strata of the working class," Kogan offers.

Lewis is puzzled. Why would the fate of the Jews be of such intense interest to this steely-eyed, über-Slavic Young Communist? What is she doing in the hideaway of two old goats and a Negro? Can she be trusted?

"You shouldn't worry, Kima," says Kogan. "It cannot happen."

"It cannot!" Levinson confirms.

"Even if it's being planned, Stalin will not allow it," declares Kogan with certainty.

"Please don't try to shield me," she says with frustration.

"What are you really afraid of, Kima?" asks Kogan.

She says nothing, only her chin juts upward, away from Kogan, away from Levinson. At a perfect forty-five-degree angle, she looks at Lewis yet past him. Tears well in her eyes as though against her will, as an unwanted consequence of an internal battle she seems to be slowly, painfully losing. Lewis contemplates her tears. They would be cold, malformed, he thinks.

He wants to touch her, not at all out of anything prurient, but out of an irrational belief that a touch could console her profound sadness.

"I know a lot more than you think," she blurts out, childlike, then, getting up, storms out, slamming the door.

"*Sirota* . . ." Kogan shrugs his shoulders. An orphan.

To him, this fully explains Kima's outburst. Lewis needs something more tangible.

Why are the old goats trying to negate the information that she had brought to them?

Certainly, deportation is plausible. Comrade Stalin had performed several, starting with wealthy peasants in the twenties and thirties. Having learned from Hitler's experience during the war, he started to target entire nations: the Volga Germans, the Crimean Tatars, the Chechens, the young Lithuanian men. These deportations were manmade cataclysms from which there was no shelter.

"Comrade Stalin will not allow it?" asks Lewis after Kima slams the door.

"He will not!" repeats Levinson, pointing at the heavens in a merciless parody of himself. "Not our Iosif Vissarionovich!"

The goats veer off into one of their customary absurdist impro-
visations.

KOGAN: What does Comrade Stalin teach us about anti-
Semitism?

LEVINSON *(with a Georgian accent)*: Anti-Semitism is a form of
cannibalism.

KOGAN: Its lowest form? Please explain this, Iosif Vissarionovich.

LEVINSON: No, comrade, you are mistaken. Anti-Semitism
is the *highest* form of cannibalism!

KOGAN: Iosif Vissarionovich, if anti-Semitism is the highest
form of cannibalism, what is its lowest form?

LEVINSON: Surgery, comrades, is the *lowest* form of cannibalism!

LEWIS: I have some questions.

KOGAN: Another concern, Mr. Lewis?

LEWIS: Yes, it's about the art of being an actor. Years ago,
when I still lived in Moscow, I heard Stanislavsky himself lecture on acting. I listened carefully. He said that
an actor draws on his experiences in order to craft the
character he depicts onstage. It was presented as something objective, measurable, reproducible. A method.

KOGAN: That's the science they are cooking at the Moscow
Arts Theater.

LEWIS: But isn't it perilous?

KOGAN: Yes. If you depict Spartacus, or Bar-Kokhba, or
what's your Negro's name?

LEWIS: Nat Turner.

KOGAN: If you think you are Spartacus, Nat Turner, or even
our Lenin, you can get yourself into considerable trouble in the street. So what's your question, Lewis?

LEWIS: My question is, how do we know that an actor leaves his character onstage after the curtain falls?

KOGAN: Would you like to answer Lewis's question, *komandir*?

LEVINSON: No.

LEWIS: Then, here's a more troubling question: Does *der komandir* have the ability to distinguish his real self from the character or characters he plays or those he thinks he plays?

KOGAN: Onstage or in real life?

LEWIS: Either.

KOGAN: You mean, for example, right now?

LEWIS: Yes. Does he think he is onstage? Or let me put this differently: is he living in the world of real things?

KOGAN: Let's ask him.

LEVINSON: Ask me what?

LEWIS: Let me try, Dr. Kogan. *Komandir*, are you able to distinguish reality from stage? Are you playing the part of the leader of a plot, or are you indeed *being* the leader of a plot?

LEVINSON: It's a theoretical question. I've heard this kind of *narishkeit* for thirty years.

KOGAN: You have, I would imagine.

LEVINSON: No, this is serious: I look at it like a battle, Lewis. I go out there, hacking away, doing my best. All this Stanislavsky thing is just talk. I'm sick of it.

LEWIS: That's what I feared.

KOGAN: So, Lewis, if this is indeed a plot, are you with me and with *der komandir*?

LEWIS: Am I in the plot?

KOGAN: If that is what it is.

LEWIS: I guess I am. *Zol zayn azoy.*

LEVINSON and KOGAN *(in unison)*: *Zol zayn azoy!*
It shall be so.

And if this were a play, the curtain would descend, and Act I would conclude.

Act II

1

Before the war, Arkady Leonidovich Kaplan wanted to become a diplomat, modeling himself on Maxim Litvinov, the Soviet Ambassador to the United States.

At school, he was learning German, but to be a stronger candidate for the diplomatic corps, he wanted to learn English as well. Studying on his own, he realized that he didn't have a prayer of getting the pronunciation right, but he also knew that he was resourceful enough to clean it up later.

Arkady—everyone called him Arkashka—was eighteen when the war began. For reasons he never understood, he was made a medic and was sent to the front lines, where he remained for four years. "I crawled from Moscow to Berlin" was his line. It was hard to imagine how someone this lean and tall could get on the ground and crawl, but if there had been an Olympic event called Nordic crawling, Arkashka would have been a strong contender for gold.

After battles, Arkashka and his comrades crawled out of the trenches, dragging stretchers, looking for wounded Soviet soldiers. He had no training in medicine, but quickly became a master of applying tourniquets to near-severed limbs, whispering words of comfort to dying soldiers, making instant triage decisions, and identifying land mines and unexploded ordnance in pitch darkness.

He never carried a weapon. The stretcher, tourniquets, and

medical supplies were load enough. Nobody cared what he did, and he felt cleaner without a gun. Whenever possible, Arkashka avoided wearing a helmet as well. It interfered with his ability to hear the moans of the wounded. The Germans didn't hold fire when they knew medics were in the field, and neither did the Soviet Army. The chance that a new battle would start was always there.

His worst injury was a chipped tooth, a shrapnel wound from Stalingrad.

Often he came within a few meters of the Germans. When he got too close and was challenged, he was able to respond in a faux Bavarian accent. In German, his pronunciation was exemplary.

The orders were to bring back only the Soviet soldiers, but once he brought back a German medic, who had been shot once through the back, presumably by a Soviet sniper. There was something student-like about that young man. Arkashka couldn't bear to leave him to bleed out in the mud. The medic was barely breathing by the time he dragged him in to the Soviet positions.

In his rucksack, the young man carried a separate waxed canvas bag that contained a copy of *Der Process*, by Franz Kafka, in German. A corner of the tome was blown off by a sniper's bullet. The text survived for three reasons: (1) the medic kept the book in the rucksack, (2) the sniper's bullet pierced the medic from the back, producing a crater-like exit wound in the abdomen, and (3) causing him to fall forward and bleed out into the snow. Had the medic been hit in the chest or the abdomen and fallen on his back, the blood would have surely destroyed *Der Process* in a manner Kafka would have appreciated.

Arkashka read that book in one sitting the next day. Realizing that a book this important must be passed on, he gave it to a surgeon he didn't know well, but nonetheless trusted. He had to be careful, because the Special Department could have easily classified *Der Process*, a book in German, as Nazi propaganda, which would have resulted in an investigation, trial, and execution.

After the war, Arkashka abandoned his dreams of diplomacy and enrolled in the First Medical Institute. There, by a massive formaldehyde vat containing body parts, a professor of surgery greeted him with a proper military salute. Generally, colonels do not salute privates, but in this case rank was beside the point. They were civilians now.

This professor was none other than Aleksandr Sergeyevich Kogan, the army surgeon to whom Arkashka had entrusted a copy of *Der Process*.

They spent the evening drinking vodka at Kogan's apartment on Ulansky Street. *Frontoviki*, men who were at the front, are a brotherhood. That night, they read their favorite passages from *The Trial*. For both men, these included the opening and the very end: *Like a dog.*

Five years later, on February 16, 1953, at around 3:47 a.m., an ambulance was summoned to the apartment of Admiral Pyotr Abrikosov on Frunzenskaya Embankment.

The complaint: the admiral's seventy-eight-year-old mother, who was paralyzed on the right side a year ago, had become unresponsive.

On ordinary nights, the ambulance crew included a doctor, a driver, and a medic. However, the medic was ill, and only the doctor and the driver were available to make the call.

"Did you know that Jesus Christ was a Yid doctor?" asked Dr. Arkady Leonidovich Kaplan, the doctor on call, as the driver, Spartak Islamov, stepped on the gas pedal and lazily turned on the siren.

It took a man like Arkashka—someone who required neither

a weapon nor a helmet at Stalingrad—to make a joke of this sort. A month ago, on January 13, the newspapers had reported arrests of top-ranking Soviet doctors, including many of the Kremlin doctors:

THE ARREST OF A GROUP OF KILLER DOCTORS

Some time ago, organs of state security uncovered a terrorist group of doctors who planned to shorten the lives of leading figures in the Soviet Union by harmful treatment.

Among members in this group were: Professor M. S. Vovsi, a therapist; Professor V. N. Vinogradov, a therapist; Professor M. B. Kogan, a therapist; Professor B. B. Kogan, a therapist; Professor P. I. Yegorov, a therapist; Professor A. I. Feldman, an otolaryngologist; Professor Y. G. Etinger, a therapist; Professor A. M. Grinstein, a neuropathologist; and I. Mairorov, a therapist.

Documents and investigations conducted by medical experts have established that the criminals—hidden enemies of the people—carried out harmful treatment on their patients, thereby undermining their health.

The investigation established that members of the terrorist gang, by using their position as physicians and betraying the trust of their patients, deliberately and maliciously undermined the health of the latter, intentionally ignored objective studies of the patients, made wrong diagnoses that were not suitable for the actual nature of their illnesses, and then, by incorrect treatment, killed them.

The criminals confessed that in the case of Comrade A. A. Zhdanov they wrongly diagnosed his illness, concealed his myocardial infarction, prescribed a regimen that was totally inappropriate to his grave illness, and in this way killed Comrade Zhdanov. The investigation established that the criminals also shortened the life of Comrade A. S. Shcherbakov, by incorrectly treating him with very potent medicines, putting him on a fatal regimen, and in this way brought on his death.

These criminal doctors sought primarily to ruin the health of leading Soviet military cadres, incapacitate them, and thereby weaken the defense of the country. They tried to incapacitate Marshal A. M. Vasilevskiy, Marshal L. A. Govorov, Marshal I. S. Konev, General of the Army S. M. Shtemenko, Admiral G. I. Levchenko, and others. However, their arrest upset their evil plans and the criminals were not able to achieve their aims.

It has been established that all these killer doctors, these monsters who trod underfoot the holy banner of science and defiled the honor of men of science, were in the pay of foreign intelligence services.

Most of the members of this terrorist gang were associated with the international Jewish bourgeois nationalistic organization "Joint," created by American intelligence ostensibly to provide material aid to Jews in other countries. Actually, this organization, operating under the direction of American intelligence, carried out widespread espionage, terrorist, and other subversive activities in several countries, including the Soviet Union. Vovsi told the investigation that he had received a directive "to exterminate the foremost cadres in the USSR from the 'Joint' organization in the United States through Dr. Shimeliovich in Moscow and the Jewish bourgeois nationalist, Mikhoels."

Another news report:

SPIES AND MURDERERS UNDER THE MASK OF DOCTORS

The unmasking of the band of doctor-poisoners dealt a shattering blow to the American-English instigators of war.

The whole world can now see once again the true face of the slave master–cannibals from the USA and England.

The bosses of the USA and their English "junior partners" know that success in ruling another country cannot be achieved by peaceful means. Feverishly preparing for a new world war, they urgently sent their spies into the rear of the USSR and into the countries of the People's Democracy; they attempted to implement what the Hitlerites had failed to do—to create in the USSR their own subversive "fifth column." [...] It is also true that, besides these enemies, we still have another, namely, the lack of vigilance among our people.

Have no doubt but that when there is a lack of vigilance, there will be subversion. Consequently, to eliminate sabotage, vigilance must be restored in our ranks.

Spartak, the ambulance driver, didn't give a rip about Jesus, or Lazarus, or Yid doctors. He had read something about that in the newspapers, but thought it had nothing to do with him or any Jews he knew.

"I didn't know Jesus Christ was a doctor," he replied to Arkashka's quip.

An Azeri, Spartak would have been a Muslim had he not been an atheist like Arkashka.

"Remember Lazarus? The dead guy he brought back? Now, that's a *doctor*!"

"Was Lazarus a Jew also?"

"Good question, Spartakushka. Yes, I think so. Probably."

"Would he have raised a dead Russian?"

"That's an even better question, but it's uncharted territory. To know conclusively, you would have needed to show him a dead Russian and a dead Jew and see which one he selected for raising."

Arkashka let the train of thought develop silently in his mind, then burst out laughing.

"Or better, a *group* of dead Russians and a *group* of dead Jews . . ."

Arkashka paused again, letting the thought roll on in seclusion, then reported back, "There were no Russians two thousand years ago, we should note to be completely accurate. There were hunter-gatherers or some such, sitting in the trees, maybe, but in those dark, distant times, Yid doctors were already raising the dead!"

"You people are the best," muttered Spartak.

Spartak didn't see why this might be amusing, nor did he care, but he was glad to see Arkashka entertain himself. They were grunts from the front, *frontoviki*, members of a brotherhood, driving through nighttime Moscow with a siren on. It was a say-what-you-want situation. No politics in that ambulance.

Arkashka would have graduated at the top of his class, except for being nearly flunked by the idiot professor of Marxism-Leninism-Stalinism. He was unable to spew out a satisfactory analysis of Comrade Stalin's latest work, *Marksizm i Voprosy Yazykoznaniya. Marxism and Problems of Linguistics.*

Arkashka had flubbed that course godlessly. He had no problem grasping Marx, Engels, and dialectical materialism. Even Lenin was mostly understandable when taken in small doses. But the words of Comrade Stalin made no sense at all, no matter how many sleepless nights he devoted to chewing them.

Besides, being a Jew in 1953, Arkashka was lucky to have any gig, and riding with the ambulance was more than good enough.

A maid wearing a dark blue dress and a light blue apron opened the door. She was a young woman, roughly Arkashka and Spartak's age—late twenties, if that.

They walked through a big, cavernous hallway, Arkashka carrying his doctor's bag, Spartak carrying a stretcher.

With the medic missing, they would both need to carry out the old woman to get her to the ambulance. Some doctors weren't strong enough for this task, but Arkashka was fine. With no one shooting at you, with no land mines to trip, carrying out the sick seemed so easy that it felt like cheating.

Arkashka instantly grasped the incongruence of the situation.

"Why are we even here?" he asked himself, looking around. "These folks should be using the Kremlin hospital." Theirs was a simple, regional ambulance, the kind that took care of stroked-out old ladies who had no admiral sons or Kremlin connections. Besides, at the Kremlin hospital they had a ventilator—American.

The maid opened the door to a large room, where a middle-aged man sat in a massive armchair in front of a bed, watching an old woman.

The man was wearing a white undershirt and uniform pants with a thick red stripe along the side, indicating that, even in his undershirt, he was an admiral. He was also wearing a black patent leather belt, the sort one would wear to review parades or have an audience in the Kremlin.

Arkashka knew the admiral's name from front-line gossip. He had been in command during the defense of Leningrad. There, he deployed something called "the floating machine gun nests." These were, essentially, rafts, each holding a machine gun and a hapless lone soldier or sailor. The rafts were anchored at various points in the Gulf of Finland, around the city. If a gunner saw the Germans, he was expected to open fire, thereby giving away his position, and since there was no way to escape, this led to certain death. These were literally floating coffins.

Arkashka reminded himself that he was no longer a grunt, no

longer the guy who dragged maimed soldiers through the mine-
fields. He was a Soviet physician and, virulent nonsense in the newspapers notwithstanding, he was proud of his rank.

The old woman lay on the bed, beneath a large painting of two
deer by a stream. It would have been a peaceful scene, had it not
been life-sized and framed in gold. The artist was German. Obviously, this was a "trophy" from the war. The admiral had to have
commandeered a railroad car to get this monstrosity from Berlin
to Moscow.

The armchair looked like another trophy, a throne grand enough
for *der Führer.*

Arkashka nodded to the admiral but introduced himself to
the patient, whose name he had seen on the complaint: "Ol'ga
Petrovna, I am Dr. Arkady Kaplan. I am here to make you better."

The patient was taking rapid, shallow breaths. She was dishev-
eled, obviously dehydrated, unresponsive. Her mouth drooped on
the left side, a sign of a past stroke. According to the call, the stroke
occurred a year ago.

"Looks like she has been experiencing Cheyne-Stokes respiration for at least twenty-four hours, more likely forty-eight," Arkashka
estimated silently. "Almost certainly, she needs to be hospitalized—
or, perhaps, it's time to say good-bye."

Spartak gently set down the stretcher and left the room. He
would be called in later, to help carry the woman to the ambulance.

"Repeat your last name, young man," ordered the admiral, and
the combination of the tone of his voice and the smell of alcohol
on his breath told Arkashka that this wasn't going to go well.

After years as a medical student, Arkashka grew accustomed to
being addressed formally, as *vy.* This man used the familiar, *ty.*
This was a sign of contempt, which could only get worse after this
man got to contemplate Arkashka's last name. (It's unlikely that
non-Jewish Kaplans exist anywhere in the world.)

"Kaplan, Arkady Leonidovich," Arkashka repeated. He gave his full name.

"Ot vashego brata ne ubezhish," said the admiral. There is no escape from you.

Arkashka left this unanswered. "May I examine your mother, Comrade Admiral?"

Arkashka's preferred way of dealing with ethnic slurs and other forms of insult was to ignore them. This is an accepted approach in the medical profession, because a doctor who is regularly insulted may eventually start to believe in his own inferiority.

Kogan called it a mind-fuck, *mozgoyebaniye.*

Self-confidence is a component of clinical judgment, and a doctor whose clinical judgment is compromised is harm waiting to happen. Kogan had been getting this nonsense throughout his career, and to protect his patients, he had completely desensitized himself to it.

Or so he claimed over vodka one night. Imagine a surgeon infected by belief in his own inferiority.

"Now, *Abram*, this is my mother, understand?" said the admiral.

"Yes, Comrade Admiral. I understand this. Now I will measure her heart rate and listen to her heart."

Arkady let the slur pass. He picked up the old woman's right hand, the one not affected by the stroke. It felt limp.

"Ol'ga Petrovna, can you squeeze my hand?" he asked, knowing that she couldn't.

While her hand was in his, Arkashka took her pulse. It was around 120 beats per minute, about twice the normal. Respiratory rate was about thirty-six breaths per minute, about six times the normal. Blood pressure was eighty over forty, reptilian low.

"There are many of your brothers in Kremlyovka," said the admiral as Arkashka grabbed the stethoscope out of his doctor's bag. "You'd feel at home there."

Through the stethoscope, Arkashka heard scattered, rattling noises. That was the sound of rhonchi, a fancy way of saying junk in the airways.

"May we discuss the status of the patient, Comrade Admiral?"

"Kaplan, Kaplan. Abrasha."

The admiral pronounced the *r* in an exaggerated way intended to mimic Yiddish. It came out on a spectrum between *r* and *h*. "And during the war, where were you, Kaplan?"

"I was in Stalingrad, Comrade Admiral."

Arkashka's pronunciation was clear, as Moscow as it gets.

"Stalinghad . . . ," repeated the admiral in mocking accent. "I'll tell you where you were! In Kazan', behind the Ural, drinking Russian blood."

He was drunk, of course, but Arkashka was no stranger to drunks. The only thing to do was to go through the case, make the decisions that needed to be made, and get the fuck out.

"Comrade Admiral, I know this is very difficult . . . ," Arkashka carried on. "Your mother is breathing the way she is because her body isn't absorbing oxygen the way healthy bodies do. As carbon dioxide builds up, she compensates by breathing more rapidly. This is called Cheyne-Stokes respiration. I know it's difficult to accept, but this is how death begins."

"Molchat'!" shouted the admiral. Silence!

"The situation may not be hopeless, however," Arkashka soldiered on. "Your best course of action would be to take Ol'ga Petrovna to the Kremlin hospital, where they will be able to do a chest X-ray, do blood work. If appropriate, they may use a respirator, a machine that will help her breathe, at least for a while. Municipal Hospital Number One, where I work, doesn't have a respirator. My ambulance can transport her to Kremlyovka. You can come with us in the ambulance while your staff makes appropriate arrangements."

The admiral's hand grabbed Arkashka by the lapels of his white coat. The hand was strong, beefy. The palm was so large, it seemed to cover half of Arkashka's chest.

"Now you listen to me, Rabinovich. This is my mother. Mother! Understand?! She will not be going to Kremlyovka. Who do you think got her paralyzed to begin with?"

"There are excellent doctors . . ."

"Yids! Bloodsuckers! Murderers!"

Clearly, a calm, professional approach was failing Arkashka. He was alone in a room with a man whose grief was fueled with alcohol.

Yet, the bit about the Kremlin hospital couldn't be ignored. The idea that this man would deprive his mother of access to a ventilator was starting to make sense. He believed the Yids at Kremlyovka would kill her.

That was consistent with what was being published in the newspapers. The stories were mostly about Kremlyovka. The list of arrested doctors includes Stalin's personal physician, Vinogradov, one of the few non-Jews on the list.

Arkashka realized that the admiral was confused, alone, unclear about what his next strategic move would be. Unable to trust anyone as his mother lay dying, he had commandeered an ambulance much like he had commandeered the railroad cars to bring his loot from Germany.

This was madness, of course. What was Arkashka to do? Was there a way out of this trap?

He threw the question to the admiral.

"What do you suggest we do, Comrade Admiral?"

"We cure her right here."

Abrikosov slowly got out of his chair and brandished a short dagger that was hanging on his belt. It was a shiny ceremonial weapon, called *kortik* in Russian and a dirk in English. This weapon had an ivory handle. It was gold plated. Unsheathing it, the admiral placed its point against Arkashka's nose.

Arkashka didn't blink.

"Now, Abramovich, this is the *kortik* of a Soviet admiral. By this *kortik* I swear that nothing will stand between my mother and full recovery. You will stay here for as long as it takes to improve her breathing, and I will sit here with you for as long as it takes to make sure that this fine Russian woman walks again."

With these words, the admiral placed the unsheathed *kortik* across his knees.

Often you need time to make an irrational family member come to his senses, Arkashka decided.

He must do something, anything, to create an appearance of a therapeutic intervention.

He reached into the bag and produced a glass bottle containing saline solution, connected it to a catheter, and carefully inserted the needle into the woman's vein. Then he placed the bottle on the table next to the bed, well above the patient.

"Ol'ga Petrovna is severely dehydrated. This should help her for the time being."

The admiral's gaze remained focused on the *kortik*.

"Comrade Admiral, please understand that you called an ambulance. We would be happy to stabilize Ol'ga Petrovna and transport her. This is our job. But we are unable to stay here, because this woman needs to be in a hospital. We cannot give her the hospital care she needs. We need to make a decision."

He sat down and looked at the admiral, whose face remained placid. Arkashka looked at his watch. Family members frequently threaten doctors. Making good on the threat is something completely different. If this man had any sanity left in him, he would not act on impulse. He would recognize the consequences. He would recognize that killing doctors was still punishable by law, almost certainly, even if they were Jews, even now. Arkashka decided to give the man enough time to decompress. If this didn't work, nothing would.

Exactly fifteen minutes later, Arkashka looked at his watch again, got up, and, saying nothing, headed toward the door.

"By the honor of a Soviet officer," said Admiral Abrikosov, rising from the armchair and, before Arkashka reached the door, inserted the *kortik* in the doctor's back, then calmly returned to his mother's bedside.

Arkashka walked into the kitchen, where Spartak was drinking tea served to him by the maid.

"There is a knife in my back," he said.

Kogan was on service that night. His notes from that surgery are unusually detailed, even by his standards:

> **Preoperative Diagnosis:** Right hemothorax due to penetrating trauma with exsanguination.
> **Postoperative Diagnosis:** Same with intraoperative death.
> **Findings:** Massive hemothorax with stab wound to the pulmonary hilum primarily affecting the right superior pulmonary vein adjacent and into the pericardium. The wound was inflicted with a ceremonial dagger, 19.5 cm. long. The dagger has an ivory handle bearing the inscription: "To Admiral Abrikosov for bravery and inventiveness in the defense of Leningrad, I. Stalin."
>
> The hilt of the dagger is cast in gold. On both sides, the hilt is marked with the words: "In Reward."
> **Indication for Procedure:** This 35-year-old, previously healthy and active ambulance physician presents with

marked dyspnea, tachypnea, and hypotension with a blood pressure of 70/40 and heart rate of 160.

An emergency chest X-ray demonstrates a large right-sided pleural effusion coincident with an entry wound just lateral to the spine in the fifth inter space and medial to the posterior axillary line.

The entry wound measures only 1.5 cm. The patient displayed a decorative dagger, which the ambulance attendant had removed at his direction after the patient was stabbed. This event occurred approximately 27 minutes prior to the initiation of the procedure.

Description of Procedure: IV access was obtained and light general anesthesia was administered and deepened as tolerated after ongoing fluid resuscitation. Orotracheal intubation was performed and the patient was placed in the full lateral position. The chest was rapidly prepared with Betadine and a fifth inter-space incision was made anterior to the entry wound.

Several liters of clotted blood were removed rapidly and minimal ventilation was performed in order to rapidly assess the mechanism of injury. Irrigation was used to remove the deeper lying thrombus. The lung parenchyma was essentially spared. Attention was then turned to the hilum.

Inspection of the anterior vessels showed no evidence of pulmonary or bronchial artery injury.

The lung was then reflected medially and an area of posterior thrombus was identified well behind the phrenic nerve.

This area was suspicious for a pulmonary vein injury and was approached as carefully as possible.

A large defect was seen in the right superior pulmonary vein continuing from the pleural space into the pericardium.

The pericardium was lacerated inferior to the venous laceration.

Once the defect was visualized, a light 4-0 silk suture line was begun to close the defect. Unfortunately, several minutes were needed to find the suture and while the chest was flooded with irrigation the patient arrested.

An arterial air embolus was suspected. Open chest cardiac massage was begun and the defect was closed with good hemostasis. The pericardium was then widely opened and no further injuries were seen.

Continued resuscitation was performed for another 30 minutes. Despite these measures, the heart continued to fibrillate and a proper rhythm could not be established.

The patient was pronounced dead in the operating room at 5:53 a.m.

The retractor was removed and the incision was closed with interrupted suture.

Kogan's objective here was to create record, to show who killed his friend and to document the extent of injuries.

If you are a homicide detective, you want notes these good, but you rarely get them.

Kogan felt pride every time he walked through the entrance of Pervaya Gradskaya. The hospital was built in 1832 at a time of Russia's great imperial ambitions. It was a grand place with massive columns, a cupola, and two small bell towers rising incongruently but charmingly from the sides of the portico at the main entrance.

Kogan often noted that the building looked even more impressive than Johns Hopkins Hospital in the city of Baltimore, state of

Maryland. He chose Hopkins as a benchmark because it's such a storied place, especially for surgeons.

On February 23, seven days after his friend died on the operating table, Kogan was summoned to the hospital's Special Department.

Kogan's strategy in dealing with the Special Department was the same as his strategy in dealing with fellow doctors, nurses, and janitorial staff: listen well, tell the truth, show respect.

The director's office was small, carved up in more than a century of reorganizations. It looked like a small sliver of a ballroom. The walls were green; a tilted portrait of Stalin looked down at the visitor's chair. The ceiling was impossibly high, and the lone, uncovered window took up the entire side of the room, giving the hospital's most ominous department the feel of a glass palace.

The man running the Special Department was rumored to be a colonel of national security. Most people in that rank will not give you their last names. This man was different. He used only his last name: Zaytsev.

Zaytsev didn't get up when Kogan walked in. When Kogan extended his hand, Zaytsev's hand remained on the massive, pre-revolutionary walnut desk.

Zaytsev drilled Kogan with his wide blue eyes. The two men were about the same age, early fifties, except Zaytsev was pudgy and looked officious in a blue gabardine suit and even a tie. Kogan was in his white coat. He would be returning to work, God willing.

"I will not play games, Sasha," Zaytsev began. "We have a problem here at Pervaya Gradskaya."

Kogan knew that when men like Zaytsev promised to refrain from playing games, they were, in fact, starting a game.

The doctor cringed a little after being addressed by his first name. This man wasn't a friend, and decorum in medicine was important. Such were his manners; everything about Zaytsev was backward.

Zaytsev pointed to a chair, and Kogan settled in.

"A young doctor here, Arkady Kaplan, now deceased, was conducting religious propaganda with an ambulance driver. He said Jesus Christ was a Yid doctor. Were you aware of this?"

"No," said Kogan.

This was no surprise. They got to Spartak after the stabbing, and with his friend dead, he had no reason to protect Kaplan.

Kogan had no idea precisely what was said in that ambulance, but it had to have been funny. He smiled. Arkashka would have wanted him to.

"What can you tell me about him, Sasha?"

"Nothing to tell, Comrade Zaytsev. I thought he was a talented young doctor. I met him before he enrolled in the medical institute. It was in Stalingrad. He was a medic. I was hoping he would get additional training and become a surgeon."

"Stalingrad. Medic. Interesting . . . When he was evacuating the wounded, do you believe he got close to German positions?"

"I presume. This is one of the dangers of the job, being in no-man's-land."

"Do you believe that he may have come *very* close, close enough to get recruited by the Germans?"

"Why would that happen? And how? He was Jewish, by nationality, as you should be able to see in the dossier."

"Exactly! Who would suspect him? Next question: do you believe Kaplan had the skills required to operate a radio?"

"I don't know. What makes you ask?"

"I am not at liberty to discuss. The investigation is ongoing. Have you known this man outside work?"

"Well, yes, he was a frequent guest at my apartment."

"Did he speak German?"

"Yes."

"Do you?"

"Yes. You know from my dossier, I studied in Berlin."

"I wanted to hear that from you, man to man. The professors you had in Berlin; were they German?"

"Some were. I ask that you familiarize yourself with my dossier, Comrade Zaytsev. I studied in Germany in 1926 through the end of 1928. I was sent there by the Commissariat for Health. It was official business."

"And your professors, where are they now?"

"Some died in the war, some in the concentration camps; one practices in London, another, I believe, in America."

"Where in America?"

"Boston."

"Where in Boston?"

"Harvard University."

"Are you in touch with them?"

"No. Not at all."

"It says in the dossier you have relatives abroad . . ."

"Yes, I do. My parents left Odessa in 1918, just as I was joining the Red Army."

"Are they living?"

"I don't believe they are. Though I have never been informed of their deaths."

"And you have siblings?"

"My sister was in Denmark, and my brother is in New York."

"Are you in touch with them?"

"No."

Of course, Zaytsev knew that maintaining ties with relatives abroad was suicidal. Fortunately, he didn't seem to have been informed about Aleksandr and Vladimir's only post-emigration meeting, in Berlin in 1928.

"Do you believe Kaplan would have been capable of a provocation against a Soviet officer?"

"No, why would he do that? He was a decorated veteran of the Great Patriotic War."

"As I said, the matter is under investigation, I am not at liberty to discuss the details."

"Well, no, I don't believe that. If he was with a patient, he would have been focused on discharging his duties as a doctor. I know this because I trained him."

"Did he have religious, fanatical views that would have prompted him to sacrifice himself in order to dishonor a Soviet officer?"

"Nothing in our interactions would have suggested that, and I am afraid I am unable to speculate. I wouldn't want to lead you in the wrong direction. What does all of this have to do with me?"

"You were his friend, and he died on your operating table. Your notes from that surgery have been examined thoroughly, and they are *too* thorough, as though someone is trying to cover tracks."

"Cover tracks? What tracks?"

"I read that document myself, and I can tell you what I thought: I thought that you killed him, Sasha. The admiral, Admiral Abrikosov, said that Kaplan declined to provide treatment for his mother and kept looking at his watch, causing the admiral, who was grief-stricken, to inflict a superficial wound. Sasha, you are a doctor, can you imagine a doctor refusing to help a dying patient? The ambulance driver confirmed that his wounds were superficial when he arrived in the hospital, and then he ended up on your operating table."

"What are you saying?"

"That Kaplan's wound, as described by witnesses, was not as severe as the wound you say he died of. It's so laughable that we returned the dagger to Admiral Abrikosov, with our sincere apologies."

"Are you really saying that *I* killed him?"

"Yes, actually, we are starting to come to this conclusion."

"I did nothing of the sort. Why would I do that?"

"Because it was a part of your long-standing plan, dating back to Stalingrad."

"But, Comrade Zaytsev, I remind you again that Dr. Kaplan was of Jewish nationality. The newspapers tell us that Jewish doctors are killing people of *Russian* nationality. In this, shall we say, hypothesis of yours, why would you think I killed another Jew?"

"Simple! Sometimes you have to kill one of your own, so people won't think you are killing only Russians."

"To cover tracks?"

"To cover tracks."

"I see. So you hypothesize that Kaplan and I were German spies, recruited in Stalingrad?"

"It does look as though you were, when you put all the pieces together. They recruited Kaplan when he was pretending to evacuate the wounded, and he recruited you."

"Would it be helpful to you if I reminded you that Germans killed millions of Jews, presumably including Dr. Kaplan's family, plus about forty of my distant cousins? It should be in the dossiers."

"Yes, and this is exactly what gives you cover."

"That's preposterous."

"And we cannot, at this point, rule out the possibility that other intelligence services were involved."

"Really? You can't rule this out? Which ones?"

"America, England, the usual."

"May I remind you that they were our allies during the war?

Why would they be working with the Germans to recruit Dr. Kaplan?"

"Yes, we thought of that. Because even then they could foresee that the wartime alliance was fleeting."

"So the Americans were in a *secret* alliance with Germany to recruit a Soviet medic in Stalingrad?"

"And pass on messages to you, from Jewish agencies in New York. And Denmark was collaborating with Germany, I should remind you."

"Oh my . . . I don't even know what to do with Denmark. I am not clear on my sister's whereabouts, alas, so I can't help you. What do you think my motivations would be in doing all this?"

"To undermine the Soviet Union."

"There is only one flaw that I see: you have left out the whirling dervishes. I don't know how you can work them in, but I think you can. Let me ask you this, admittedly from a doctor's perspective: do you actually believe all of this, Comrade Zaytsev?"

"Does it matter what I believe?"

"I guess not. Will you be arresting me now?"

"No, not now. We want to give you the opportunity to confess your crimes and surrender publicly, at the hospital staff meeting, which will be attended by journalists and members of the public.

"You will come to the meeting as though you are a member of the audience, then you will rise and take the podium and you will make a full confession, and you will point out other members of your secret organization, who will be there."

"I don't have a secret organization, so I am afraid I can't help you."

"We will refresh your memory. We will have the names of individuals involved. We will share it with you before the meeting."

"You want me to falsely accuse good people. That's indecent. And I don't understand why you wish to make a spectacle of this.

Why wouldn't you handle my arrest in a customary way, by sending a Black Maria to my apartment in the middle of the night? Is this something new? I've never seen this before."

"You are very perceptive, Sasha. Yes, we want this case to become more open, more visible than it has been. As you've read in the newspapers, we are unmasking conspirators, but it's all been done in secret. We are uncovering conspiracies, but the people don't know what we are doing. Now we are in a different place in this operation. We want the people to see us at work. We want their support, even their participation in defending the motherland from outside elements. And, Sasha, you are going to see many things you haven't seen before. The situation is about to change dramatically."

"I am sure I will. But just to make sure I understand, what am I being offered, should I agree to take part in this spectacle?"

"I am not authorized to make any offers. But you are welcome to take a week to think."

"What if I say no?"

"Then you will be letting me down. And yourself. I said you were a sensible man. I vouched for you."

Kogan thanked him. At home, he packed Dusya's suitcases—she had two—and when she returned from work, he told her to go.

There was no point in having her share his future, like the wives of the Decembrists. Kogan urged her to testify against him—even plead for his execution—when the time comes, i.e., if the organs of state security choose to produce the dance of jurisprudence. *Tanets umirayuschego evreya.* The dance of the dying Yid.

The idea that the wife must share her husband's fate is utterly absurd to begin with. It might have been easier to convince her to reject the idea of self-sacrifice had their marriage been good. She would have accepted this as a token of love. Alas, their love was a thing of the past.

Their marital fidelity was among the victims of that war, but that wasn't the worst of it. He had a succession of "front wives"; she a succession of "front husbands." The war ended, but normalcy didn't return. Or maybe it did return, but in a changed form, with neoplasms hanging off its innards.

There was a long tail of complexities, but they still took care of each other, out of duty, perhaps. And now he told her to go, liberated her. He knew exactly where she would go, and it was, oddly, just fine with him.

"Run, Dus'ka, save yourself. I am a dead man," he implored, and this time she left.

"Perhaps they will leave her alone after they come for me," he thought as she closed the door of their apartment on Ulansky Street. "Thank God, at least she is Ukrainian."

In his transition from machine gunner to surgeon, Kogan learned that the way you feel about death is determined by where you are.

Killing is a natural act when you are nestled behind the shrapnel shield of a Maxim. Your compassion is suspended; your victims are dehumanized. When you are a surgeon whose job it is to save the life of a wounded soldier, life acquires paramount importance.

Dr. Kogan feels no regret about the deaths caused by machine-gunner Kogan. For whatever reason, the boundary between these two men is solid. Never has Kogan contemplated crossing back.

"Aleksandr Sergeyevich, if you had a chance, would you have killed Hitler?" Arkashka Kaplan asked him over vodka a couple of years ago.

Arkashka was the only man who had the ability to get him to confront so fundamental an issue. His integrity and intelligence were unmatched. More important, Kogan trusted the younger man's intellectual rigor, his willingness to hold himself accountable.

He trusted Levinson's integrity and intelligence, too, but as an ethicist Levinson was a disaster. Levinson's thinking always defaulted to strategy. He set goals and plotted the best way to attain them.

"I did have a chance to kill Hitler, I think," Kogan responded to Arkashka that night. "I think I saw him at a beer hall in Munich, before he was *der Führer*. Or, at least, I was told that we were sitting near some corporal, Austrian. He was surrounded by thugs, I was told. When he became more prominent, I thought he looked sort of familiar."

"You could have laced his beer with something bad. You knew how."

"I suppose I could have."

"Isn't it tantalizing to think that you could have saved the lives of millions of people?"

"Yes, that's one way to look at it. But I didn't have any basis for believing that this thug would become *der Führer*. I would have had to kill many thugs, and I still wouldn't know whether the right one was among them."

"We are not talking about diagnosis."

"Are you trying to narrow the question?"

"Yes. In an abstract hypothetical situation, would you, as a physician, have been able to justify killing that man if you knew he would ultimately become *der Führer*?"

"For the sake of argument?"

"Yes, for the sake of argument."

"What about the consequences to me?"

"We aren't talking about the consequences tonight."

"I don't know," said Kogan, and that was the truth.

Now Kogan is facing a difficult ethical quandary. His arrest, in the midst of a spectacle, is days away. Likely, pogroms are next. Hypothetically, if one individual can be, as they say, "liquidated" to save millions of lives, would he, Dr. Kogan, have the resolve to do it?

Alas, Kogan's answer is unchanged. He has no idea.

Had the answer been yes, the rest would be strategy.

2

The evening of February 24 is well suited for disposing of corpses and Black Marias.

The frost is at once fresh and dry, the sort that stopped Charles XII, Napoleon, and Hitler. If you are a soldier in a stranded army, fear that frost. But if you have a thick white sheepskin coat, a high collar, a proper hat, and good felt boots, the frost will be your keeper.

For the burial, Kogan chooses a well at the dacha of Professor N, whose scientific work fuses the disciplines of tumor biology and Marxism-Leninism. According to the esteemed professor, human malignancy is the result of poor moral-ethical upbringing among cancer sufferers. This unified theory of cancer opens possibilities for ideological interventions.

It's not to Kogan's credit that he could barely suppress the delight he felt, three months earlier, when he learned that the professor was taken away in a Black Maria from his Moscow apartment.

"What about his wife?" asks Levinson.

"Vermin also," Kogan assures him. "It runs in families. Let's be fair: in our country, you don't have to be a decent person in order to get arrested."

"You surgeons would like the world to believe that you are detached from death," says Levinson. "Actually, you love the dead."

"And actors? You love the living?"

"You, Kogan, are a surgeon without an OR," says Levinson.

"And you, Levinson, are an actor from a burned-down theater."

"And who am I?" asks Lewis, climbing behind the wheel of the Black Maria.

"My friend," says Kogan, getting in on the other side.

"And the only family I have," says Levinson, getting in after him.

The doors are slammed shut, and the Black Maria pulls out of its hiding place, heading toward Zapadnaya Street.

"Do you think your friend suspects anything?" asks Lewis.

He remembers her name well, very well, but there is no reason to let the old men know that, despite his efforts, thoughts about the girl have been creeping into his mind, interfering with his never-ending assessment of his exceedingly complicated, one might say hopeless, situation.

"Kima?" asks Kogan. "I am sure not."

Lewis waits. Surely Kogan, a compulsive storyteller, will let some information slip.

"You can't tell by the way she talks, but she has a clear head, like her father," says Kogan.

Lewis waits.

"The Commissar," Kogan continues.

Lewis looks up inquisitively.

"A hint: the name Kima."

Kima is a woman's name based on the acronym Communist International for Youth, KIM. Had Kima's parents had a son, his name, presumably, would have been Kim.

"Her father was in the Comintern for Youth?"

Kogan nods.

"Comintern for Youth was Zeitlin . . . Yefim Zeitlin."

Lewis makes no effort to remember the names of Soviet officials. They enter his memory effortlessly, on their own, joining a hall of fame next to the ballplayers of the Negro Leagues. The latter gallery was boarded up abruptly in 1931, as Lewis left America.

"Exactly!" shouts Kogan. "Hence, Kima Yefimovna."

"Her last name is Zeitlina?"

"Petrova . . . her mother's name. She is listed as Russian. This might save her."

"Zeitlin was executed in 1938," says Lewis, whose memory extends to statistics of terror, too. "What about her mother?"

"Mysterious death, in 1942," says Kogan. "Most people who blow out their brains can't help leaving a gun nearby . . ."

"She didn't?"

"No. And the suicide note was a carbon copy. The girl was ten. She grew up in an orphanage in Karaganda."

"Did you know her parents?"

"Met her father a few times in 1918. Solomon knew him better. I first saw her here, in the dungeon beneath GORPO, in bottle redemption. Do you expect to encounter an enlightened face when you redeem bottles? But there she was, her eyes burning in the dungeon."

"And you became her friend."

Now Lewis knows where she works, at the GORPO, an acronym for City Consumer Organization, a cooperative.

"Mentor, for the lack of a better word," says Kogan. "An intelligent young woman would not get much of that in Karaganda. I invited her to tea; I prescribed Akhmatova."

To Lewis, this is a familiar choice.

"From Akhmatova, I moved to Tsvetaeva and Mandelstam. Always start with the moderns. If your student is a woman, appeal to the lyrical. Ask her what she thinks, and when she is ready, cautiously mention feelings. Then, after a few months, if signs of feelings are observed, prescribe Zoshchenko and Babel, to develop a sense of the absurd and a sense of history."

"Absurdity and history . . . aren't they the same, in your country?"

"Yes, Comrade Lewis, definitely, proudly, yes!" says Kogan. "But that's something you learn at home, not at an orphanage. If you see signs of feelings and instill the sense of the absurd, you work back to the foundation: Pushkin. Starting with Pushkin is wrong. Without proper preparation, Pushkin is nothing but pretty verse and cheap melodrama.

"Think of *Onegin*: Tatyana loves Onegin. Onegin doesn't love Tatyana, but changes his mind later. He does . . . he doesn't . . . he does . . . *oy*! He shoots a friend at fifteen paces. Bang-bang . . . *basta*! Write a dim-witted opera, stage a ballet. *Narishkeit!* But if you are able to feel and laugh, you've beaten history at its game, and then the real Pushkin awaits you in his debauched glory."

"I am familiar with the curriculum," says Lewis.

He is, after all, a walking testament to its effectiveness.

The Black Maria pulls up to the darkened dacha of Professor N. Since the houses on Zapadnaya Street stand vacant and shuttered during the winter, there is no reason to hurry.

Kogan bounces out of the cab, opens the gate of Zapadnaya Number Four, and climbs onto the running board.

Tied with the chain that under normal circumstances suspended a bucket, three partially clad white corpses are laid out next to the well.

Sadykov is positioned three meters from the well, a chain looped twice under his arms. The nineteen-year-olds lie closer to the well, the chain passed once under their arms and tied in knots under the armpits. All three are in undershorts, their milk-colored skin on the verge of transparency.

"Commanders first," says Levinson.

The skin of that which once was Lieutenant Sadykov is cold and slippery. Lewis fights the gag reflex.

The lieutenant is propped up, folded over the edge of the well.

"Let him drop," says Levinson to Kogan, who is holding the winch handle.

Sadykov's body goes over the edge, dangling on the chain. The chain tightens, and one of the nineteen-year-olds starts to slide toward the well, pulled by the descending Sadykov.

"Help him to the edge," commands Levinson. Lewis feels queasy. Levinson and Kogan are unmoved.

"This is the land of the dead," Lewis declares to himself. Frozen, like a corpse dangling on a chain. The nineteen-year-old is doubled over, his arms and face hanging over the water.

"Now, send him," commands Levinson, taking the right leg and motioning to Lewis to take the left.

"I didn't come to arrest *him*," says Levinson, sensing Lewis's reluctance to take part. "He came for me."

"I know . . . it was war," says Lewis, taking the left leg and easing the corpse over the edge.

A moment later, the boy is dangling above Sadykov, and the third corpse moves sled-like toward the well.

"Kogan," says Levinson curtly. "Hold it. Don't let the handle spin."

"Yes, *komandir*."

"Let's help him," says Levinson, and he and Lewis position the boy over the edge, his blank eyes turned to the comrades below.

As the last corpse goes over the edge, Kogan drops to the ground, letting the handle spin. The bodies hit the water with three distinct splashes.

"The beauty of this is that we can always fish them out and bury them," says Kogan as Lewis bends over the edge to let out a stream of vomit.

"I've seen this reaction in first-year medical students," says Kogan, his hand resting on the back of doubled-over Lewis.

"And I've seen it in actors," counters Levinson.

"Actors? I've seen it in the audience," says Kogan.

"When?"

"When *you* were onstage!"

Indeed, halfway through his career at GOSET, Levinson became known as "the janitor of human souls." It's also true that sometime in the thirties, the theater wags had stenciled his name on the janitor's closet and on every bucket therein.

Many stories were told about the Levinson-Mikhoels *broyges* (rivalry). Here is one: in a nasty, public altercation in 1932, at a time when Mikhoels suffered from a crippling depression, which Levinson regarded as a sign of weakness, *der komandir* shouted: *"Gey shpil Kinig Lir, Khaver Direktor!"* Go play King Lear, Comrade Director!

Translation: Your career is done, perform your dance of the dying swan, make us cry if you still can, and, please, *zayt azoy git*, have the decency to stiffen after the curtain falls.

This attack occurred at a theater-wide meeting. Some people laughed: a few disgruntled actors, the janitor, the fireman.

In an article about the staging of *Lir*, Mikhoels attempted to obfuscate this ugly moment:

"My life in 1932 was filled with grief. Over a very short time,

I lost several people who were dear to me. These great losses affected me so profoundly that I started to contemplate leaving the stage altogether. The prospect of going onstage to play my former roles became intolerable. These roles contained comic episodes, which amused the audience. To me, laughter was alienating. I was envious of people who could laugh, since at the time I was internally deprived of this ability. I had made a firm decision to abandon stage. But my theater comrades had resolved to return my interest to life and work, and with increasing frequency they said, 'When you play *Lir* . . .'"

Mikhoels accepted Levinson's challenge.

He performed that swan song, and he kept its beat, and he didn't die for another decade and a half, an era when people vanished by the million.

In the same article, Mikhoels describes Levinson as a hardworking mediocrity with a "nasal voice, lower than average musicality, and less than a natural sense of rhythm."

Worse, "fate didn't give him the opportunity to obtain proper training," Mikhoels wrote. "As compensation, he was given immense determination, stamina, and an overarching drive to prevail by force. That's how he educated himself. Everything he knows he picked up on his own, by overpowering his nature. Now his knowledge is considerable, albeit empirical, forced and disjointed. Like most actors in our theater, Levinson is a passive thinker. He lacks the capacity to generalize."

In his universe, Mikhoels was both the Creator and the Master.

Not only could he direct the director directing him as an actor, but he could write a review, publicly humiliating members of his own ensemble, on the pages of the journal *Teatr*.

These were the kindest words Mikhoels could squeeze out of himself on the subject of Levinson.

To be an actor, especially if your main interest is comedy, you have to read voraciously, and voracious reading was not for Levinson, not because he couldn't read, but because he couldn't sit. He needed to be engaged, he needed something to do. His brain was powerful, but not nimble. He had only one joke. It was done with a straight face and was rooted in his character. Zuskin was much funnier. Mikhoels was in a different league altogether.

GOSET employed a plethora of actors who had been instructed in a variety of training schools, but the majority had no training at all.

Levinson was squarely in that majority.

He was an autodidact, and autodidacts are rarely nimble thinkers. They can amass facts—vast storerooms of facts—but they are too uncertain of themselves to get comfortable with doubt, humility, and nuance. Indeed, the more their storerooms of facts expand, the less flexible they become. They start believing that no one understands them, that their critics are conceited fools.

Anyone can amass facts, but it takes wisdom to connect them.

Mikhoels saw *der komandir* as his responsibility, his potential vulnerability.

Why did this soldier need theater? And why did he have to end up at Mikhoels's theater?

Clearly, Levinson wasn't, strictly speaking, an actor. Was he even—*truly*—a soldier? Levinson's stubbornness—punctuated by infrequent eruptions of genius—could reduce directors to tears. Was this man ever able to take orders from a higher-ranking officer? He may have been highly effective in the forest, as Robin Hood, but not reporting to Robin Hood. He would have excelled in the Paris Commune, on the barricades.

And surely he was just the sort of *royte komandir*—red

commander—you would want to terrorize the White Army and its foreign sponsors along the Trans-Siberian Railroad, as he so famously did.

Who would give you orders in the Siberian taiga? The howling wind? The wolves? The hibernating bears? It had to be Levinson versus the world, Mikhoels presumed.

At another time, Mikhoels might have added that a man of Levinson's makeup would have done exceedingly well leading death-defying feats of ragtag fighters in the Jewish ghettos of Central European cities and—of course—the forests, but that calamity was a few years away at the time Mikhoels wrote his vicious screed in *Teatr*.

Since Levinson and Mikhoels were the sort of adversaries who hardly speak to each other, Mikhoels had no way to determine whether Levinson was (1) the kind of brigand who seeks glorious death in battle, or (2) the kind whose objective is to kill and flee. How do you ascertain whether you are dealing with a Type 1 or Type 2 lunatic, except by spending time with said lunatic, observing him in action, perhaps even drinking vodka with him in order to make a conclusive diagnosis? This Mikhoels couldn't force himself to do.

What Mikhoels understood was indeed troublesome. What if something in Levinson's head went cosmically wrong and he started to act? What if he decided to form a terrorist group or ignite a slave rebellion? Wouldn't he (Mikhoels) be held accountable for this act of madness?

To analyze Levinson, Mikhoels resorted to the shortcut of the Stanislavsky Method, a philosophy of sorts that directs the actor to apply his entire being to portray the characters that appear onstage. Mikhoels didn't use the method. He shaped characters out of aspects of himself, just like God created Eve out of one of Adam's ribs rather than the entire Adam. With leftover ribs, an actor can shape a variety of very different characters. Mikhoels had a storeroom of characters which he could combine as he saw fit. He knew Stanislavsky well enough to accept his assurances that there was no such thing as a single Stanislavsky method. He had taught different approaches at different times and in different settings.

Still, Mikhoels found it useful to consider whether Levinson's experience informed the characters he portrayed onstage or whether the characters he portrayed informed Levinson's experience.

In his case, it was clearly the latter.

Let us unpack this dichotomy. When your characters inform your experience, you are intent on making the world conform to your will; you are creating the universe in your own image; you become the Creator. Only a playwright is entitled to such power.

If your experience shapes your characters, you are safe. You know where the stage ends. You realize that after you go home, you stop being Kinig Lir and become yourself. Your door is firmly closed to allowing characters to shape experience, and you will have no trouble refraining from slaying villains on Groky Street.

If you are allowing the characters you portray to shape your experience offstage, could it be that you are also invisibly allowing your experience to shape your characters? You could be locked in a cosmic spiral—cosmic because, having relinquished gravity, you are unable to distinguish your up from your down as you speed through the dimensions of madness.

In 1936, while *Lir* was still running, Levinson heard a rumor that his nemesis had authorized a series of concept drawings of King Richard.

Skeptical of putting on another play about a monarch, Levinson went to the Lenin Library and located the text of *Richard II* in a prerevolutionary translation into Russian. He was preparing a case against the play, which he was going to present to the meeting of the GOSET collective, in conjunction with a motion to relieve Mikhoels of his duties as artistic director.

The translation was stilted and academic, yet the story sent chills down Levinson's spine: a usurper and his satraps murder an ineffectual monarch.

Surely, Mikhoels would cast himself as the bumbling, doomed king. He would inject his character with complexity, faith, and moral superiority over his killers.

That would leave Mikhoels in need of a strong Bolingbroke, the leader of the revolution, someone who understood that objective laws of history inevitably demand regicide, a *komandir* from another time. Was any member of the ensemble better schooled in the art of prevailing by force? Who at GOSET could play *der komandir* better than *Komandir* Levinson?

After reading the play, Levinson went up to Mikhoels's office, the sanctum he had avoided for over a decade. The reception room door was ajar. In the inner office, Mikhoels lay on a leather sofa. His shoes were in the center of the room, atop a small pile of manuscripts. He was writing on a pad.

Mikhoels seemed startled, obviously annoyed.

"I know we haven't been the best of friends . . ." said Levinson in Yiddish. "But I have to agree with your choice of Shakespeare."

Levinson stood in the doorway to avoid towering over the sofa.

"Thank you, *Khaver* Levinson." Comrade Levinson. Very formal.

Mikhoels sat up. Height was unavoidably an element of their interplay.

"I've read the play," said Levinson. "It's really about our revolution."

"*Our* revolution?"

Yes, strong leaders like Bolingbroke were the stokers of our worker-peasant revolution. That matter was beyond dispute. Levinson had come to Mikhoels to negotiate a peace treaty, to trade concessions, to secure the part of a heroic leader, not to be put on the spot.

"I can't recall a revolution . . . how does it end?"

Levinson recited his own translation:

Ikh for bald opvashn, inem Heylikn Land
Dos merderishe blut
Fun mayn zindiker hant,

Mikhoels repeated the line, his mind bouncing it into Russian or German.

"Yes, *Richard II* would be an excellent selection," Mikhoels said. "Of course, in Yiddish, the Bolingbroke conspiracy would be reminiscent of the Protocols of the Elders of Zion, and that final declaration would be, I'd say, passionately Zionist.

"I don't think the audience will have the courage to applaud. They'd be looking around to make sure that no one is watching. Then they would go home, lock the doors, and cry. I am not critical of that play, *Khaver* Levinson, because we are, first of all, educators, but I have no plans to stage it."

Levinson stood silently.

"You've probably heard of concept drawings for Richard, but you've read the wrong Richard. I was thinking *Richard III.*"

Mikhoels's left hand rose slowly to his forehead. His index finger tapped against the bridge of the nose, with two more fingers landing behind it to transform his soaring forehead into a blackboard.

"*Richard III,*" Mikhoels repeated. The subtext was hard to miss:

Count them if you are able, Levinson: not two, but three. *Richard Three.*

Levinson turned around and left the room. In the hallway, he expected to hear an explosion of hysterical laughter, yet he heard nothing. Mikhoels was done.

"Look, comrades, why don't you walk back to the house, and I'll get rid of the truck," says Lewis.

"As the commander, I agree," says Levinson. "One young man can do this better than two old ones."

"Take this," says Levinson, handing Lewis a heavy, meter-long sword, its scabbard attached to a wide, well-oiled belt.

The blade is curved, the handle long enough for the sword to be held with two hands. Lewis can't resist the temptation to let the sword pivot from side to side. The handle is so perfect a counter-weight to the blade that the sword seems to move on its own.

"*Krasnaya kavaleriya,*" he says, his hand gliding over the curve of the scabbard. Red cavalry.

3

Iosif Vissarionovich Stalin devotes his early morning hours to watching children play.

His children are not flesh and blood. They come from illustrations from magazines he hangs on the once barren walls of his study. These are idyllic scenes: a girl picking flowers, a boy holding a model plane.

His mind is reaching heights of clarity he hasn't known before.

He goes to bed in early hours of the morning, after guests stumble out the door (the dacha has one low step) into the massive limousine.

At night, in solitude of his private quarters, he hears the floorboards creak. The sounds resemble footsteps, albeit disjointed, like little jaunts to no particular place. Before he falls asleep, he hears a sound akin to purring. It gives him warmth, and in the early hours of the morning, he sees the children step off the illustrations and play in the sunlight of the coming day.

Thus, on the morning of February 25, he sees a girl pick flowers on the carpet in the Big Dining Room. A boy puts wings on an airplane in the Small. Day after day, he adds children to his displays, and in the mornings, they stir. At dawn, the children are his companions, and then they vanish, to give him room to wield affairs of state.

Sleep no longer matters to the Czar. Two hours out of twenty-four are quite enough, even too long. Less may be better if clarity is his goal.

At night, he thinks that he can feel the breath of history. His cause is just, his victory assured. The Czar's orders fly to every corner of his czardom. He needs freight trains, as many as can be spared, but he stops short of choking all production.

And what if choking occurs? What would he rather have, a Yid-free land, where children play, or wagons of rusting iron, big mountains of coal, and great corrals of sheep and goats?

The Czar knows all one needs to know about the Jews. They kill each other for a cause. There is no better sport to watch. Remember that treacherous Yid Zinoviev, grabbing his executioners' feet, licking their boots, shouting something about *shema* and *Adonoy*, their God? Forget your God; your *Adonoy* is mine, Zinoviev! He serves the Czar! He works for Stalin. And he is naming names.

The lists are often on Stalin's mind. He can imagine the multitude of Jewish, foreign-sounding names, and he can see the gallows he'll construct for killer doctors who had the gall to plot against him.

He'll stand where Czar Ivan stood to watch beheadings.

Barbaric? No! When teaching is your goal, more blood is better. Hang some, behead a few. Then, stand upon a tower and watch the start of lynching, the pogrom, the biggest of all time, a Kristallnacht times ten, or times a hundred! Americans will telegraph a protest, but what strength do they have? Bogged down in Korea, they have no real army. His army is the biggest the world has seen. Let's say Americans blow up the atom. He'll blow up hydrogen then!

His soul dances amid the flames . . .

As the pogroms slow down to give the weary Muscovites a chance to sleep and to recover from days of murder, fire, and rape, surviving vermin will start emerging from their holes and run in the direction of the waiting trains. Their own Lazar Kaganovich, a product of deicidal seed, Stalin's Minister of Transportation, is making preparations.

Should Foul Lazar be placed on the last train, as captain of a sinking ship? Perhaps. And yet a bullet in the head is more dependable than rails. Give Beria the pistol . . . then Beria will get his bullet from someone else. It's time . . . use Zhukov? And dispatch Molotov . . .

In morning solitude, the Czar sucks life from happy children and makes his plans.

After making rooster in the violinist's brass bed, Tarzan rolls off Kent and falls asleep.

To avoid forming the impression that they are living like a man and a woman, Tarzan never talks after rooster. A long and rewarding day of adventure has come to an end.

There is a roof over their heads. Not just any roof, but a big log house full of oak furniture, crystal vases, even two verandas for drinking tea. Looking at a painting in the living room, Kent and Tarzan can see that the owner of the dacha is a nosed one, *zhid*, or at least an Armenian.

In bright aquamarine hues, it depicts a violinist facing a powerful wind gust, pointing his instrument toward its origin. A shock of white hair trails the entranced musician, then widens, smoke-like, behind him, flying off the canvas.

Since this is February, it doesn't look like the musician will be returning soon, and if he does, Kent and Tarzan are going to make a run for it. A militia investigation would produce nothing.

Bottles, candy wrappers, and empty tins have accumulated

next to their bed as evidence of prosperity and bliss. Kent likes to watch Tarzan unwrap hard candy with his strong, tattooed hands. The word *"privet,"* greetings, inked in unevenly between the knuckles of Tarzan's right hand, is intended to be the last thing you see before you black out. The word *"tovarischam,"* to comrades, is squeezed in between the knuckles of his left hand. Viewed together, the two fists extend greetings to comrades.

Kent can't resist reflecting on his life. Through his adolescence, he knew that he was born to hunt, to take everything he needed to sustain his life. His instincts have been tested in the streets, in prisons, on prison trains, in colonies for young criminals. He does well on his own, and when his skills are insufficient, he does the bidding of stronger, older men, which can involve sucking a wafer, bending over for rooster, or shaking down a political. Once, on a prison train, somewhere around Kalinin, he planted a sharpened carpenter's nail deep in the neck of some *intelligentik*, a man who looked like the nosed violinist.

Though he was treated like an animal for most of his life, Kent is fully a human. Tarzan, who spits through his teeth, sends snot as projectiles through his nose, and defecates standing up, is a human as well. Indeed, Kent and Tarzan believe themselves to be more human than any nosed musician.

Animals may understand the concept of belonging to a pack, but the concept of motherland is beyond their reach. Kent and Tarzan passionately love their country, are proud to be part of the Great Russian People, and accept the burden of ruling the less significant peoples.

The ability to honor martyrs similarly distinguishes them from the animals. Kent and Tarzan revere Aleksandr Matrosov. In 1943, Matrosov covered a Nazi gunner's pillbox with his chest, and this feat of bravery enabled his unit to carry out the commander's order and capture a nearby village. For this, he was posthumously awarded the Gold Star Medal of the Hero of the Soviet Union.

Every Soviet citizen knows of Matrosov and his feat. Streets are named after him, as are schools and young pioneer palaces. Even the horrible colony for young criminals where Kent met Tarzan is called the Matrosov Colony for Underaged Criminals.

In the thirties, Matrosov, too, spent four years there for attempted theft. They said he tried to pick a pocket but was stopped. How is that possible? Either you pick a pocket or you don't. Of course, he was railroaded, picked up for being a wandering, homeless youth like Kent and Tarzan.

At the colony, they said that Matrosov led a daring escape, digging a tunnel out of the furniture factory that operated in the zone. It would have worked, but somebody snitched. Even at the colony, Matrosov sacrificed himself for the good of all. Would a nosed one be capable of such a feat?

Is the motherland about to summon Tarzan and Kent for service as well? Will they get their chance to gum up the enemy guns with their fragile, tattooed bodies? Will they be given an opportunity to demonstrate their love for their people? Will they, too, bathe in blood and glory?

Kima Yefimovna Petrova is unable to fall asleep.

She lives in a corner of an eight-square-meter room, which she sublets from one of the many war widows in the barracks.

The corner is blocked off with an armoire and a curtain. Inside, there is room for everything Kima needs: a cot with a straw mattress; a cardboard suitcase atop a chair; a sack with laundry, which also serves as a hiding place for the thin, pamphlet-sized books lent to her by Kogan, most of which are banned; and, in the corner, another borrowed treasure—a pair of Finnish skis that she presumes belong to Kogan's wife.

Her section of the wall is bare, except for a pinned photo of Zoya Kosmodemyanskaya, a Red Army commando who went out into the snowy night almost exactly eleven years ago to demolish a Nazi stable. She was captured, tortured, and hanged.

Railroad workers all over the USSR have a nickname for themselves—*mazutniki,* axle grease people. Heavy black grease saturates their clothing and covers their hands and faces. A worker at one of the depots of the Kazan railroad line is just as likely to call himself a *negritos,* a slang word for Negro. At nights, as *negritosy* in the barracks cook their grub, drink, quarrel, and curse the Jews, Kima finds peace by gliding through darkness in the woods, or—lately—alongside the gorge, within sight of the railroad tracks.

In the past, Kogan joined her. His skis are of American Lend-Lease vintage, put to good use in the war, then sold on the black market.

When they were side by side, they talked about literature, medicine, wars.

One evening, in the forest, at the base of a steep hill, Kogan recited Akhmatova:

It is good here: rustling and crackling;
It freezes harder every day,
The brush bending in a white blaze
Of dazzling, icy roses.

Taking a deep breath, he broke away, sprinting madly to the top, then slowing down, allowed her to catch up, then shouted out the rest of the poem:

And on the splendid, magnificent snow
There are ski tracks, like the memory of how,
In that somehow far-off century,
We passed this way together, you and I.

Some of his stories and most of his poems cause her chin to jut forward to that forty-five-degree angle that she thinks suppresses and disguises tears, yet Kima is always eager to join Kogan in the woods and, to Kogan's amazement, never turns back when conversations cause pain.

Once, after a Sunday in the woods, Kima offered herself to him. It was a verbal offer, a gift, really.

"I am an admirer of a different sort," he said, and quickly returned to Akhmatova.

She kissed him on the cheek, and he teared up when she left his house that night, and that was the full extent of their physical contact.

Kima is a formidable challenge for Kogan. He has no training in psychology or psychiatry. Everything he knows about Freud and psychoanalysis has to be gleaned from ideological screeds attacking this approach. Its focus on the individual, as opposed to class, is deemed anti-Marxist and therefore appeals to Kogan immensely. Interpretation of dreams in 1953 brings a death sentence.

Though Kogan has never seen Kima's corner of the barracks, he would understand why the photo of Zoya hangs above her bed.

He would see the evolution:

In 1942, Kima would have wanted to be like Zoya, and by offering her life to the motherland, she would have hoped to demonstrate that, her enemy lineage notwithstanding, she was a patriot. She wanted her country to love her.

In 1953, it's about something else: confronting evil and savoring martyrdom.

Undoubtedly, this path of change would make Kogan cringe, for it represents a journey from one form of pathology to another, a psychiatric equivalent of the nasty mutations he can so adeptly identify with his microscope. (He has a lab and is interested in pathology.)

Kogan is subtly didactic in his treatment plan. The ski outings and poetry are intended to allow the patient to abandon fear of her feelings, particularly grief. Surely, he knows that his attention will inevitably lead Kima to sexualize their relationship. A polite, firm rejection is intended to illustrate that his attention to her is not a form of courtship and will continue, just as it did before, without sex.

Now Kogan is holed up in his house, staying out of sight, and Kima takes her ski runs alone, usually alongside the gorge. There is no more poetry. She is counting trains, observing them, like the martyred Zoya observed the Nazi troops in the forests around Moscow.

She has heard and watched them come for weeks, a freight train every hour, maybe more, usually heading toward Moscow, rarely back. She knows those trains from the inside. She has been cargo time and time again. Now, they are back, to take away . . . She learned that concept in 1937, the night they took her father.

His image is now dim: thick glasses beneath a karakul hat, a leather overcoat.

Night. Strangers in the house. A slap across his face, his broken glasses. A woman screaming. Her mother. Then, hours alone in a small room. A pantry? She thinks she drew snakes on walls. It was dark. Drawing with fervor, her life at stake. A song was the last thing she heard. In a language she would later recognize as Germanic, it projected pain, condemnation, power. Was this her father's final message to her? How would she recognize that song again?

When the door opened, her father was gone. No farewell. His books, his papers, gone. Mother collapsed on a settee. The wood on it was red. She would never see such wood again. A big, over-heated hand on her small back . . .

Is this a fantasy? Did this happen? Maybe. Why now the tears? She knows how to hold back that sort of thing. To live this life, you can't have tears. Never a sob, not even when she found her mother's corpse four years later, with half a face. No tears while reading the blood-soaked, typed note. One sentence was about "unbearable remorse for having borne an enemy's child." She begged the state to raise her daughter. The suicide note was a carbon copy. There was no gun and no typewriter.

If they have killed your parents and raised you like a cub, it may be better to find a way to set it all aside, to pack it, seal it, and throw it in the river, or snakes will eat your guts.

Oleg Butusov, a night guard, spends much of the early morning of February 25 on the steps of the dry goods store near the *kolkhoz* market.

It's unclear what he is guarding, from whom, and why. But being a night guard is sacred work, for it gives men like Butusov a purpose in life and a reason to consider themselves guardians of order and superiors to the average passersby.

While it is impossible to determine with certainty what Butusov is doing in front of the *kolkhoz* market, it is clear what is on his mind at 2:38 a.m., February 25, 1953. Butusov is immersed in deep pondering of the Jewish Question.

Every summer for as long as anyone can remember, Jews have been everywhere you look in Malakhovka. But where are they after the November snowfalls? Like birds, they fly to warmer places. To Moscow, to their apartments, to central heating. Butusov used to see them around the Jewish orphanage, before it was abandoned. Do they care about our Russian orphans? No, only their own.

What do we, the Russian folk, the working class, get for sheltering them? We get poisoned! They say one Jew doctor was caught injecting the pus from cancer patients under the skin of healthy Russians. He was doing it on buses, trolleybuses, and streetcars, and Russian people all over Moscow were getting sick with cancer. Butusov believes that he knew one of the victims.

Butusov views his people as strong, passive, good-natured dupes perpetually outwitted by conniving outsiders. The idea of a smaller nation attaching itself to the Great Russian People strikes him as intolerable. The Jews are trying to get a free ride to Communism, without working up a sweat. They strap themselves to Russia, then strap black boxes to their bodies and summon the powers of the Evil One to defeat us. That's why everything we touch turns to shit, Butusov reasons.

People say one Jewess was arrested for killing a girl in a communal flat in Moscow. They say the Jewess used the blood in bread they make for their Easter. This happened in a courtyard off Chaplygin Street, just after the war. The invalids were sitting outside when the killer was led away. They say the Jewess was nearly torn to pieces. We spilled blood in the war, and our children are getting bled in rituals.

And where were the Jews in the war? They stayed in safe places. In Kazakhstan, in Uzbekistan, in the Perm Oblast, fattening up on American corned beef in cans, wiping the fat off their rosy cheeks, while he, Butusov, was sloshing through mud and snow, coming out of the trenches, blasting away the Fritzes, getting shot at every day for three years straight. Indeed, it should not be forgotten that Butusov slogged through the whole war.

More than anything, Butusov wishes he had been present to see them load that killer Jewess into a Black Maria. He would have spat in her face, and the *chekisty* would have done nothing to him because they were soldiers, too.

Butusov knew one good Jew: Venyamin Goldfarb. They met on the Byelorussian Front. Now, that was a man! Stronger than a bull! Drank vodka! Played anything Butusov wanted on the accordion! He'd never kill Russian children for blood. He'd never spread cancer pus, like that doctor.

The two walked through the war side by side, until Goldfarb was shot through the chest by a sniper from a rooftop in Kovno. So there are some good ones. Really good ones, like Goldfarb. But not often.

Surely you've noticed that Butusov's thoughts are a jumble. Ideas move in random patterns, their multiple threads dangling over the proverbial abyss. But who is to say that a man must be coherent?

Our purpose is to describe these events with accuracy, coherent or not.

At 2:38 a.m. Butusov sees two headlights. Not many people have a reason to drive at such a time. The sound of the engine tells Butusov that he is about to witness the approach of a light military truck.

As the truck comes closer, he recognizes a Black Maria. The truck plows into the snowbank that separates the sidewalk from the street. In the morning, it will partially block both pedestrian and automobile traffic. A man jumps out of the cab and starts running toward the underpass.

Why is there just one man in a Black Maria? Why isn't he wearing a military coat? Where is his hat? Why is he running?

"Stoy!" Butusov commands.

The man keeps running.

"Stoy, zhidovskaya morda!" he shouts again. The man Butusov calls a Yid-face refuses to stop.

Butusov follows. He cannot see Yid-face's face. A dark figure is all he can discern.

Butusov wishes he had a gun. He hasn't breathed so deeply since May of 1945, the final days of the war, when victory was near.

The war is the overarching theme of Butusov's jumbled thoughts. If you were in Germany then, as Butusov was, you could take all the women you wanted and kill them afterward. That's how it was: you walked all the way to Berlin, spilling blood on every kilometer, so who was there to stop you from blowing off some steam?

Butusov's Yid-face doesn't try to run across the underpass. Instead, he darts to the left, to the railroad platform. This Yid-face is a coward. Butusov will catch him, work him over, hogtie him.

Butusov doesn't think of the reward, the glory, his picture in the papers. Vigilant Night Guard Arrests Zionist Spy. Fame doesn't motivate him. The chase is the reward. Butusov loves his work.

"Sdavaysya, suka," shouts Butusov into the howling wind. Surrender, traitor.

Yid-face remains unseen.

"Sdavaysya, blyad'!" Now he calls Yid-face a slut.

Still no surrender. Only snow and wind surround Butusov.

He walks halfway to the edge of the platform, thinking of the weapon he carried all the way to Berlin, his PPSh machine gun.

Butusov turns around suddenly and sees a man, his sheepskin coat open, his hand raised. It is his prey, the Yid-face. They stand six paces apart. Without a word, the Yid steps forward.

What is the shining object in his hand?

It causes no pain. Just an irretrievable flash of cold beneath Butusov's lower right rib.

As steel pierces the delicate white sheepskin and begins to separate his abdominal muscles, Butusov's arms shoot upward, his fingers curved. The blade makes a direct route through the tangle of his intestines, piercing the sheepskin once again, this time from the inside.

A competent forensic pathologist would have determined that the entry wound was significantly below the exit wound. That would indicate that death occurred as a result of injury with a curved, sharp instrument, akin to a saber carried by the cavalry at a time when there was a cavalry. The victim's injury was characteristic of the Civil War.

The sword retracts cleanly.

Butusov's arms drop to his sides as he stands balancing at the edge of the railroad platform, his eyes transfixed in wonder by the figure before him.

"Paul Robeson!" he utters, as though staring at an apparition, for the American singer, actor, and fighter for justice Paul Robeson is the only black man whose existence is known to night guard Butusov.

"Prosti, bratishka," says Lewis in Russian, bringing the sword handle to his shoulder. Forgive me, brother.

Then, with a rapid, broadside swipe of Levinson's sword, Lewis severs the cluster of veins and arteries in the night guard's throat, causing what pathologists would call rapid exsanguination.

Though crime statistics for Moscow in 1953 are grossly unreliable, anecdotal accounts suggest that murder is not rare. True to tradition, inebriated peasants favor axes. Street thugs use short Finnish knives; narrow homemade blades with handles wrapped in twine; and various spikes, including large, sharpened nails and screwdrivers. War veterans, yielding to the urge to settle scores, use their bare hands. Scientists, engineers, pharmacists, and physicians gravitate toward toxic substances, and writers report their rivals to the organs of state security. Deployment of a Japanese cavalry sword would be puzzling in the extreme.

While forensic experts would have been confounded by Butusov's wounds, the simple folk would not. The night guard's slit throat points to the Jews. The Jewish Easter is close. They need Christian blood, the simple folk would say.

Never mind that the version of the blood ritual story most popular among the Russian folk suggests that a child's blood can be used. The Jew who killed night guard Butusov could not find a child, so he slit the throat of an adult instead, the folk would reason, and Butusov, had he lived, would have concurred.

"Paul Robeson," Lewis echoes, beholding Butusov's body as it tumbles between the rails of the Moscow-bound line. "Paul Robeson has never killed a man."

At that moment, Lewis wants to feel regret, guilt, grief. He wants the skies to part, a full-blown tempest, with howling wind, with deafening blasts, with blinding flashes. The snow is all he gets. A face-full. No remorse. No flash. No sound effect whatsoever. Only his hands shake a little.

A few minutes later, as he runs toward the dacha, Lewis hears the sound of a Moscow-bound train.

He does not hear the whistle, which means that there is none.

He does not hear the engineer pull the brake, which means that he does not.

At night, with snow blowing toward the headlight, the engineer sees nothing but large white darts.

That night, Kima learns that the heroes are not all gone. Some still fight bravely.

What will she do now, as the trains encroach on Moscow, like Hitler's hordes?

She will stay close to Kogan, and Levinson, and that short, funny Negro who bows like a fool and stares at her. He is a hero, albeit not like Zoya, for he survived and ran.

As Kima crouched behind a snowdrift earlier that night, she saw the night guard tumble onto the tracks, and, after making certain that Lewis had escaped, she crossed the tracks, brushed blood-soaked snow off the platform, and laid the body across the tracks.

This took five minutes, maybe ten, and to make certain that all went well, she went back to the snowdrift where she had left her skis and waited for the train. The schedule is firm: a freight train every hour.

Butusov's body was torn to pieces. There was no abdomen, no rib cage, no throat, just morsels of muscle mixed with intestines, splintered bones, and blood that soaked into the snow, transforming it into ice. The story told by these remains is simple and compelling: a drunken night guard slipped on the railroad platform and fell onto the path of a freight train.

Would anyone in their right mind challenge such a story?

The steam locomotive that dismembered Butusov's corpse was anything but ordinary. It was an IS 2-8-4.

The full name of this magnificent machine was spelled out atop a massive red star at the front of its tank: I. Stalin.

I. Stalins are generally used to pull passenger cars. Freight cars are more likely to be pulled by SO-type locomotives, which memorialize Bunyan's patron, Sergo Ordzhonikidze, the commissar of heavy industry.

The IS locomotive that ground up Butusov pulled a long garland of freight cars.

4

After Levinson's departure, Moisey Semyonovich and Ol'ga Fyodorovna no longer need to be discreet.

Nonetheless, at 4:30 a.m. on February 25, she gets out of bed and disappears into darkness. They never say good-bye. She simply gets up, pulls on her white slip and her woolen robe, and goes across the hallway to her room.

Of course, Levinson knows about their affair. He had to have been dead not to guess, but nothing is acknowledged, nothing discussed.

The affair began in 1950, shortly after Ol'ga Fyodorovna ended her equally clandestine liaison with Levinson.

Moisey Semyonovich did nothing to court her, but one February night, he woke up to find her next to him, her head on her elbow, her razor-cut bangs weighing playfully to the right. It took him a moment to awaken fully. She put her finger to his lips. Silence. Then she kissed his forehead, briefly his mouth, then his chin.

She looked up as her lips reached his penis to begin a *minet*, a sexual practice familiar to him only from overheard crude conversations. His wife, who left in 1946 after nineteen years of marriage, had taken no interest in his pleasure. He felt bashfulness at first but surrendered to the new sensations.

"Now, do me," she whispered, guiding his hand downward, directing his head past her small breasts.

"I will not be your mistress," she said hours later, as the sun intruded upon them. "I will come here when I want to, and if you knock on my door, I will stop coming here altogether. By day, we are cordial near strangers."

He was the best lover she'd had since Levinson, but her rules were never to be bent, and they were not.

On the morning of February 25, 1953, Moisey Semyonovich watches her leave and, playing by her rules, gets up only after the door closes.

He opens the window to let in the frost, puts on his riding breeches, and positions his twenty-kilogram weights for his daily hour-long workout.

At 5:45 a.m., he emerges from the entryway at 1/4 Chkalov Street, takes in a deep nose-full of February air, and, carefully analyzing the scents, looks around. People who live secret lives borrow behavioral characteristics from wolves.

Those prone to stop and ponder our place in the universe should be intensely interested in the powerful perturbations Moisey Semyonovich began to experience sometime before dawn, an hour or so before Ol'ga Fyodorovna stealthily left his room.

Though tone-deaf and completely lacking musical education, Moisey Semyonovich would describe his condition as an ever-intensifying musical barrage. He is more familiar with marches than symphonies, yet that morning a symphony in his head is bursting out beyond the intensity of any known concert-hall-bound crescendo.

It is said that religious fanatics can whip themselves into similar frenzy through a combination of fasting and devotion, but

Moisey Semyonovich is innocent of mortification of the flesh and agitation of the soul.

The night before, he had a satisfying meal of herring and boiled potatoes. After his wife, an army hospital physician, left him, Moisey Semyonovich became so skillful a cook that he looked forward to preparing meals and rarely missed one. Any notion of communication with a higher power would cause him to smile dismissively. He is proudly earthbound, ideologically lashed to the ground.

The sound is soft at first. He is aware of it before he fully awakens that morning. It continues to gain in intensity as he works out with his weights, takes a sponge bath, brushes his teeth with chalky powder, and dresses.

It's the same sound that visited him when he was fifteen, in 1913, in the shtetl Morkiny Gorki. The self-defense committee was diverse. There were Marxists aided by Zionists, thieves, butchers, tailors, tradesmen, and young Moisey Semyonovich, an apprentice to a druggist in Mogilev, who devoted his nights to the study of natural sciences. Their goal was limited enough: when the bandits come, fight back.

The band requisitioned knives and axes from all the Jewish homes, and the butchers in their midst contributed all their tools.

That night, as he crouched behind a bench by the synagogue's stoop, Moisey Semyonovich ran his index finger along the blade of his cleaver. He felt a tremor, a spasm, really. It had a peculiar, oscillating quality, intensifying, weakening, reaching an extraordinary peak, then, topping it, another. Was it fear? He didn't know how this state of mind would affect him when the *pogromschiki*, the bandits, came. Would he be left incapacitated by these terrifying blasts within his skull?

The mobs were led by a Russian nationalist group called the Black Hundreds, which was connected to the Czar's secret police.

When the Black Hundreds came, his hand did not tremble.

Though it had the dynamics of a seizure, the feeling was its direct opposite. The druggist's apprentice fought his way into the thick of the mob, learning that his calling to ease suffering was counterbalanced by an extraordinary capacity to maim and kill.

Later that night, he stood on the bloodstained cobblestones in the shadow of the synagogue, feeling the dissipation of the glorious crescendos. The new sensation, whatever it was, deserved a name, he thought, and the name came to him the instant he began to seek it: *gerechtikeit.* Justice.

Involvement with militant Jews led Moisey Semyonovich to a wider group of young men and women committed to building a separate Jewish future within the greater social democratic world. They called themselves the Bund, short for *de Algemeyner Yidisher Arbeter Bund in Litve, Poyln, un Rusland.* Over the years, the Bundists sided with various Marxist radical factions. Since this was a Jewish radical group, everyone fought. The principles were worth fighting over. Moisey Semyonovich sided with the terrorist wing.

He was never caught, but he was the man who set the explosives that wounded a second-tier czarist official in Mogilev. He received neither blame nor credit for that action, which was just as well. The Bund didn't formally endorse terrorism but didn't condemn it in individual cases.

Later, Moisey Semyonovich joined the Mensheviks in their battle against the Bolsheviks. They confronted Zionism as a harmful escapist movement. Some members of the Bund—including Moisey Semyonovich—advocated imprisonment as punishment for the act of speaking Hebrew, the language of escapism (that is, the rabbis and Zionists). He was a member of a nation within a nation: progressive, Yiddish-speaking workers and peasants. Of course, he was a Marxist, and as such believed that we are defined by our relationship to ownership of the means of production, but as a practical matter, why not allow these people to identify themselves as, say, Jews? Inevitably, their national identity will wither away, but why must there be a rush to reach that day?

Moisey Semyonovich wasn't seeking a separate, safe future for himself and his fellow Yiddishists. He threw himself into every conflict he could, and whenever fate tested him, which it did on many a death-defying charge and hopeless retreat, Moisey Semyonovich became composed, machine-like.

Too often, Jews are described as victims of historical calamities. Moisey Semyonovich was not a victim. His goal was not to survive. It was to prevail.

Alas, Bolsheviks prevailed, Mensheviks were slowly slaughtered, and the Bund was classified as a counter-revolutionary organization. It wasn't enough to say that you were wrong and apologize for your ideological mistakes. There was no tolerance for deviation, past or present. If you apologized, you hastened your demise. Moisey Semyonovich knew that evidence that would tie him to the Bund existed somewhere on Lubyanka and yet, for some reason, the unexpected remission of his deadly political disease continued.

During the Great Patriotic War, he believed that he was at greater risk of being killed by SMERSH—the Soviet organization charged with rooting out spies—than by the Germans. He was wounded twice, and he lost much of his family.

His necrology was typical. His parents and his sister were killed in late July 1941, soon after the Nazis captured Morkiny Gorki. The Nazis deployed a classic method for the liquidation of relatively small groups of rural Jews. A long trench was dug in the forest clearing outside the village, the Jews were pushed into it, and the ditch was covered with dirt. This approach enabled the preservation of bullets for the front, as only those Jews who had the capacity to climb needed to be shot. The peasants said the ground over the ditch rose and fell for two days, as people tried to dig out or perhaps just continued to breathe.

Moisey Semyonovich had a wife and children, too. But they didn't survive the train journey from Moscow to evacuation in Siberia. When German planes attacked their train and it stopped, his family was mowed down as they ran toward the woods.

Wounds and losses unchained Moisey Semyonovich from concerns about his life, limbs, and family, freeing him to make his machine gun into a sword of justice that meted out punishment consistent with the crime.

In February of 1953, with the newspapers declaring war on the international Jewish conspiracy, a sense of history ingrained in his bones tells Moisey Semyonovich that a scheme similar to Hitler's Final Solution of the Jewish Question is about to be revealed. He senses that—just as was the case with the Black Hundreds in his pre-terrorist, pre-Bund days—the mobs will be deployed. The next war on the Jews will be a people's war.

Why arrest those clueless doctors? Why this anti-Semitic frenzy? Why the outbursts of blood libel?

And why the knock on Levinson's door instead of his? Only one explanation satisfies Moisey Semyonovich. It was a clerical error. Someone misfiled his dossier.

Walking out into the cold morning on February 25, Moisey Semyonovich turns left, toward Drugstore Number Twelve, which he manages.

He heads for the store's stoop and, standing there, surveys the small park. A group of drunks sits uncomfortably on cold benches, waiting for stores to open. *Alkashi, dokhodyagi,* men on the edge between withdrawal and the next dose. Vodka, that luxury of luxuries, is out of the question for these poor devils. Most of them drink Svetlana, a cologne, or Valocordin, a stinky alcohol-based anti-anxiety drug sold without prescription. It does neither harm nor good.

Moisey Semyonovich isn't going to the drugstore. After ascertaining that he isn't followed, he heads toward the Kazan Station. The sun has not yet risen, and the trolleys have not yet begun to roll.

His destination is Malakhovka, the home of Dr. Aleksandr Sergeyevich Kogan.

He walks into the Kazan Station at 6 a.m., half an hour ahead of the first electric train of the morning.

As he lies beneath his sheepskin coat on his cot, staring at the light that floods the dacha, Lewis thinks of the final words of the man he murdered.

"Paul Robeson," he repeats, trembling.

In Magnitogorsk, in 1932, Lewis was proud of having stood up to that new aristocrat.

Take my advice, Comrade Mikhoels. You go get yourself a bug-eyed, toothy Jew and paint him black.

After putting Mikhoels in his place, Lewis returned to the scaffold. He did his best thinking up there, on iced-up wooden planks, swaying with the wind, hanging on like a cat.

Why was he in Magnitogorsk? Why did he, a progressive, a revolutionary, lack a party ticket? Why hadn't he renounced his seemingly redundant American citizenship? Why were the same questions that haunted him in the land of Jim Crow resurfacing in the context of Comintern?

He loved the idea of defining himself as a member of a class—a proletarian—and, to the extent possible, forgetting the rest. But Negro comrades in America warned him to watch out for Jews, Russians, Lithuanians, Irishmen, and WASPs. Can anyone tolerate being called a baboon while trying to teach Hegel's dialectic to fellow enlightened workers? And what if Russian comrades of Jewish origin refer to you as an *orangutan*, presumably not realizing that the word is the same in English?

Perhaps this was something about America, a remnant of slavery that afflicted the Right and the Left alike, Lewis thought. Surely, this wouldn't exist in the Soviet Union, a country where racial differences didn't mimic America's. Other Negro cadres were being sent to the USSR for Party work, but Lewis couldn't get close enough to the Party, let alone rise high enough to be sent officially to the land of victorious revolution.

Finally, he joined McKee as a welder, and in a matter of months, he was bound for the land where race was purportedly negated, irrelevant. It wasn't hard to find that job. At a time when capitalism was trudging through an economic crisis, Russia was gearing up for its great leap forward, selling meaningless treasures—melted-down gold, outmoded art—and pumping hard currency into the construction of heavy industry.

He was the first American worker in Magnitogorsk. Bunyan, an engineer, was already there, living in American City, a cluster of bungalows on the city's edge. Another worker, a radical college-educated white youth named John Scott, would arrive six months after Lewis. Lewis's first shelter was a tent, where sheepskins made the difference between life and death.

He learned Russian quickly and easily. After less than a year, his ability to join steel earned him the respect of his comrades, and Bunyan's intervention made him a *brigadir*, the brigade leader.

So why did people like this Mikhoels seem hell-bent on treating him like a younger brother? They were embarrassingly ignorant, clumsy, and no less evil than their American counterparts. For his own sake, for the sake of the Soviet Union, Lewis was determined to stand in their way.

That night, Lewis took a circuitous route to his room in the barracks.

He stood in line to pick up a loaf of black bread, which was all that could ever be found in the cooperative store.

In line, he ran into Scott, a fellow welder, who was heading to classes at Komvuz, the Communist institute, where he studied Marxism-Leninism alongside future Party workers. A lanky graduate of the University of Wisconsin, Scott had fantasies of becoming the John Reed of the Great Leap Forward. Years later, he would write *Behind the Urals: An American Worker in Russia's City of Steel,* a splendid book.

"They call it the 'nationalities question,' right?" said Scott, chuckling at Lewis's Comrade Jim story. "If you are a strict Marxist, it's all about class, no nationalities, no race."

"You can't have your world revolution if you perpetuate that same old shit," said Lewis.

"Comrade Jim is not much better than Nigger Jim. Is it?"

"Comrade Tom's no good either."

"It's all in the name of reaching the stage of social development where there are no Negroes, no Jews. Just the proletariat, colorless, interbred, free of the prejudice of the past," said Scott.

"And you believe this, John?"

"Less and less."

Lewis walked into the barracks, whistling Dixie, of all things. As he inserted his key in the door, he felt a tap on his shoulder.

"I am sorry, Comrade Lewis, but I was unable to get myself painted," said the girl in a peculiar, vaguely British accent that has evolved at the English departments at Russia's institutions of higher learning.

"Sorry, ma'am, I can't help you none," said Lewis, smiling broadly and blinking in a manner the movie script surely required. "I be just a simple niggah weldah."

"Will you invite me in?" she asked.

"To help you write a report for the Comintern?" Lewis was no longer in character.

"I don't work for the Comintern."

"Then whoever . . ."

"I don't write reports, Comrade Lewis."

"Then what do you write?"

"I am a literary translator," she said. "Invite me in, please."

"Well, come right in, ma'am," he said, opening the door (he did have a heated room with a door) with a doorman's sweep of the hand.

"Call me Miss Goldshtein, if you insist on formality. Tatyana Goldshtein," she said, squeezing past him through the narrow doorway.

It should be noted that at the meeting with Mikhoels, Lewis realized that the girl in front of him was already his, and—this is even less rational—at that very instant Tatyana Goldshtein came to a corresponding realization.

This notion—this flash of insight—was a formidable puzzle to Lewis. Be it a hunch or a revelation, he shook his head in disbelief and returned to the scaffold. Not being as committed a rationalist, the girl found this occurrence less puzzling.

Let us return to the question Mikhoels posed to Lewis: "How do you like our women?"

Surely by the time Mikhoels understood that the answer was sitting to his right, he developed a craving for tea, but it was too late. The girl missed the entire conversation, except for Lewis's triumphant finale, his teaching moment.

"To what do I owe the pleasure, Miss Goldshtein?" asked Lewis, closing the door.

"I can't explain," she said, and at that instant, they moved toward each other and their lips met.

After some time, she pulled away.

"I hope you don't think that I do this all the time. I never have. Not like this," she said, and their lips met again.

Though no official tallies of such things exist, most sexual encounters in Magnitogorsk were vertical: in the bushes, behind the bread store, leaning against a shed. There were no trees.

The city was a construction camp, an amalgamation of barracks, tents, and prison zones. The foreigners lived better than the Russians, but Lewis didn't have a room until Bunyan's intervention made him a *brigadir.*

That night, their lovemaking was horizontal, atypically unhurried. He woke up before dawn, before the sound of the combinat horn that punctuated his life.

She would leave for Moscow later that morning.

He ran his calloused fingers through her thick, dark hair. He kissed her eyelids, first one, then the other.

"Paul Robeson," she said, waking up. That would become her name for him.

Paul Robeson. A Russian-speaking Negro who gave his voice to the working men. A Yiddish-speaking Negro. A hero of the Left. An athlete, actor, musician, champion of the oppressed, a Red Othello. There were worse names to call a man—and in America, Lewis was called those names, as was Paul Robeson.

After seeing that responsible comrades at the Regional Committee of the Party gave him a motorcycle for the five-kilometer trip to the airstrip, Mikhoels slathered a thick layer of TeZhe cream onto his face, to prevent frostbite. In his shoes, which were more appropriate for the boulevards of Paris than for the snowdrifts of Magnitogorsk, he was at the very least guaranteed a cold.

Tatyana returned to the hotel after dawn. They had two adjoining rooms, for they had been, for quite some time, intimate.

Tatyana's role in preparing the production of *Kinig Lir* was never acknowledged. She was the last person in the translation process. The Yiddish text was completed by the poet Shmuel Halkin. Halkin's verse tended toward elegant Hebraic form. Academic translations of Lear into Russian were dead, unacceptable. Poetic translations were textually unreliable. Halkin spoke Russian, but no English or German. (There were many excellent translations of Shakespeare into German.) Mikhoels spoke German, but no English. The director, Sergei Radlov, spoke some English, but only a little Yiddish.

"Halkin had to be watched closely, in part because his excessive fondness for 'biblical stylistics' threatened to overwhelm other important characteristics of Shakespeare's style," Mikhoels wrote in one of his many essays on the subject of his own achievements.

Working from Russian translations, Halkin refused to distinguish Shakespeare's prose from the iambic pentameter, and had to be stopped from converting the entire play into verse.

Phrase by phrase, the three men fought their way through the text, transforming King Lear into *Kinig Lir*, keeping what they could, sacrificing what they had to. Not even Halkin and Radlov were told that at night, Mikhoels sat down (and, yes, sometimes reclined) with a language student, and went through the play line by line, comparing the Yiddish and English texts.

In those days, the trip back from Magnitogorsk could take days, largely because the single-track railroad was chronically bottlenecked. After obtaining a mandate from Yefim Zeitlin, head of the Comintern offshoot for youth, Mikhoels commandeered a military plane to simplify his hunt for Comrade Jim.

Much is said about high party officials who used their positions for personal enrichment or for fixing problems for their friends and family. Commissar Yefim Zeitlin was not like that. Finding a military plane for Mikhoels and a collaborator was part of Zeitlin's official duties to facilitate production of propaganda materials aimed at America's Negro population.

The pilot, Grisha Gershenson, greeted them in Yiddish. Grisha grew up in Boston, speaking English, Yiddish, and Russian. When he emigrated to the USSR with his parents at age seventeen, he had dreams of becoming a test pilot, but instead became a glorified taxi driver on Comintern missions.

The scene he witnessed that morning figures in his unpublished memoir.

Tatyana opened an old tome of the Falstaff edition of Shakespeare. Mikhoels opened the manuscript in a yellow folder.

"Me hot zi ufgehangen," he read. They've hanged her.

"It's not in the original," said Tatyana.

"How does it begin?"

"In English: 'And my poor fool is hanged: no, no, no life?'"

Tatyana translated these words literally into Yiddish.

"Too much all at once," said Mikhoels.

"Halkin gives us a simplistic declaration not rooted in the text."

"Yes, but it gives us an image we can relate to. They've hanged her! And we see that she has indeed been hanged! Her body is right there. Onstage. And we think of people we knew who have been hanged, and of people who arc being hanged, and of those who will be hanged. And we imagine ourselves trading places with them."

"Yes, but you aren't doing Shakespeare."

"Maybe you are right. And if you are, so what? I set my stage for the audience I have. Translate what Shakespeare wrote, and the audience will think my character is insane."

"He is."

"Not in this scene! Here, he experiences grief, actively, painfully, slowly. Rush through it, and he'll become what? English?"

Gershenson writes that at that point Mikhoels wiped off a tear, which the pilot attributed to the cold winds of Magnitogorsk.

"*Mayn narele, mayn lets, dos lebn hot / Shoyn mer keyn vert far mir,* " Mikhoels continued. My little fool, my clown / Life has no longer any value to me.

"This, too, is not in the text," said Tatyana. "Here, he uses the diminutive suffix for fool, *narele*, instead of *kleine nar*, little fool. Then he repeats himself by calling his *narele* his clown, *lets*. We already know that Nar is a clown. That's his job. By now we've seen everything but the concluding scene."

"I like the sound of it," said Mikhoels. "It repeats the point . . . *narele* . . . *lets* . . . diminutives accentuate the weight of his loss. Little is big. Big is little. I don't know how the English feel their losses. This is for us:

"Me hot zi ufgehangen.
Mayn narele, mayn lets, dos lebn hot
Shoyn mer keyn vert far mir."

He continued reading:

". . . A ferd, a hunt,
A moyz—zey lebn oykh, un du, mayn kind,
Du otemst nit, du vest shoyn mer tsu undz
Nit umkern zikh keynmol . . . keynmol . . . keynmol.
Ikh bet aykh, Ser, tseshpilyet mir ot do.

Azoy. A dank. Ir zet? O, tut a kuk.
Di lipn ire . . . zet . . . nu . . . kukt zikh ayn . . .

"'I feel my losses slowly, I give myself permission to dwell on them,'" Mikhoels continued.

"Like Kinig Lir," she said.

"Like Kinig Lir."

"And then he dies."

"And then I die . . ."

Gershenson notes that Tatyana and Mikhoels were in tears by the time his plane touched down for refueling in Sverdlovsk. He attributes this to the power of Mikhoels's first performance of the final words of *Kinig Lir*.

Through Tatyana, Lewis accepted a new language, another family, life beyond pigmentation.

Tatyana introduced him to Moscow: stage, directors, writers, actors. Lewis discovered—and met—Meyerhold, Stanislavsky, Bulgakov. He met Zuskin, and Tanya's uncle Solomon Levinson. He saw *Kinig Lir* on opening night in 1934, the two hundredth performance in 1938, and many performances in between.

In 1938, after Lewis completed training in engineering, he received a package from Magnitogorsk: a box of twelve shirts, six white and six blue, made of sturdy American cotton. Also, there was a new black tie and a note:

Make them look up to you, Mr. Lewis. It's important. Your friend,
Charles.

Soon after that, Charles Bunyan vanished without a trace. The Party and the organs of state security were purging the country of bourgeois specialists and internal wreckers. Even foreigners—especially pale-skinned foreigners—were no longer guaranteed safety.

There was no report of Bunyan's departure via Black Maria. Even his company Ford remained in place in his driveway. The mystery of his disappearance remains unsolved.

In 1941, after the Nazis invaded, Lewis volunteered to join the army, but he was sent east instead. The blast furnaces he had helped construct were working around the clock, producing steel for the war.

Tatyana went with him, completed a nursing course, and was sent to the front. She perished with the Second Shock Army, killed in the swamps of Vereya in June of 1942, a casualty of a criminally botched attempt to break through to the besieged Leningrad.

On the morning of February 25, 1953, more than at any other time over the decade that has elapsed since he and Tatyana parted at a railroad station, Lewis longs for her. Is she leading him on another adventure beyond his horizon? Was it not Tatyana's mad uncle who had handed Lewis the sword with which he spilled the blood of a man who called him Paul Robeson?

Outside, Lewis hears the sound of clanging sticks. Levinson and Kogan are once again conducting war games.

That morning, Kogan doesn't fight like a goat. He is Levinson's equal. The two spar verbally as well.

"You, Kogan, fight like a *goy*."

"A *goy*? Explain, My Lord, how fights a *goy*?"

"A *goy*, *briderlakh*, aims for the chest."

"Where should *I* aim?"

"A Yid has but one place to aim: the throat. Be true to what your audience expects."

"Why do what they expect? Why not surprise them?"

"I answer with a question: Why do we kill?"

"We kill to teach."

"How will the audience learn, unless they get the realization of their biggest fear? What do they fear, Kogan?"

"They fear ritual murder. Is this what you suggest?"

"I suggest nothing but what they fear. They write the play: a ritual murder. Or maybe just ritualistic."

"And a conspiracy?"

"They fear it, which means they've earned it."

Lewis steps up to the ring.

"Last night I killed a man."

Levinson and Kogan interrupt their match of swordsmanship.

"How do you feel?" asks Kogan.

"Much better than I'd like."

"I understand. The first time I killed was in 1918, the day I met *der komandir.*"

"That was war," says Levinson.

"War is relative. I hate killing, but I don't hate myself for having killed."

"You haven't asked me who he was," says Lewis.

"I didn't think I had to," Kogan replies.

"He was a night guard."

"Butusov, then," says Kogan. "May he rest in peace."

"You haven't asked me why I did it. And how."

"I didn't need to ask," says Kogan. "He saw you get out of the Black Maria, and then he saw your face."

"It was a case of him or me."

"And then you killed him with my sword, and let him drop onto the tracks," says Levinson.

"I did. Tell me about him, Kogan."

"No sense in it. He was an anti-Semite, but a good man."

"Do such things happen?"

"Often," says Kogan. "He hated us in the abstract. He hated the idea of our being. But one-on-one, he was a decent man. I've fought beside men like him, and I would again.

"I would have trusted him with my life."

"The old Bundist couldn't stay away," says Levinson as a short, muscular man with a prominent chin walks through the gate of the dacha.

"How much does he know?"

"He cleaned up my room. He knows."

Levinson first introduced Kogan and Moisey Semyonovich before the war, at a performance of *Kinig Lir*. The two renewed their acquaintance near Stalingrad. Though they spoke Yiddish whenever they were out of the earshot of others, they eschewed the informality of Yiddish culture, addressing each other as *Doktor* and *Khaver*. Moisey Semyonovich was technically a major; Dr. Kogan, a colonel.

After the war, *Doktor* Kogan and *Khaver* Rabinovich developed a separate, professional relationship. Whenever Moisey Semyonovich needed to refer a patient to Pervaya Gradskaya, he called Kogan, and whenever Kogan needed to obtain medication for an acquaintance, he called Moisey Semyonovich, who took out his own scales and measured out the required substances.

LEVINSON: To what do we owe the honor?

MOISEY SEMYONOVICH: You needed me, and I came.

LEVINSON: We whispered into the wind and you heard?

KOGAN (*extending his hand*): Nonsense, *Khaver* Rabinovich. I
    invite you now.

MOISEY SEMYONOVICH: Thank you, doctor.

LEVINSON: Lewis, Moisey Semyonovich has a function in God's creation. He illustrates a principle: an old conspirator invariably thinks he smells the revolution—even when something completely different is in the air. Just think revolution, just whisper the word into the wind, and next thing you are staring at an old Marxist like this one, smelling of mothballs and thinking bloody thoughts. Just whisper ever so softly, and they will come, lone wolves, wizened sparrows.

KOGAN: I thought it was the other way around. First, you have the revolutionaries, and, second, they make the revolution.

LEVINSON: Reading Lenin? Stop! He was then. We are now.

MOISEY SEMYONOVICH: *Genig, khaverim.* Enough. They can occupy themselves like this all day.

LEWIS: And if you let them, revolution is *kaput.*

LEVINSON: Let's get our terminology straight, Lewis. There is no revolution. We will do what history calls for.

LEWIS: And it's calling for a single, isolated act of terror?

LEVINSON: Lenin was wrong. It's a mistake to negate the individual's role in history. Class isn't everything. Revolution isn't always the answer. There are times when simple terrorism is good enough.

5

A yearning for solitude descends on Lewis suddenly.

What is he doing in this cold, impoverished, barbaric land? The Moor of the World Revolution, a Yiddish-speaking Moor who killed one man and dumped three dead ones in a well.

The newly acquired status of murderer hasn't begun to bother Lewis, and the only remorse he squeezes out of his soul that day is the remorse for feeling no remorse. While logic is commanding him to sense eternal doom, he stubbornly continues to feel hopeful, energized, free.

Are Levinson and Kogan serious about their plot to assassinate Stalin, or is this a theater game staged by infantile old men? Has Lewis really joined the plot, or the farce, or whatever it is?

Levinson and Kogan are real-life Red partisans, real guerrillas from the Civil War, yet they are nothing like the characters from Soviet war epics or the heroes Lewis imagined at the outset of his obsession with Russian Communism.

These men are profoundly disorienting. Did they fight wars in this ambiguous state of mind, between pursuit of victory and utter nonsense? How can they switch so easily from killing to absurdism, from swordplay to wordplay? With all that smoke, do they have the capacity to understand each other?

Has Lewis agreed to follow these clowns in a horrific, heroic, hilarious dive off the trapeze? He has just killed a man. Was this in self-defense, for a cause, or for a gag?

Humor plays no role in Lewis's life. Certainly, he can never acquire the ability to treat death—especially death he caused—as a lighthearted matter.

This disconnect has nothing to do with language. He speaks Russian like a Russian and Yiddish like a Jew. Lewis understands all their humor, registers it, even plays along with it sometimes, but after receiving aggravation or pleasure from it, moves on to more important matters. Men like him learn to laugh much later in life, if at all. Lewis has only one way to find out what is real: by testing.

"It would be nice to have some help," he suggests later on the afternoon of February 25.

"From whom? Americans?" asks Levinson. "You know any?"

He looks serious. But, of course, he is an actor.

"Not anymore. Do you, gentlemen, know Zionists?"

"I knew Mikhoels," says Levinson.

"I heard that after the war, a group of religious fanatics took a trainload of their people across the border," says Kogan. "I think they crossed it, but I know one who stayed."

Kogan seems serious, too. That is, perhaps, a little more meaningful than Levinson's perpetual straight face. Of course, Kogan has been around theater for so long that he may be in character as well. And the compact of their friendship seems to require Kogan to play a supporting role.

"And how, may I ask, would a Bolshevik like you know religious fanatics?" asks Levinson.

"I live next to the Jewish cemetery. I know every Yid around."

"Including some traitors," Moisey Semyonovich interjects.

This offends Lewis. He has heard that some exotic factions of the Bund were so loyal to their mother countries that they regarded emigration as treason.

He knows that some of these zealots advocated imprisoning their brethren for speaking Hebrew, the language of the rabbis, instead of Yiddish, the language of the workingman. Could such absurd beliefs have survived this deep into the revolution, to be encountered in February 1953? Now a living, breathing answer stands before him.

"If I know my fanatics, he will tell us to go take a shit in the sea," says Levinson.

"Maybe he will," says Kogan. "But maybe we can give him a present."

"What present do we bring to a fanatic?" asks Levinson.

"We have weapons," suggests Lewis. "Three pistols. I can give him mine."

"For what does a fanatic need a pistol?" asks Kogan. "Whom will he aim it at?"

"God," says Moisey Semyonovich.

So this unflappable man has a sense of humor, albeit indistinguishable in tone, content, and delivery from political information lectures.

"Lewis, you've just witnessed a moment of Bund humor," says Levinson. "This is exceedingly rare, so savor it. I have known this man for thirty years, and in that time he hasn't even smiled."

"Your religious friend will need a pistol when it begins," Lewis concurs.

"And what will you use?" asks Levinson.

"I'll use your sword."

Intuition tells Lewis to relinquish doubt: This is indeed a plot.

Technically, Kogan knows several Americans—members of his own family.

In the autumn of 1927, when he was studying in Berlin, he came across a news story that mentioned a man who was almost certainly his father. The story mentioned him as an executive of a New York shipping company that was doing battle with striking dockworkers.

Kogan dropped a postcard to the company, mostly to tell the family that he was alive, that he had finished an accelerated medical course for veterans, that he had been practicing medicine in a regional clinic, and that the Commissariat of Health had sent him to get surgical training in Berlin.

Three months later, a tall young man in a fedora and a trench coat came to the hospital and asked for Dr. Aleksandr Kogan. He identified himself as Dr. Kogan's brother.

Kogan was assisting one of the hospital's luminaries in scraping out a tumor that originated in a child's bone. That day, the decision was made to amputate. Kogan was present during that discussion before he went to the cafe across the street from the hospital where his brother waited.

What do you say to the brother you haven't seen in over a decade? Vladimir was fourteen years old when they parted. Now he was twenty-four, a tall American who spoke Russian perfectly, but with a slight accent. He had graduated from Yale and was now doing something remarkably strange for an advertising company with offices in New York and Chicago.

The family had reestablished itself nicely. Being a shipping entrepreneur with money in Switzerland is a wise strategy if your goal is to ride out humanity's greatest perils. The family lived on Park Avenue. His mother had a Steinway again (the one left behind had been commandeered by the Odessa Opera). "She can play Chopin and glance at the park," Vladimir said, and Aleksandr was happy to hear this.

Vladimir's job sounded vaguely interesting. Sitting in an office on Madison Avenue, he read every tidbit of information emanating from the Comintern, the Soviet bureaucracy created to stoke the flames of world revolution. Kogan had no problem with the Comintern, even when it engaged in espionage. Countries do engage in such pursuits. And, of course, he personally knew Zeitlin.

"What relevance does it have to your American life?" Kogan asked with genuine surprise.

"You would be surprised. Speaking broadly, your Comintern is about social engineering. My job is to try to find ways to adapt your experience for commercial purposes."

"For businesses?"

"To engineer their relationships with the public."

"You are trying to create *business* out of our pursuit of the overthrow of capitalism?"

"Exactly. That's what I do all day every day."

"I will be sure to bring this story to Moscow. I am sure my friends at Comintern will be amused."

"Tell them I can get them good jobs in the advertising industry."

You might think that discussion of the emerging American business of public relations is a strange topic to come up at a meeting of brothers who hadn't seen each other in a decade. Kogan realized that, of course, but Yale and the Red Army are universes apart, as are surgery and advertising. The fact that the two young men had anything to say to each other was to be accepted for what it was.

Vladimir was sent as an emissary from their parents. He had an offer: if Aleksandr wished not to return to Moscow after his training in Berlin, the family would support him as he obtained American credentials. Kogan was touched, of course, but the idea of leaving his country struck him as unthinkable.

It seemed to violate some fundamental principle—a commandment—something akin to "Thou shalt not kill" and *Primum non nocere.* He will not kill. He will do no harm. He will not run to the United States. He will remain in Russia, doing his part, as his young country rises from the rubble of the Civil War that he helped win.

Kogan's response to the family's generous offer was a polite no.

And now, as steam engines pull cattle cars toward Moscow, as mobs of street thugs and Red Army units are being organized to carry out a coordinated action, as the prospect of public executions looms, does Dr. Kogan wish he had accepted that offer? Does he wish he were performing appendectomies in Cambridge, Massachusetts, or teaching anatomy at Yale, or listening to rich patients whine on a couch somewhere on Park Avenue, or—more likely— taking care of Negroes in Harlem?

No. Kogan made his choices decades ago. Whatever comes, he is where he wants to be.

When she stops at the dacha, Kima looks like she has been running. Lewis surmises that she has important news to report.

The cautious stares Kima exchanges with the stranger—Moisey Semyonovich—betray an instantly formed feeling of mistrust.

"Kima Yefimovna, this is our comrade, Moisey Semyonovich Rabinovich." Kogan makes his usual formal introduction as Kima stands uncomfortably by the door.

The balding, middle-aged man with a measured, procuratorial demeanor has silently extinguished the enthusiasm of the young woman excited by her role as the bearer of urgent news.

Moisey Semyonovich slowly sets down his glass of tea, raises himself briefly out of a chair, and nods in Kima's direction, a probing elder asserting rank over a young comrade.

"Your last name?" he asks.

"Petrova."

"And your real name?"

"Her name really is Petrova," says Kogan.

"That would have to be her mother's name. What about her father's?"

"What is this? An interrogation?" asks Kima, retreating into the tense demeanor that for her is never far away.

"Her father's last name was Zeitlin," says Kogan. "You knew him. Yefimchik."

"That's why I ask. They look alike."

"Let me guess, you think he was a traitor, too," says Levinson, seizing the opportunity to stick in a needle.

Moisey Semyonovich nods.

"Because he went with the Bolsheviks in 1906, when your Bund took a turn with the Mensheviks?" asks Kogan. "So how does this make him a traitor? He did in 1906 what a lot of others have done since. You, for example, don't go around advertising your belonging to the Bund."

"He doesn't?" says Levinson. "Why, just the other day I saw him in the Bund parade, marching on Gorky Street."

Levinson is now in the middle of the room, goose-stepping in place, pretending to catch imaginary bouquets of flowers, blowing kisses to the adoring crowd.

"The Bund saves Mother Russia from her legendary, monumental idiocy! And, listen here, Lewis, the loudspeakers on rooftops are blaring 'Di Shvue,' the anthem of the Bund. Let's see if I can . . ."

Continuing his march, Levinson belts out:

"Brider un shvester fun arbet un noyt,
ale vos zaynen tsezeyt un tseshpreyt,
tsuzamen, tsuzamen, di fon iz greyt."

(Brothers and sisters in labor and fight,
Those scattered far and wide,
Assemble, assemble—the banner stands poised.)

"Shut up, *komandir!*" shouts Kogan as Kima turns around and starts to open the door.

Alas, Levinson seems unable to stop short of completing the verse:

"Zi flatert fun tsorn, fun blut iz zi royt.
A shvue, a shvue af lebn un toyt."

(It flutters with woe, with blood it is red!
We swear. A life-and-death oath we swear.)

"Kimochka didn't come here to watch your Bundist parade, you idiot!" shouts Kogan as Kima closes the door from the outside. "Now I have to convince her to come back."

As Kogan leaves coatless to try to convince Kima to return, Moisey Semyonovich takes a sip of tea and, without a trace of either insult or amusement, says to Levinson, "Solomonchik, you of all people should know that I don't respond to provocations."

After she is convinced to return, Kima reports that earlier that morning, one Nadezhda Andreyevna Khromova had stopped by the **GORPO** cellar to redeem the bottles emptied by herself and her husband, a regional militia commander, Lieutenant Mikhail Petrovich Khromov.

The number of bottles—seventeen—strikes Kima as unusual. It suggests that the lieutenant has spent nearly his entire monthly salary on vodka.

"*Rodnya s'yekhalas'*," Nadezhda Andreyevna volunteered an explanation. Family came to visit.

Then, without a pause, her breath still smelling of alcohol, she whispered: "*Zhidov to nashikh skoro ne budet. Tyu-tyu. A v domakh ikh budet zhit' Russkiy narod.*" Our Jews will soon be gone. Bye-bye. And their houses will be occupied by Russian people.

"*Chto, nachalos'?*" asked Kima. Has it begun?

"*Pochti chto,*" replied Nadezhda Andreyevna. Almost.

With the understanding that the young Russian woman employed in bottle redemption could be trusted with such information, she proceeded to explain that Lieutenant Khromov was having a difficult time preparing the lists of Jews and half-bloods.

It's not hard to see why half-bloods would be a problem. In their identity papers, nationality can be listed as, say, Russian.

Even in the case of half-bloods whose fathers have Jewish names, the situation is far from clear. What if their fathers are half-bloods as well? Should quarter-bloods be on the list? Should octoroons be given a pass? And what about half-bloods listed as Russian under Russian names? They can evade detection, unless other criteria for ascertaining nationality are introduced. Are such criteria possible? Can such criteria be sensitive, specific, and reproducible?

These questions are so vexing that Nadezhda Andreyevna apparently doesn't consider that the Slavic-looking woman before her could be, in fact, a half-blood.

Also, Kima reports that two days ago, the night guard Oleg Butusov fell into the path of an oncoming train; an unlocked, empty Black Maria is permanently parked near the *kolkhoz* market; and two elderly Jewish women were murdered over the previous two nights. The victims were tortured with hot metal and hanged.

"This is a grim picture, overall," says Kogan. "But, remember, these events can be unconnected. I have doubts about the significance of the lists. This may be an unfounded rumor. The Black Maria at the *kolkhoz* market probably holds no special meaning. What if it broke down? Butusov's death was accidental, and the two murders, though tragic, were most likely the result of simple robbery."

"Kimochka, you needn't worry," says Kogan.

Kimochka, you needn't worry . . . "They are trying to protect her, the old goats," Lewis thinks. "Do they not realize that if the plot is uncovered, which it surely will be, everyone with even the most cursory connection to the plotters will face the firing squad?"

Lewis realizes that by comparison with the Doctors' Plot, an international Jewish conspiracy that is currently the top-priority state security case on Lubyanka, the Levinson plot may seem insignificant.

Yet, even before they conspired to assassinate Comrade Stalin, the participants of the Levinson plot spilled more blood than the doctors, who spilled none.

The murder of Lieutenant Sadykov and his men constitutes a terrorist act, as defined in Article 58-8 of the USSR Criminal Code: "The perpetration of terrorist acts, directed against representatives of Soviet authority or activists of revolutionary workers and peasants organizations, and participation in the performance of such acts, even by persons not belonging to a counterrevolutionary organization . . ."

Since Levinson, Kogan, and Lewis act as a group organized for the purpose of carrying out said plot, theirs is, in fact, a "counterrevolutionary organization," defined in Article 58-11 as "any type of organizational activity, directed toward the preparation or carrying out of crimes indicated in this Article, and likewise participation in an organization, formed for the preparation or carrying out of one of the crimes indicated . . ." The appearance of the

American citizen Friederich Robertovich Lewis and the Bundist-Menshevik Moisey Semyonovich Rabinovich in their midst gives the conspiracy a more ominous politico-historical sweep.

Since members of the conspiracy carried out an armed attack on officers of the organs of state security, their plot constitutes "an armed uprising" under Article 58-2: "armed uprising or incursion with counterrevolutionary purposes on Soviet territory by armed bands . . ."

Even Kent and Tarzan can be regarded as individuals who are aware of the group's counterrevolutionary activities and therefore subject to prosecution under Article 58-12: "failure to denounce a counterrevolutionary crime . . ."

There will be no trial. Lewis's new motherland has liberated itself from the notion that convicts are entitled to an appearance of an investigation and an appearance of due process of law. There are show trials; there are secret trials; there are deportations of entire ethnic populations, such as Chechens, Crimean Tatars, and young Lithuanian men. Now, an entirely different form of extra-legal repression is starting to emerge. This is mob rule. Unburdened by civilization, it is tribal.

No, Lewis will not play Levinson and Kogan's hypocritical game of protecting the young lady from the madness of their time.

"Perhaps we should monitor systematically what kind of railroad cars are going toward Moscow and what kind of railroad cars are leaving," he suggests.

Kima looks up with surprise.

Lewis continues. "We shouldn't worry about *all* railroad cars."

Kogan nods, and most people would have stopped at this point, but Lewis thinks and speaks methodically and therefore needs to complete his idea.

"We shouldn't worry about tank cars or open platforms. In

other words, we should examine the composition of trains going in and out."

Kogan shakes his head. This is frustrating, but nothing can be done.

LEWIS: If trains bound for Moscow are predominantly pulling cattle cars, and if trains going out are predominantly composed of tank cars and platforms, we may be in for some trouble.

LEVINSON: The spare lines, too.

LEWIS: We could check them out. If there are freight trains standing off the main tracks, it's a bad sign. And if they are made up exclusively of cattle cars, our situation is even worse.

KOGAN: This doesn't rule out a fluke. I'd have a greater degree of certainty if we could consider the train depots.

LEWIS: That's right. If we see nothing but cattle cars, and no tank cars, and no platforms, we are . . . What's the Yiddish word . . .

KOGAN: What's the English word?

LEWIS: Fucked.

MOISEY SEMYONOVICH: *Farflokhtn?*

LEWIS: Sounds right.

KIMA: I don't know Yiddish. What is it in Russian?

KOGAN: *Nam khudo.*

The goat is protecting her from profane language, too, Lewis concludes.

KIMA: I'll go to the depot.

KOGAN: I'll go with you.

LEWIS: As will I.

LEVINSON: No, Kogan, let her take Lewis. He's younger and faster, and he's been cooped up too long.

KIMA: Tonight.

LEVINSON: Tomorrow. Tonight, we visit a friend.

Late in the evening of February 25, the members of the conspiracy walk out into the blizzard. Their destination is the house of Meyer Kuznets, a seventy-nine-year-old follower of a religious leader based in Brooklyn, New York.

According to a Malakhovka rumor carefully circulated only among the most reliable people, seven years earlier, together with other religious Jews, all of Kuznets's family vanished from Leningrad. The younger Kuznetses took a westward-bound train and now resided beside their leader.

Is it possible that at that time the Iron Curtain had a hole large enough for a train to pass through? Did every Hasid on that train have false papers? How were these documents made? By whom? Did the Hasidim have protection from above? Was it Kaganovich? Molotov? Beria?

In 1947, secret police grilled Kuznets, but the old man spoke in riddles, and in response to threats, wove tales of inspiration. It is said that during a daylong session, he tricked a captain of state security into acknowledging native command of Yiddish.

On their two-kilometer journey alongside the railroad tracks, Lewis, Levinsion, Moisey Semyonovich, and Kogan encounter a train pulling cattle cars toward Moscow. Lewis sees no platforms and no tank cars.

"They are having a big agricultural fair, Kogan," says Levinson. "Prize-winning goats from Kazakhstan! Sheep from Abkhazia! Bulls from Ukraine!"

Kogan, Lewis, and Moisey Semyonovich walk in silence.

"Kogan, listen, I said goats," Levinson tries again. "You thought your family was killed by Hitler? Not true! They are being brought to Moscow, to the agricultural fair! My family was mostly people. They are dead. Kogan, you are lucky to be a goat! Did you hear me?"

"Don't respond to his provocations," advises Moisey Semyonovich.

Kogan doesn't require advice.

He is busy with calculations.

What is the Jewish population of the USSR? About 2.2 million. It's possible to deport them. Hitler killed about three times this number. Of course, he did this over seven years, building an infrastructure for transportation and liquidation.

How many people can you squeeze into one cattle car? About sixty, if you don't care how many of them are still breathing upon arrival. A train pulling fifty cattle cars can move three thousand people. Let's say you are trying to move four hundred thousand people from Moscow alone. (This is Kogan's best estimate.)

You need about 130 of these trains, if you pack them tightly, no luggage. The trains have to stand ready, because the deportation will have to be carried out quickly, while the pogroms continue to spread across the country.

You round up the majority of obvious Jews immediately and mop up the secret Jews later. You get them to the stations, have them waiting under guard.

Assuming absolute efficiency, you'd need about 730 such trains to transport the entire Jewish population to Port Nakhodka, the railhead of the Trans-Siberian Railroad. Kogan's rough calculations don't include cars for the guards, who would keep the deported Jews in the trains while making at least some effort to hold back the marauding mobs.

Of course, things will get muddled in the provinces. You will be running trains from one regional center to another, wasting coal, causing tie-ups. And, inevitably, some trains will be captured by the mobs, their passengers slaughtered.

How do you supply this number of deportees with water? Food? What about sanitation? Are the transit prisons large enough to accommodate them along the way? Will the system overload? Will it collapse? What will they do with the dying and the dead? Throw the corpses into the taiga, to fatten up the wolves? And what about those who survive?

And then comes the biggest obstacle of all: the rails take prisoners only as far as Port Nakhodka. If Kolyma is the destination, the rest of the journey will have to be done by barges, which carry a thousand or so prisoners at a time. Have new barges been built? If not, the concentration of deportees will become so heavy that selections for liquidation could be required.

Excessive calculation was Hitler's principal miscalculation. This operation will be carried out the Soviet way: improvised, cheap, vicious.

KOGAN: Levinson, you do know who will conduct the round-ups?

LEVINSON: Red Army.

KOGAN: *Our* Red Army? We fought for this?

LEVINSON: What *did* we fight for?

KOGAN: Can you remember?

MOISEY SEMYONOVICH: I fought for the cultural autonomy of the Jewish people, and I would again.

LEVINSON: Lewis, he is a Martian.

MOISEY SEMYONOVICH: Another failed provocation, Solomon.

KOGAN: Speaking only for myself, I don't know what I fought for. It must have been the spirit of the times. The wind of history.

LEVINSON: The wind of history?

KOGAN: Yes, Levinson, divine wind!

LEVINSON: You want the spirit of the times? You want divine wind?

After carrying out this time-honored setup, Kogan places a gloved hand over his nostrils. "You are farting into the blizzard, *komandir.*"

Shooting sideways glances at a slowly moving freight train, Lewis surrenders to deep, dull anguish. He will die here, in this dark, cold, impoverished land. In Omaha, he learned to associate death with the smell of burning houses, marauding mobs, humiliation. This will be different. There will be no hangman's noose, no posthumous castration. Only a hail of bullets, a burst of pain, then irretrievable silence . . . surrender.

To chase away these images, Lewis looks back at the train. He stares intensely, to escape from his memories, from his fantasies, too. This fails to produce respite. Yet, he could swear that, for an instant, he catches a glimpse of wretched, pale faces staring at him from the slowly moving cattle cars. Are they real? Is this a flash from the past? A harbinger of the future? And why is his hand caressing the handle of the pistol that once hung on the belt of Lieutenant of State Security Narsultan Sadykov?

After the freight train crawls out of sight, three men cross the railroad tracks. Within minutes, they stand at Kuznets's unpainted picket fence. Smoke is rising from the chimney.

Kogan knocks, then knocks again.

"Maybe he is hard of hearing," says Levinson.

Kogan pushes the door. The doorjamb is shattered, the wood splintered.

"Reb Kuznets . . . ," says Kogan from the threshold.

Inside, Kuznets's meager, principally black wardrobe is strewn about the room. The drawer of the kitchen table is opened, its contents dumped out.

A stack of firewood lies next to the stove.

Kuznets hangs head-down off a large hook on the wall. Ribs protrude through the tight skin of his slight body, and wide red stripes run from his shoulders to his belly.

"Fascists," says Kogan, lifting Kuznets's hand.

There is no pulse, just cold, eternal stillness.

"He's been dead for an hour, give or take," says Kogan. "Note the long, wide burn marks on the torso. Looks like they used a fire poker. It's a quaint folk torture method. Drag a poker along the skin slowly."

Atop a pile of Kuznets's belongings, Lewis notices a thin leather belt. He bends down and pulls.

The belt is over a meter in length. Attached to its other end is a half-broken, empty leather box. Next to it, Lewis finds another, similarly mutilated box.

"Tefillin?" he asks.

Kogan nods.

"Why would anyone gut tefillin?" he asks.

"Who do you think killed him?" asks Levinson. "State Security?"

"No, they'd do it in their own lair," says Moisey Semyonovich. "This is neighbors."

"Why?" asks Lewis.

"They may have thought the old man had gold," says Kogan calmly. "Or dollars. And who would catch them?"

"Maybe it has begun," suggests Lewis.

"Maybe it has," says Kogan, bending down to close Kuznets's eyes.

"Levinson, do you still remember the Kaddish?"

"I do, but I don't say it," says Levinson.

"And you, Moisey?"

"Never."

"Am I asking you to read *Mein Kamf*?" asks Kogan. "It's for him, not for you. *Shmoks . . . Yisgadal veyiskadash shmey rabo . . .*"

He pauses, realizing that someone is saying the words of the prayer for the dead with him. He nods at Lewis with admiration, and the two continue:

"beolmo di vro khirusey . . ."

A self-described atheist, Lewis is not at all interested in Jewish religious observance. However, before the war, someone gave him a record of Robeson's version of "Rabbi Levi Yitzchak Kaddish," a song loosely inspired by a great Hasidic master, which contained the opening of the prayer for the dead. A few years later, after receiving a *pokhoronka*, a yellow scrap of paper informing him that his wife, Tatyana Abramovna Lewis, fought bravely in the Second Shock Army and was killed in the vicinity of Vereya, a colleague volunteered to transcribe the entire prayer in Russian transliteration.

The colleague was not at all religious, either.

He was a young engineer who understood instinctively that expressions of respect for the dead constituted a weapon against Fascism. Though Lewis made no effort to memorize that prayer or to learn its meaning, the unfamiliar words made a permanent home within his memory.

6

Strapping his leather boots into the ski bindings provokes a complex response in Lewis. It is double-edged patriotism. Like Lewis, the skis are American, and, again like Lewis, they spent the war years in the service of the Red Army.

There is more to it: America's army is segregated, and no black man, no matter how brave and athletic, would be allowed to wear the insignia of America's elite mountain troops. The Red Army is a disappointment, too. No longer a liberator, it stands poised to conduct massive roundups that will sweep up the people who so cheerfully and unconditionally accepted Lewis as one of their own.

What is he now? Still the Moor of World Revolution?

On his twenty-second year in the USSR, Lewis is embroiled in an entirely different struggle. The enemy's face is before him, and it is unmistakably Fascist.

"A buffalo soldier," he says to himself as he takes a turn toward the workers' barracks by the railroad station. Indeed, he has become a buffalo soldier in a fight against Fascism. How did the earth's political polarity flip so completely in so brief a time? Were battles lost along the way? Was he, Friederich Robertovich Lewis, hiding in Siberia as those battles were lost?

Kima waits by the side of the road. He nods to greet her without interrupting the pace. She slides into the track behind him.

They move silently for half a kilometer to the railroad crossing. This is the most direct route to the Kratovo depot six kilometers away.

Along the way, they will pass spare spurs, taking the opportunity to analyze the composition of waiting trains.

Levinson's order is clear: stay in the shadows. The pistol in Lewis's pocket is to be used only in extreme peril.

"No more night guards," Levinson said, handing him the revolver. "And control her."

That will be difficult, Lewis realizes, casting glances at the girl. He understands her a little better now, and, gliding swiftly under the stars, he extrapolates the rest.

He has seen many women like her. Her kind volunteers to do the most physically challenging, most dangerous work. These Kimas dig frozen dirt in Magnitogorsk, lay railroad tracks through the tundra, and carry explosives behind enemy lines. Lewis knows the type in more intimate situations as well. These women don't fuck you. They take you on for reasons other than the pursuit of pleasure. Their objective is to outwit, overpower, outman, and, leaving you for dead, disappear into the forest.

The girl is on his heels now, pushing him to speed up. And another thing about Kimas: they are programmed for self-sacrifice. For her kind, survival can only be accidental.

Tatyana was more complicated. Most of the time, she was actually a woman, not a would-be man in a skirt. But in the end, the inner Kima won, and Tatyana was, as a consequence, gone, blown to bits in a swamp. Lewis volunteered for the war as well, but he wasn't born to be a soldier. He is a maker of things, not their destroyer, and he was relieved to hear his new motherland politely decline his kind offer of self-sacrifice. His place was in the Ural, on the production front.

———

They follow in the tracks of a truck that passed a few hours earlier.

The girl is alongside him now, setting the pace effortlessly, just a touch beyond his comfort level. He is starting to run out of breath. This is a race between the sexes, her game.

"Another kilometer to the spur," she says. "At this rate, we'll see another train before we get there." There is a soldierly efficiency about her.

Heading away from Moscow, toward Kratovo, Kima and Lewis cast glances to the left, toward the railroad.

A student of the train schedule, Kima knows exactly when to expect the next Moscow-bound train. Lewis realizes it as well. In the moonlit night, they see an approaching aura of lights, the steam rising above the horizon. They move forward, pondering the same questions: Will it be made up of freight cars? Will there be tank cars? Platforms? Will passenger cars be mixed in as well? Will the locomotive be a Sergo Ordzhonikidze or an Iosif Stalin?

As the train passes them, the engineer blows the whistle wildly. Does he catch a glimpse of the nighttime skiers? Is he drunk? Is his celebratory mood triggered by anticipation of some great national event? The composition of his train is unusual in the extreme. There are no tank cars, no platforms, only freight cars and two passenger cars. The train is pulled by an Iosif Stalin.

"I counted forty-nine freight and two passenger," says Lewis.

Kima says nothing.

"Were you able to read the inscription on the passenger cars? Someone forgot to take it off."

Kima nods, her chin jutting at that forty-five-degree angle. Lewis gives her a few minutes to seize control over her feelings.

"I couldn't read it," he says eventually, a subtle reminder. "The cars looked prewar."

"Omsk-Novosibirsk," she says.

"Why are they here? That's halfway through the Trans-Siberian."
He knows the answer, of course.

"Dlya okhrany," she answers. For the guards.

Of course. The entire railroad system is being taxed to produce freight cars and assorted passenger cars in preparation for
some event taking place in Moscow and, presumably, other major
cities. Is it possible to accept that preparations for a mass deportation of Jews are indeed afoot? Can competing hypotheses be
finally dispensed with, eliminated?

"Now, the locomotive, that was clearly something else," notes
Lewis. "An IS! Iosif Stalin! Have you ever seen an IS pull freight?"

Kima nods. "I have." Then, looking into Lewis's eyes, she adds,
"Once."

As a spare spur branches off to the right, Kima and Lewis follow.
There is no longer a road. They stomp slowly through the brush
in a new-growth forest.

After half a kilometer, Kima and Lewis reach a waiting train.
Smoke is rising from the chimney of a green caboose. A group of men,
at least four of them, can be seen playing cards by kerosene light.

Lewis raises his finger to his lips and points toward the woods.
They are now fifty meters from the train. The going is slow. No
more easy gliding. Snow is making its way into their boots, and
sharp brush blocks their way. They are making entirely too much
noise, but they move forward toward the locomotive.

"Forty freight cars, one passenger," whispers Lewis.

"No platforms, no tank cars," says Kima.

"We are fucked," says Lewis in English.

"Khudo nam," Kima translates into Russian, and for the first
time Lewis sees the outline of a smile on her face.

"Farflokhtn," says Lewis.

Once again, Lewis raises his hand to his lips. He hears footsteps. It could be a guard or a railroad worker. He carries no lantern and has a look of a drunk.

"So when does it begin?" asks Lewis.

Kima is silent.

"It can't be too far away," he continues in a whisper. "Do you know what I have to go through to get a few lousy freight cars? I have to beg somewhere, know somebody, make promises. And here they are, standing idle, an entire train, waiting for the devil knows what."

Lewis thinks he understands the reasons for her silence.

He suffered from a similar affliction until his mid-twenties, before he joined a circle of enlightened workers that met at various spots in Chicago to argue passionately about the correctness of competing revolutionary ideologies.

"What we need is the routing chart," he says.

Is he trying to impress Kima, to break through to her that it's okay to talk? Or is her silence making him nervous?

"It would tell us where they came from, their destination, their time of arrival . . ."

She stares at him now, saying nothing, letting her burning cobalt eyes do the work of making him squirm.

"And their time of arrival would likely tell us the very thing we need to know . . ."

"What?" she replies loudly, confirming Lewis's fear that he has gone on a reconnaissance mission with a partner who lacks caution and is, in her heart of hearts, looking for a bullet.

"What would it tell us?" she repeats in a voice that seems to boom in the quiet of the night.

"It would tell us when it begins," he whispers.

With no warning, before Lewis is able to stop her, Kima unstraps her skis, stands up, and, stretching to her full height, unhurriedly steps out of the snowbank and heads toward the locomotive.

"Oh, fuck," whispers Lewis in English, then, after taking off his skis, he pulls the pistol out of the pocket of his sheepskin coat.

Crouched and running toward the locomotive, he repeats the word rhythmically, like a chant. "We are fucked . . . fucked . . . fucked . . ."

"*Ty chto, okhuyela?*" he whispers, catching up and grabbing her by the shoulder. Now they stand by the bumper of the locomotive. Have you gone fucking nuts?

The locomotive is an SO 1-5-0. Kima's actions continue to be consistent with Lewis's diagnosis. She pulls her shoulder out of his grip, grabs onto the ladder, and climbs into the engineer's cab.

Cold sweat streams from every pore of Lewis's skin.

He fears death, of course, but there is something he fears even more. He fears dying stupidly, gratuitously, Russian style.

Consider Tatyana. How much technical knowledge did it require to realize that ice melts in the spring? Wasn't it obvious that after the swamps melt, an army loses its capacity to either advance or retreat? It bogs down, literally, without food, water, or ammunition. Had the Second Shock Army been allowed to break through to Leningrad or, failing that, pull back before the thaw, Tatyana might well have survived.

"Americans have their baseball, their greed, their nigger bashing. Russia's national sports are alcoholism, violent idiocy, and Jew baiting," Lewis thinks as he crouches alongside the mighty tank of the SO locomotive, pistol in hand.

The girl is inside the locomotive now, and by the time he climbs in, she is fiddling with the lock of a large steel box next to the engineer's seat. The box is locked.

"*Dayte pistolet,*" she orders. Give me the gun.

Who the fuck does she think she is? Worse, she is addressing him formally—*dayte*, not *day*—like a child addressing an elder.

"Get out," he shouts in Russian. "Have you fucking heard of ricochet? This place is all steel. I'd need to hit the lock."

As they get out of the cab, Lewis aims and shoots. The bullet ricochets madly. He shoots again, then again, finally hitting the lock.

She hops inside, reaches into the box, grabs the logbook, and rips out a half-dozen pages.

Surely the shots were heard in the caboose, but that's forty cars away, far enough to allow Lewis and Kima to disappear into the night.

They run toward their skis, and a few minutes later, they are on a road gliding away from the tracks, toward Malakhovka's lake.

Glancing at the stars and the full moon, Lewis thinks of a text that crept into his memory years ago. This isn't a prayer for the dead, but something closely related.

It's a small provision of Article 58 of the USSR Criminal Code: "the undermining of state production, transport, trade, monetary relations or the credit system . . ." The punishment is, of course, the firing squad; it would be one of a series of death sentences so squarely earned by the conspirators.

They don't speak on the run back to Malakhovka, and as they reach the barracks, Kima silently hands him the sheets of paper and turns off the road.

He takes it as a fuck-you. There can be no good-bye. Though the operation was a success—information was obtained and no one is dead—Lewis seethes at the young woman he now calls the suicidal little bitch.

Inside the dacha, he throws the papers on the table, in front of Levinson.

"From a locomotive?" asks Levinson, contemplating the graph paper in front of him.

Lewis nods, looking over Levinson's shoulder. It appears that the train has come from Omsk, and its crew has orders to arrive at the Kazan station. Imagine that: a freight train arriving at a passenger station. Whatever for?

LEWIS: This tells us when . . .
LEVINSON: That it does.
LEWIS: When it begins . . .
LEVINSON: Looks like it's March fifth for the pogrom. March sixth for deportations.
KOGAN: Alas, this rules out a fluke.
MOISEY SEMYONOVICH: We have exactly seven days.

Levinson cooks porridge and scribbles frantically in his notebook.

The porridge is generously lubricated with *shkvarkes*, melted fat with browned onions. *Shkvarkes* can be made with an animal fat of one's choice, and—as one would surely guess—Levinson likes lard, both for its strong taste and its symbolic value. Pork has been his meat of choice for quite some time.

Next to the bowl lies an extraordinarily large salted pickle, the kind you pull out of a barrel at a market and eat on the way home. The aroma of garlic and dill overpowers the smell of wood burning in the stove, and pickle juice is bleeding godlessly onto the table. A greenish puddle encircles Levinson's inkwell.

"Lewis, what do you think of blood rituals?" asks Levinson without looking up. He is back to his absurdist games.

"They are pleasant," says Lewis. An idiotic question warrants an idiotic answer.

"*Vos!*" Levinson slams his hand on the table. "Blood rituals are pleasant. *Drey nit ba mir di beytsim!*" Don't twist my balls. There is no better way to tell your interlocutor to be forthright and brief.

"You keep your *beytsim*, many thanks," says Lewis.

"How deep a cut?"

"A cut in what? Your *beytsim, komandir?*"

"No, the throat!"

"Whose throat?"

"The victim's, idiot!"

"Of what?"

"The ritual sacrifice!"

"You Jews have those after all? I thought you didn't."

"No! We do not! That's why it's so difficult. How deep a cut?"

"About halfway."

Too late, Lewis realizes, he is drawn in, if only for a moment.

"I see . . . You hold them by the hair," says Levinson, pulling back his own head. "And . . . slash! Halfway . . . *azoy* . . . Like this . . . and then you let it drain."

"If you wish. I'm going to bed."

"This is not useful." Levinson returns to the table, muttering, "*Shlof zhe, shlof* . . . I ask an engineer . . . That's what I get . . . Halfway . . . Pleasant . . . *A sheinem dank* . . . *A kluger* . . . Why couldn't she find an actor? Paul Robeson, for one . . ."

"*A gute nakht, mayn tayerer komandir,*" says Lewis in Yiddish. Good night, my dear *komandir.*

It makes no sense, perhaps, but just before he drifts off to slumber, he sees Levinson dance slowly, alone, singing something about blood, a bucket, and a sword, then continues to dance as his words dissolve into a *nign.*

Lewis could swear that Kogan, returning to the hut, sets down the firewood and sings and dances, too. Their *nign* is quiet. Their dance consists of slow, exaggerated, sweeping moves.

It is conceivable that this is a dream, but if it is indeed, what can it signify? And how does it differ from the other dreams Lewis has that night, dreams of flashing swords and half-severed heads and blood that gushes into a dirty bucket?

Throughout that night, Lewis hears a *nign.*

7

A deep, fresh coat of snow falls during the night and, on the morning of February 27, Kogan walks out into the yard to shovel out a path.

He stabs the snow with his old, well-worn shovel. The birch wood of the handle is oiled with sweat and worn to make grooves for his strong hands. This is his sweat, his little mark upon this planet.

Aleksandr Sergeyevich Kogan loves to shovel snow. The songs that people sing as they shovel are telling of what they hold sacred and, by inference, who they are.

Kogan sings Red Army songs. These are not the authentic songs of the Russian Civil War. Levinson's partisan detachment was decidedly nonartistic. No one sang. In Kogan's view, Civil War songs were written for agitation and propaganda purposes years after the battles ended. He knows the "Internationale" in French, Russian, German, and Yiddish, and he knows every piece of music ever performed by GOSET. Yet these songs do not stir his soul.

His soul is touched by a song from a propaganda musical called *"Traktoristy,"* in which tractor drivers attest to their readiness to switch to another piece of heavy machinery—a tank:

Gremya ognyom, sverkaya bleskom stali,
Poydut mashiny v yarostnyy pokhod
Kogda nas v boy poshlyot Tovarishch Stalin
I Pervyy Marshal v boy nas povedyot.

The translation that follows sacrifices the song's minimal poetic value in favor of optimizing the accuracy of the text:

(Thundering with fire, shining with the glimmer of steel,
The machines will advance into a ferocious campaign
When we are sent to war by Comrade Stalin
And the First Marshal leads us into battle.)

As a Red Army veteran and a thinking man, Kogan surely knows that the First Marshal, Kliment Voroshilov, is a particularly thick-skulled cretin, who—had he been left to his own devices—would have lost many a war.

Why is this musical idiocy on Kogan's lips shortly after dawn on February 27? Out of respect for Kogan's profession and his historical significance, a reader may be tempted to regard him as a Western-style, leftward-leaning small-d democrat.

In reality, Kogan is very much a product of his time and place, and the sense of belonging to something greater than himself gives him comfort.

Even when the snowfall is light, it takes Kogan an hour to make a narrow path from the porch steps to the gate. He starts shoveling at seven. A little after eight, he reaches the wooden bridge over the drainage ditch that runs alongside the road.

He looks up to mumble a greeting to two young men who are

sliding along the gouge a passing truck made in the middle of the lightly traveled road.

"Tarzanchik, smotri, vot zhid nash," says one young man to the other. Tarzan, look, here's our Yid.

"Da, i vparavdu nash," says Tarzan. Our Yid, indeed.

"Tovarishchi, ne zhid a yevrey," says Kogan with pride. Comrades, I am Jewish, not a Yid.

As a physician, Kogan believes that projecting a sense of dignity and inner strength has the capacity to thwart would-be assailants. In reality, of course, dignity and inner strength, no matter how powerfully projected, are not protective in the least.

Consider Solomon Mikhoels. Could his world-renowned projection of dignity and strength hold back a truck?

"Khorosho govorish, zhidishka," says Tarzan. You speak well, little Yid.

"Kent, are you afraid of him?" he asks his comrade.

"I'm shaking."

"Me, too."

Before Kent grabs him from behind, and prior to Tarzan placing brass knuckles on his hand and taking a wide swing, Kogan raises his hand to loosen his precious dentures.

At the moment Tarzan's fist makes contact with the right side of Kogan's face, his dentures—both lower and upper—shift to the safety of his stretched-out left cheek.

Not only does this maneuver preserve the dentures, but the young men feel great satisfaction when Kogan spits out a stream of blood and artificial teeth into the snow-filled ditch.

"Where are your dollars?" asks Kent. *"V filine?"*

"Filin?" Kogan is puzzled. An owl? No, it cannot be. In Russian, the word *filin* means an owl; nothing else.

Why are they asking whether I keep my dollars in the owl?

I have no dollars. I have no owl.

What else can they mean by *filin*? It could be something that sounded like the Russian word for owl . . . *filin* . . . *filin* . . . *tefillin!* Free associating, Kogan's mind races to Kuznets, hanging head-down, the marks of a hot iron on his feeble torso.

"Should I tell these fools that the Russian word *filin* is not the same as the Hebrew word *tefillin?*" Though Kogan views himself as an educator, he resolves to remain silent.

"*Vrezat' eshche?*" asks Tarzan. Slam him one more time?

"*Davay!*" says Kent. Go ahead.

Kogan is in no position to describe the ensuing events, but an observer would have seen two thugs, each holding Kogan's foot, drag the surgeon along the cleared path toward his dacha.

In the blinding morning light, Lewis sees two young men drag Kogan along the path he cleared earlier that morning.

"Wake up, *komandir*," he whispers, handing Levinson a revolver.

There are occasions when a sword is better than a pistol. Lewis has a score to settle.

It's unlikely that the fraction of a second that elapses between the kick on Kogan's door and the swift realization that a bullet has entered his eye and his brain has erupted from the crater that was the back of his skull gives Tarzan enough time to fathom the magnitude of his strategic miscalculation.

Kent, by contrast, learns that retribution has the capacity to hide behind closed doors and lurk around blind corners. As his comrade falls backward onto the steps, a blade digs lightly into the skin beneath Kent's Adam's apple.

"*Stoy, suka,*" says a Negro, edging a massive sword into Kent's skin and letting out a light trickle of blood. Don't move, bitch. In Russian, the word "bitch" connotes treachery.

"You know who I am? I am your Yid. You chased me down. You punched me in the face. You kicked me in the back."

Regaining consciousness, Kogan finds himself head-down on his porch steps. Next to him, also upside down, lies a corpse. Their clothing and the porch steps are splattered with spongy fragments of pink and gray material that Kogan recognizes as human brain.

The two are face-to-face, and Kogan feels no joy in his recognition of the young man who slugged him what seems like days ago.

He feels a pair of hands behind him.

It's Levinson.

"My dentures," says Kogan, with a panic that old men know. "In the ditch."

"I'll bring them," says Levinson.

After helping Kogan get to a cot, Levinson picks up a ladle and the pig-iron cauldron in which he cooked the porridge and melted lard for *shkvarkes* the night before. Methodically, with the ladle, he lifts the bloodstained snow.

He returns to the house, holding Kogan's dentures in one hand and a cauldron in the other.

Has Kent chanced upon a nest of conspirators, wreckers, terrorists, and spies?

Whoever they are, these people don't appear to be common criminals. They don't speak the right language. They have the look of politicals, educated people who held important jobs before arrest. Alas, these politicals aren't under arrest. They act like soldiers.

Kent's first tactic is to scare them.

"Mikhail Petrovich Khromov knows where we are," he says.

They say nothing.

The ability to gauge the fear of others is the most important and best developed of Kent's survival skills. Now he senses none.

"Mikhail Petrovich will come," Kent adds, knowing that it is futile to threaten these men with retribution. "Mikhail Petrovich will avenge us."

"Lieutenant Mikhail Petrovich Khromov knows where *you* are?" asks the short nosed one whose bloody dentures Tarzan sent into the snow.

Kent vows to break away from these men, to run to the *chekisty* and tell them that he saw an underground organization that liquidated Tarzan.

He must remember the descriptions of these men. He will give them names to distinguish them from each other.

There are four.

There is the tall one the others call *Komandir*.

There is *Negritos*.

Also, the small, muscular one with a massive chin. Kent names him *Bul'dog*.

And then, the one with the dentures. Kent names him *Protez*, the prosthesis.

Kent hears *Komandir* pose a question in a language that sounds like German. Are these spies or homegrown wreckers? Or both? No, these are clearly spies.

Are these spies German?

Has he stumbled upon an international conspiracy uniting the Fascists with the nosed ones?

"Lieutenant Khromov is the chief of our heroic militia and a Gogolesque crook, whose wife is nonetheless a lovely lady," *Protez* explains in Russian.

"You think he really knows?" asks *Komandir*, then adds ominously, "Let's see what we can learn . . ."

As *Negritos* stays behind with the ailing *Protez*, Kent is pushed out into the courtyard.

His hands are tied behind his back, *Bul'dog*'s hand on his shoulder.

Komandir has his pistol cocked and pointed at Kent's head. He looks like the sort who wouldn't miss. At least for now, escape is out of the question. What are they going to do to him?

They are now in the shed, next to the uncovered remains of his friend Tarzan.

Kent fights off tears.

It is said that the dead can look as though they have gone to sleep.

But as he lies on the dirt floor, a large portion of his face missing and shards of his skull exposed like a broken jug, Tarzan looks definitively dead.

Is this the way his father looked after his final battle, in Kursk?

"No," thinks Kent, "my heroic father was a tankist, and the tankists' bodies get blown to bits and burned."

Watching war films, Kent learned that saying nothing during interrogations may be the only honorable course of action, even when they work you over with rubber truncheons, whips, or hot pokers. The same goes for situations where they hang you by your feet.

In some of those films, Reds arrive at the last minute and save their comrade from the gallows. Do last-minute rescues happen in real life? Will Lieutenant Mikhail Petrovich Khromov and Vasyok, his stepson, arrive in time to save him from *Komandir*, *Bul'dog*, *Negritos*, and *Protez*?

In the shed, Kent is ordered to sit on the floor.

"Your name?" asks *Bul'dog.*

"Matrosov," says Kent.

"First name?"

"Aleksandr."

"Patronymic?"

"Matveyevich."

"I've heard of you," says *Komandir.* "It looks like you have found your pillbox."

"Ubivay," says Kent, looking squarely into *Komandir'*s eyes. Go ahead, kill.

Kent smiles defiantly at his captors. He doesn't say, *"Ubivay, suka,"* Go ahead, kill, bitch. He says, simply, kill, for fear of death has suddenly and irrevocably vanished from his soul. From that moment on, his life is preparation for the finale.

"This is pointless," says *Bul'dog.* "Get it over with."

"Not yet." Then, addressing Kent, *Bul'dog* adds, "Why did you come here? Why did you ask about dollars and tefillin?"

"Answer," orders *Komandir,* placing the gun directly beneath Kent's left nostril.

Kent's mouth has been dry for an hour now since his capture. But as fear departs, saliva makes a comeback, and Kent accumulates it in his mouth, to spit at their bullets, into their pistols, into their faces, too.

"Your choice," says the tall nosed one, though everyone knows that nothing can be further from the truth. Kent has no choices left, nor do his captors.

LEWIS: Aleksandr Sergeyevich, are you up to intellectual discourse?

KOGAN: I am alive.

LEWIS: In America, we have something called minstrel shows. You've heard of them?

KOGAN: I haven't.

LEWIS: In minstrel shows, white men paint their faces black, and make foolery, pretending to be Negroes.

KOGAN: I think I read this in Mark Twain. Refresh my memory. What's their purpose?

LEWIS: To show that we are monkeys with bigger penises, but smaller brains than humans.

KOGAN: Fascism, then.

LEWIS: A form of Fascism. Yes. Now, Aleksandr Sergeyevich, do you recall the photo of *der komandir*, standing on his head, wearing tefillin?

KOGAN: Yes. It was in 1921. He was demobilized, his wounds were mending, and he was stronger than an ape. The play was called *An Evening of Sholem Aleichem*. A madman, Marc Chagall, designed the props and costumes. It was cubism, madness cubed. Biomechanics. Futurism. Jarring noises. I loved those days!

LEWIS: I've seen the photos from that time; sometimes the actors wore nose masks, exaggerating their already substantial beaks . . .

KOGAN: But that was cubism, nothing else.

LEWIS: And our minstrel shows? Are they about paint?

KOGAN: I see your point. I'll help you drive it home. Shortly after Levinson stood on his head in leotard and tefillin, Zuskin put tefillin on his legs and wore a dress. With this, he pranced onstage.

LEWIS: Did you laugh?

KOGAN: I laughed until I cried! In 1926—when you were very young, and living in your Omaha—the theater staged *137 Children's Homes*. A wooden play, where Mikhoels portrayed a man named Shindel, the villain. This Shindel hid contraband in . . . guess.

LEWIS: His tefillin?

KOGAN: Correct.

LEWIS: It's a strange object of fixation.

KOGAN: I wish I had tefillin for you to test. You put one box
on your head. Symbolically, this binds your intellect to
God. You put the other box on your left arm. You loop
the thin belt of the tefillin seven times around the arm,
and then three times around the middle finger. This represents your heart and soul. All men must do it. This is
in the Torah.

LEWIS: What is the text inside?

KOGAN: Two little portions about consecrating firstborn
sons in honor of the Exodus, and the Shema. You know
Shema . . .

LEWIS: Hear, O Israel, the Lord our God, the Lord is one.

KOGAN: There is a little more, but that's the highlight. Hilarious. Let's take this step by step: if you love God, it's
a good thing to bind yourself to Him with tefillin. But if
you question God, the tefillin and the bond it represents
become more onerous than a bad marriage. Next step:
if you believe religion has to wither, and with it, your
farkakte shtetl, you may take aim at the ties that bind—
symbolically—God and man. And that's the tefillin!
Simple.

LEWIS: The shtetels are gone, Aleksandr Sergeyevich.

KOGAN: Destroyed by Hitler, not by GOSET. And tefillin's
now *filin,* an owl, which, for some reason, is sought by
thugs.

LEWIS: Does this surprise you? When you desecrate the tefillin onstage, breaking with God in ways that are intense, and personal, and public, the rest of us are left
outside. All we can hear is something about a *filin,* and

something else about contraband, and jewels. Let me return to our minstrels. They envy our cocks, and when they're done performing, they go lynch a nigger.

KOGAN: And our players loathed the shtetl, tradition, family, and God. They were illuminati in cubist masks and skirts, *mit* upside-down tefillin on their legs.

LEWIS: They played the minstrels and the Negroes lynched.

KOGAN: That's Jewish luck. But what do you propose? How should we settle our grievances with God? Discreetly? Privately? Like Swedes or icy Anglo-Saxons? Can you propose weapons and a venue?

As *Bul'dog* raises his gun, Kent knows the end has come.

The words he needs are in his throat, and he lets them out fast: "You can kill me now. But you can't kill everyone!"

A hero of some sort said something like this. Poor Kent lacks the memory for who and what and when.

"We certainly can kill you now," *Komandir* says. "You were about to murder Kogan, and you may have killed Kuznets and those two women."

He nods to *Bul'dog*.

Before Kent's body slumps to the floor, Levinson feels an instinctive urge to wipe warm liquid off his left cheek and forehead. Could that be Kent's blood? It is, in fact, Kent's spit. Defiant to the end, he has become a fitting heir to both Matrosov and the German gunner who manned the pillbox.

Inside the house, Kogan and Lewis hear a muffled gunshot.

"They killed the boy." Lewis cringes.

"*Komandir* Levinson would call it an execution," says Kogan. "Old tactics never wither."

"I call it murder. Thank God I'm not *der komandir*."

8

On the afternoon of February 27, Ol'ga Fyodorovna resolves to pack her prerevolutionary leather valise.

Nearing sixty, she has the wisdom of a woman who has outlived most of her lovers. Until her postwar detour—an exploration of the Jews—she limited her amorous pursuits to Russian poets.

They never left her fully, and their final moments were poetry as well: Nikolay, daring the firing squad to set his soul aloft; Marina, hopeless and hungry, her neck in the noose.

They died in prisons, revolutions, wars, and famines; by hanging and by the despair that comes with driving taxis on Paris boulevards and selling insurance in New Jersey. They vanished, but she stood guard over the remnants of the beauty that once inspired them. It was elegance, really, the spare beauty of a girl petite and willowy at once.

Her grace is still intact, as is her strength. The low-slung bangs are there, too, still patent-leather-black and straight as wire. They now caress her thick and graying brows.

Her room is about symbols of beauty as well: a round white dining table is Biedermeier, a palatial treasure she found discarded in revolutionary Petrograd. The mirrored armoire is white, as are the walls, the sofa, and the sheer curtains. The bentwood chairs her parents brought from Prague before the revolution are bleached with age, but sturdy still. She owns one vase, a set of white plates, clear simple glasses, and absolutely no china figurines.

There is a charcoal drawing on the wall: a willowy young woman with razor-straight bangs, nude, reclining on a draped divan. Where is the boy for whom she posed? The gold mines of Magadan, the bogs of Narva, or the Auschwitz sky?

On the afternoon of February 27, Ol'ga Fyodorovna performs an act for which she is famous.

She leaves.

A bloodstain is the first thing Kima sees when she passes through Kogan's gate. The tears cease as suddenly as they begin, and only her red eyes and the bags that swell beneath them bespeak the awakening of grief that gripped her during the night.

She hears a gunshot, and sadness is instantly replaced with the steely comfort of mortal danger.

Instead of lurking in the bushes to gather information and taking a calculated risk, she runs toward Kogan's house.

"A gunshot!" she shouts, bursting through the door, and, to her relief, she finds Kogan and Lewis in what appears to be a calm conversation.

"I am afraid so," says Lewis, looking up.

"Who?"

"Levinson killed a thug."

"Aleksandr Sergeyevich, what happened?"

"I was beat up. They came to kill me."

"Has it begun?"

"I don't think so. These were simple thugs."

"I saw the Black Maria behind that hedge three days ago. I saw the corpses. The throats of two men were slit, and one was stabbed. I watched you dump the bodies."

"So you were there," says Kogan. "I'm not entirely surprised."

"You were too busy making humor of Friederich Robertovich's vomit. After he drove away, I followed on skis. I saw him kill Butusov."

"You did . . . you did . . . Now, please, go as far as the rails will take you," says Kogan. "I'll give you money."

"Aleksandr Sergeyevich, I don't need protection."

"But you are a lady!"

"Thank you for what you've done. This is enough. I am your comrade. I need some burlap sacks, a sled, and a long piece of rope."

"You'll find it in the shed," says Kogan.

"When I return, I'll want to know the plan for our attack."

"You are a copy of your father," says Kogan. "A clear head."

"I've feared too much for too long. Now I will fight. I'll join your band."

"No," says Kogan. "That was, emphatically, the answer I prepared in the fear that your determination would lead you to our plot. I have my lines, yet I can't say them. I have no right. You aren't the beaten cub who crossed this doorway seven months ago. My lines be damned. Please, join us, comrade."

"She knows," says Kogan as Levinson walks in.

"You blab again." Levinson scowls. "Soon, all of Malakhovka will know! I have a joke: Two Jews meet at the *kolkhoz* market. 'Have you heard, Levinson and Kogan have formed an underground counterrevolutionary *organizatsiye* . . . ' 'You don't say!' "

KIMA: How does your joke end?

LEVINSON: I don't know yet.

LEWIS: It may not be a joke.

KIMA: What can I do to make it real?

KOGAN: You've done enough.

LEVINSON: Not so fast. I need red cloth.

LEWIS: What for? Don't tell me there are costumes.

KIMA: How much red cloth?

LEVINSON (*counting on his fingers*): One . . . two . . . three . . .
Four or five large flags' worth.

KIMA: I'll bring a dozen.

KOGAN: This isn't the time to die. Our Kima is ready to read
Pushkin.

In the shed, Kima puts Tarzan's shattered head inside a noose. She runs the rope to his feet and pulls, until the corpse is folded in half and Tarzan's single remaining eye is left to stare at his leaden ankles.

She loops the rope three more times to keep the body folded and asks Lewis for a burlap sack. Lifting the head and ankles, she places the burlap under and asks Lewis to lift the other half.

The sack closes neatly above Tarzan's buttocks. She slips another sack on top of the first and drops a few handfuls of hay inside. The second sack closes above Tarzan's head and feet. Repeating the same procedure with Kent's corpse, she ties the sacks to Kogan's sled.

"I'll come back after dark," she says, and leaves for work.

That night, after the sled slowly pulled by Kima and Lewis disappears from view, Moisey Semyonovich sits down with a book, and Levinson approaches the stove.

"Do you have the thing that spins?" he asks Kogan, looking at the watery red fluid in the cauldron.

"My *beytsim*?"

"*Fok yu!* Laboratory thing. A dreidel that you put things in and spin, to separate the dreck. I saw you use it."

"Laboratory dreidel . . . Let me think . . . To separate the dreck. I had it . . . You mean a centrifuge?"

"That's right. You have it?"

"No."

"What should I do with this?"

"The blood? You dump it in the outhouse."

"What's a blood ritual without blood? Are you insane?"

"Remember when they stood you on your head onstage? You wore a leotard. There was a tefillin on your leg."

"I'll boil it."

"Boil what?"

"The blood."

"What are you doing, trying to reduce it?"

"I guess. To get the snow out."

"Why do you need *my* blood? Isn't the purpose to obtain the blood, to bleed the *victim*? And what about the thugs? You killed two just today."

"This is my play. When it's your turn, you'll write your own. How much should I boil out?"

"Bring it where I can see."

Kogan puts on his glasses. His nostrils rise slightly as he intensely ponders the pinkish, watery liquid.

"Why's there fat on top? And what's this? Onions?"

"A little *shkvarkes* from last night."

"You couldn't wash it out?"

"I didn't know. How much?"

"About three quarters. What was it like?"

"What was *what* like?"

"What was it like to stand on your stubborn, empty head and wear a leotard and tefillin? How did the world look?"

"The world looked almost right."

The reader knows better than to believe old men. You should have seen Levinson then, in 1921, when proudly upside down he stood, in a hall painted black.

The players who joined the troupe of Alexander Granovsky sought neither fame nor bread. If fame and bread were what you wanted, you'd surely escape from revolutionary Russia.

But if you shared Granovsky's vision of the modern world, as Levinson did, you'd dance amid the cataclysm of crumbling empires. His was the world of big equations. World equaled theater, Theater equaled World. Stage, orchestra, and seats merged into one, an entity of art, a modern unit, where acting equaled music, which was the same as props and pantomime. A leotard equaled canvas, which equaled cog, which equaled sword, which equaled turbine. All became one, a monolithic unit of justice, truth, and beauty.

In those days, Levinson learned to get out of bed in a way that symbolized cubism, extending his left leg in the direction of the left corner of his mattress, the right leg in the direction of the right. And then he stretched his arms in the same manner.

In those days, Levinson didn't give applause a thought. His modern world had no room for talent. Man's goal was to become machine, an instrument of history and of production. As industry and art became the same, the loins of art would merge with propaganda, and propaganda, being the truth, would serve as the people's education.

Old God was lowercased to god, a cosmic, powerless dwarf of heaven. And upside down, Levinson held up his godless world, like an inverted Atlas. A leotard, tefillin, an ancient prayer to mock. Would anyone dare to ask for more?

You should have asked him then, "What does the world look like?"

"The world is good," he would have said. "Because we gave it reason."

In those days, he reveled in the wholeness of an ensemble, the rush of being onstage, and—yes, of course—the laughs.

Standing over a cauldron on the evening of February 27, 1953, Levinson is beyond pondering big equations.

"It's turning brown!" he shouts to Kogan.

"What is?"

"Your blood!"

"My blood . . . oh, in your cauldron. The red blood cells are breaking down. They are weak."

"What should I do?"

"Add butter."

"I don't have butter!"

"Then use lard. It's better anyway."

Levinson lops off a thumb-sized piece of lard and throws it in the cauldron. Meanwhile, Kogan returns to the meditative state of a man who has sustained two blows to the head.

"It's still brown!" shouts Levinson.

"What's still brown?"

"The blood!"

"Which blood?"

"The blood I'm boiling! Your blood, old goat!"

"I guess that's good," says Kogan. "Let me see . . ."

Kogan waves his right hand over the cauldron, driving the fumes toward his nose. The smell of the glue-like, brown substance works like a tonic.

"It's done," he says.

"But it's still brown," protests Levinson. "You told me to add lard! The blood did not turn red!"

"I didn't say it would. Why should it?"

"What do I do with this? This dreck? I wanted red!"

"Do what you want, *mayn komandir.*"

Theater historians haven't understood that Levinson had to steal his sole artistic triumph.

After the success of *Kinig Lir,* its translator, the playwright Shmuel Halkin, was commissioned to interpret the story of Bar-Kokhba, the leader of a Jewish rebellion against Rome.

The timing infused the old story with urgency. Fascism was on the rise. Indeed, it seemed unstoppable. Young Jews, whether Communist or Zionist, were scouring history for strong leaders. The Maccabees made a triumphant return, as did Bar-Kokhba, a rebel who was pronounced the messiah by none other than Rabbi Akiva.

Of course, Levinson loved the play and the *komandir* it glorified. Alas, due to his own history of rebellion—an effort to oust Mikhoels—he was relegated to being an extra. He had two parts: As a Roman soldier, he had to walk ominously and stand silently. Then he had to make an appearance as an old Jewish sheepherder who comes to swear allegiance to Bar-Kokhba.

In this role, Levinson had to look mildly decrepit and carry a shepherd's staff. It was a harmless part. He was contained, dissolved into the crowd as Rabbi Akiva blessed the rebels.

At the premiere, as freshly blessed rebels stood in their assigned positions, Levinson threw down his ridiculous staff and grabbed a dagger out of the hands of an unsuspecting rebel, then another dagger out of another set of hands and, continuing on a mad trajectory, became airborne, then went completely motionless as the bottom of the velvet curtain touched the stage.

This acrobatic feat triggered a standing ovation mid-play. It was noted in all the reviews. Mikhoels was furious. He would have used this act of insubordination as an excuse to fire the madman. Halkin, however, thought it was a brilliant interpretation that emerged organically after the dress rehearsal.

"*Eto nakhodka*," Halkin said to Mikhoels in Russian. "This is a find."

And a find it was. Is there a better way to portray the unfurling of hidden power than an unexpected pirouette with smallswords?

The fact that many members of GOSET audiences were non-Jews is largely forgotten. They flocked to the theater because it was one of Moscow's best. Levinson's acrobatic feat transcended language.

It worked so well that Halkin convinced Mikhoels to abandon his reservations about Levinson and move him to the part of Bar-Kokhba. This couldn't happen in Moscow, but it did happen when the play was taken to the provinces.

It is no small feat that during the summer of 1938 Levinson toured the former Pale of Settlement, portraying the strongest of strong Jews, a man whose name means Son of a Star, the defier of Rome, and a messiah to boot. The play had to be altered for Levinson. The singing parts had to be dropped, because Levinson was able to carry a remarkably narrow range of notes, had no notion of tonality or rhythm, and, overall, sounded goat-like.

Spectacular stage combat beats hokey singing every time. The son of a whore made a fine Son of a Star.

When Levinson uttered Bar-Kokhba's final words—"The struggle isn't over! Forward!"—the character's and the actor's experiences became one and the same. What difference did it make what came first? What difference did it make what trumped what? Who the hell was Mikhoels, who the hell was Stanislavsky, to pronounce themselves arbiters of right and wrong when it was the leap that told the story, the whole story? Halkin understood that, God bless him.

This was Levinson's final contact with the millions of Jews who inhabited the areas of western USSR. Within three years, the people who applauded Levinson's Bar-Kokhba would think of his heroic leap as they met death at the edges of deep ditches, the omnipresent chasms where the stage ended.

And—yes—other strong Jews remembered Levinson's leap as they stormed the Nazi positions, spraying from the gut.

Levinson's battle continued as well.

A loud knock on the dacha's door makes the three men take their battle positions.

Has it begun?

The choices they make reveal their inner selves and how they feel about inflicting death.

Moisey Semyonovich reaches for a pistol.

Der komandir lets his smallswords flash, retreating behind the door. He'll be the first to greet the intruders. Kogan takes no weapon at all.

They wait silently for another knock. The person outside can surely see the smoke rising through the chimney and the flickering of the yellow, halting light of the kerosene lamp.

Moisey Semyonovich throws open the latch, then stands aside.

The door opens slowly, and, like a vision from her own youth, a woman in a shapely karakul coat strides into the center of the room, and with a smile that once could have been tragically misconstrued as seductive (it was, in fact, sarcastic), giggles. *"Oy mal'chiki, mal'chiki . . . puglivyye vy u menya?"* Now, my dear boys . . . aren't you fearful?

"Ol'ga Fyodorovna, dear, to what do we owe the pleasure?" asks Kogan.

"Vy pomnite, u Anny Andreyevny bylo takoye . . ." Do you recall, Anna Andreyevna wrote about this?

Everything has been plundered, betrayed, sold out,
The wing of black death has flashed,
Everything has been devoured by starving anguish,
Why, then, is it so bright?

Kogan is familiar with the poem, from Akhmatova's *Anno Domini MCMXXI*, and it takes considerable effort for him to refrain from reciting the rest.

"Why, then, is it so bright?" he asks instead.

"Otchego zhe nam stalo svetlo?" Ol'ga Fyodorovna repeats.

"Are you personally acquainted with Anna Andreyevna?" asks Kogan, who, alas, is not.

"Cooing like little birds," Levinson whispers to himself. Onstage, this would be an aside. Around the table, it is rude.

"Yes. She hates me with a passion."

"Something political?"

"Something amorous."

9

The night is overcast; the light from a quarter moon is filtered through the clouds. For half a kilometer, they pull the corpse-laden sled. With rope across their chests, they pull horse-like on trampled snow, with not a human soul in sight. Only the dogs howl.

"Where did you learn to handle corpses?"

"A morgue. Where else? After the orphanage, that was my job."

Compared to Tatyana, this girl seems as cold as the weather, except her bright eyes speak of something trapped within. An argument can be made that Kima is just like Lewis.

After Tatyana's death, Lewis had multiple interludes with Russian, Ukrainian, and Jewish nurses at a military hospital in Novosibirsk, but these women regarded love as a step that followed and preceded consumption of vodka, onions, and herring. It was a quasi-medical procedure, a brand of treatment for the human condition.

The majority of able-bodied Russian men had gone to the front, and many of those who returned were able-bodied no more. As an intact male, Lewis could have all the vodka, onions, herring, and love he could possibly want. Being a Negro continued to be an advantage. He represented a new type of procedure for the curious nurses.

The layers of burlap are safeguard enough. He feels no cold. He doesn't see their vacant eyes or their clear, pale skin.

Kima's movements are economical, tight. She opens the sacks and stuffs them with bricks she found in the shed next to the dacha. Four bricks for Kent, four bricks for Tarzan. Lewis takes her orders, lifting a sack onto the edge, giving a push.

He listens for a splash, then, once again, the sack . . . the edge . . . a push . . .

Two hapless thugs join Lieutenant Narsultan Sadykov and his soldiers, to stand eternal guard in frigid waters. After the second splash, Kima bows her head, not out of grief (she feels none), but as some mysterious punctuation.

Lewis lacks remorse as well. His stomach does not constrict; his vomit has been cast upon these waters. He has no more.

As the waters close above Kent and Tarzan, Lewis stares down the well. Five corpses lie beneath him. This is his moment of reflection upon their death, upon his life. He can still feel. Or can he?

The girl stands next to him in silence, so close. Her hands are on his back. He raises himself from his weird genuflection and turns around to face her. As their hips meet, her torso moves tensely back, as do her lips. He sees this as an invitation to follow her, and so he does, toward the dacha.

A good strong yank is all it takes to open the dacha's door. They are inside, their sheepskin coats still on. His hands move upward from her waist to her small breasts as her lips tremble against his. He stops the movement of his hands to let her trembling stop, and stop it does.

If you have lived unscarred, you'll have to go through some contortions to understand this, but understand you will. He feels her edge, her boundary of feeling, her shore of the unknown.

And Kima knows the boundaries of Lewis's knowledge. The void of feeling engenders feeling, too. That night, Kima Yefimovna Petrova, the daughter of a martyred Commissar, chooses to place her trust in a Negro named Lewis. A rootless Negro and an orphaned Jewess; can God conceive of a more equitable match?

And so they stand in an embrace, their sheepskin coats on, and it seems hours pass before her trembling stops, before she knows she can accept his lips upon her neck, upon her breasts, and then beneath.

The sheepskin coats are their sheets; the floor is their bed; the void is their bond.

"Why did you want me?" she asks.

"Why did you want me?"

They remain locked in an embrace.

Why is he dumping corpses? Why did he kill a man? Why is he going on a mad suicide mission, pretending to believe that he will survive? Why is he saying Jewish prayers when Jews do not? Why her? Why anyone? Why anything? Why is he rootless?

"Because you wanted me."

"How old are you?"

"I'm twenty-one. And you?"

"More than twice that."

"That old?"

That old . . . yes, old enough at last to face the cursed mob that chased him out of Omaha, staying on his tail as he escaped around the globe. He'll face it squarely now, with nothing held back.

His caution vanishes suddenly, its final vestige purged, as tremors herald the arrival of courage, not a false bravado that will leave with the appearance of a lynch mob or the first volley of enemy fire. He'll take what comes—his mob, his bullet, or his truck.

"That old," he thinks. "And when I die and face my God, I'll say, 'I held your sword. I fought for her. I fought for freedom.'"

Her question brings him back from his meditation.

"When do we strike?" she asks.

As Levinson fills the teapot with snow and places it on the wood stove, Moisey Semyonovich steps outside to smoke. He hates drinking tea and the tiresome conversations it engenders. He hates pretending, hates addressing her formally by name and patronymic—Ol'ga Fyodorovna, *vy*—instead of Olya, *ty*. Do they use patronymics in intimate situations? No, but as dawn nears, they grow more distant.

He smokes Belomor, an unfortunate habit he picked up during the war. He smoked to warm up then, to feel something other than adrenaline or boredom, to ward off sadness and fear, to vacate the mind, to make the music stop. When he smoked, he thought of nothing but his smoke.

He is out by the shed now, looking at the expanse of the cemetery, that majestic piece of Judaica in the heart of Russia. It is the physical manifestation of what he believes in, what he fights for. These are his Jewish roots, stretching deeply, intricately and far beneath a Russian landscape. This is a permanent mark, something no one will ever extract.

He hears her footsteps. Why is she here? These aren't her roots. This isn't her battle. Moisey Semyonovich has never heard of Akhmatova; he doesn't accept poetry as an explanation for anything at all.

Her hands are on his shoulders now.

"Pochemy ty zdes'?" he asks. Why are you here? He addresses her in the familiar now. He is tired of formality, tired of asking no questions, tired of secret intimacy, tired of fearing that she may not return.

Instead of an answer, her hands turn him toward her, and so they stand, like young lovers facing each other in silence for what seems like hours.

10

Militia Lieutenant Mikhail Petrovich Khromov is anything but a Gogolesque crook. Khromov, thirty-seven, is a bespectacled, independent-minded scholar of the role of opportunity in the context of the objective laws of history.

His approach to history is both internally consistent and consistent with the traditions of Marxism-Leninism-Stalinism. He understands that the Party as a whole and Comrade Stalin personally can react to only the most global of challenges, such as the struggle against bourgeois imperialism, the struggle against Fascism, the struggle against wreckers. All of these struggles have one thing in common: they occur on the ground, on the level of the army and regional militia. His domain.

War is the ultimate test of functionality of the systems of government. Did the Party and Comrade Stalin set the goal to sweep Germany clean, taking every diamond and gold watch as trophies? No. But an enterprising soldier on the ground could be more thorough, benefiting himself without jeopardizing the greater goal, or perhaps even advancing it.

Was it necessary to rape every German woman in order to subjugate Germany? Probably not. But as long as rape and looting didn't contradict the general line of the Party, it could strengthen enforcement of the laws of history.

Now Khromov clearly sees another emphasis of the Party.

The final action in the struggle against Zionism and cosmopolitism is scheduled to begin within days. The decision has been made on the appropriate levels, the lists mostly drawn up.

As the official directly responsible for drawing up the Malakhovka lists, Khromov knows this conclusively. Certainly, some problems remain. The question of half-bloods, for example, is thorny but ultimately manageable.

This insight opens extraordinary opportunities: considerable wealth is about to change hands, and from his vantage point, Khromov has the right to claim a portion of that wealth.

He can be more thorough than the Party officials in Moscow and even those at the Regional Committee level. He can make the Jews give up the envelopes they keep under the floorboards and the jars they keep in the cellars.

Just in case, he instructs two young men he calls *druzhinniki*—volunteers—to open every *filin* they can find.

Khromov is careful to target only people who are, in his judgment, unlikely to survive deportation.

The old and the infirm do badly in prison transit. Hanging may be gentler than death from dysentery in a prison train. A little torture may loosen tongues and even out the calculus of pain. Lieutenant Khromov is selective. To get on his list, you have to have relatives abroad, or to have retired from well-paying work.

Over the preceding weeks, Mikhail Petrovich comes into possession of a number of gold chains, assorted jewelry, one Star of David, a jar full of American dollars, a stack of rubles, and seven gold crosses. (He is surprised to discover that Jews own gold crosses.)

He gathers his entire family once, in celebration, buying real vodka for all. Now he considers buying a motorcycle.

Is it wrong for Khromov's volunteers to dispatch the old man Kuznets and—separately—those two old women, speeding up a few deaths and taking some valuables that would be lost in the pandemonium when it begins?

Alas, Khromov's volunteers haven't returned from what appeared to be a simple task—liquidating an old doctor who lives alone.

They haven't been seen for twenty-four hours, missing their next assignment. They are common thugs who, in exchange for protection, turn over half of everything they loot. Khromov then shares some of the proceeds with Vasyok, his wife's son from a previous marriage. (They are, after all, his friends.) Have the *druzhinniki* double-crossed him?

The situation requires Khromov's personal attention.

The dacha's door opens suddenly, letting in a burst of frigid air and nearly blowing out the kerosene lantern.

Shoulder to shoulder, two men squeeze through the door. The older man holds a pistol; the younger, an old *berdanka,* a rifle of the kind first used by Hiram Berdan's sharpshooters during the American Civil War, then adopted around the world.

"This is it. Article 58. The wall," thinks Kogan, recognizing the man with the pistol as Khromov. "Local militia arrests especially dangerous state criminals."

Levinson looks up at the armed men.

"Dr. Kogan, who are these men? Robbers?" he asks, bringing a glass of tea to his lips.

"How can this lunatic be so completely unperturbed?" Kogan wonders. It looks as though a waiter and a busboy have just appeared to clear the table. This can mean one thing only: *der komandir* is assuming his battle position. This is his command: remain composed. Nothing is lost until it's lost.

"At least technically, these men aren't robbers," replies Kogan, similarly taking a sip. "One of them is none other than Mikhail Petrovich Khromov, lieutenant of the militia, a man I have always considered to be something of a friend. The other seems to be his wife's son, Vasyok."

"Zatkni rylo," shouts Vasyok, pointing his rifle at Kogan. Shut the snout.

He is very young, his voice still high-pitched.

Disregarding the command, Kogan continues: "I can see how you might have mistaken them for criminals. Militia officers usually knock on your door, introduce themselves, and present you with an official order. Also, it's extremely unusual for militia officers to deputize members of their own families, arm them with nonstandard weapons, and bring them along."

This feels good, whatever it is. Kogan slowly accepts the idea that Levinson has a plan.

"So you are puzzled, too?" asks Levinson.

"Quite." Kogan recognizes the smirk on Levinson's face.

"Scha blya shlyopnu," shouts Vasyok, placing the muzzle of his rifle directly against Kogan's ear. Loosely translated, this means, "I'll kill you," but the verb *shlyopnut'*, literally, to slap, merits notice: it is, in fact, an affectionate term for an impromptu execution.

Kogan smiles politely.

"Pomolchi," says Khromov to Vasyok. *"Vidish, lyudi intelligentnyye, chay p'yut?"* You be quiet. Can't you see, these are refined people, drinking tea.

"What do you have here? A Jewish holiday?" he asks, moving inside the house, his pistol drawn.

"A feast," says Levinson.

He recognizes that victory has become possible. Khromov and Vasyok don't seem to have the wisdom to come in and shoot everyone. This is how Levinson would have conducted an operation of this sort. Instead, these fools have engaged in a conversation, and dialogue brings victory to the person who controls it. At least that's how it works onstage, how it should be in real life. The process has slowed down. Now the task is to keep them engaged.

"We were just talking about procuring blood, and you walked in," offers Levinson. "How fortunate!"

Sometimes you have to say something—anything—and stay with it. Keep the enemy stay in conversation and remind the ensemble that "all for one and one for all" is a game with life-and-death consequences. Force them to up the stakes.

"*Chto, vpravdu?*" asks Vasyok, now pointing his gun at Kogan. So it's true?

"*Zaraneye vam, tovarischi, spasibo,*" says Levinson, causing Vasyok to shift his rifle. Thank you in advance, comrades.

"*Za chto-zh eto yesche?*" asks Khromov. Whatever for?

"*Za krov' vashu svezhen'kuyu, velikorusskuyu. Budet chem zapivat',*" answers Levinson. For your fresh great-Russian blood. I know of no better way to end a meal.

"What's this about blood? I don't believe any of this," says Lieutenant Khromov. "Dr. Kogan and I have known each other for seven years, and I don't believe that he has ever had a sip of vodka, let alone blood."

"In that case, what brings you here?" asks Levinson. "Has a child gone missing?"

"Not a child, but we are investigating the disappearance of two individuals whose whereabouts should be known to you," says Khromov.

"Were they nice people?" asks Ol'ga Fyodorovna.

Her initial fear is gone, too, replaced by infectious defiance. The proximity of gunpowder has chased away the half-nun, giving the half-harlot the dominance she craves. She smiles at the gunmen.

"No," says Khromov. "I wouldn't say that they were nice."

"So would it be a problem if they were gone?" asks Levinson.

"Actually, their disappearance would present certain problems," says Khromov, the muzzle of his revolver drawing a slow, ponderous circle around the table. "In our country, people don't disappear."

"They don't?" asks Ol'ga Fyodorovna.

"Sasha, my initial suspicion is now confirmed: this is not an official visit," says Levinson to Kogan. "If it were, by now the good lieutenant would have asked us to show our documents. I believe that we are indeed under attack by robbers."

"Tak-taki pozovite militsiyu," suggests Vasyok with a crude imitation of Jewish speech patterns. So call the militia.

"Moisey Semyonovich, we should choose our words carefully," says Levinson. "An idiot is defined as someone who is likely to discharge his weapon accidentally. Fortunately, they don't survive long."

"Let's get the *filiny*," says Vasyok.

"*Filiny* . . . This is the second time in as many days that someone has demanded my owls," says Kogan. "I have no owls. You must be talking about tefillin."

"Yes," says Khromov. "Must be. Where are they?"

"I don't believe in God," says Levinson.

"I am a Marxist," says Moisey Semyonovich.

"I am a Christian," says Ol'ga Fyodorovna.

"I am technically a Marxist, very much a scientist, but not completely an atheist," says Kogan, addressing the barrel of Vasyok's *berdanka*. "So my faith and my philosophy—philosophies, really—are often in conflict. It's a long answer, I realize."

"Enough. Just hand over the *filin*," blurts Vasyok, nervously swinging his *berdanka*.

An observer might conclude that Moisey Semyonovich has drifted off into a private dream world, a Bundist paradise, a place without exploitation, where Yiddish is the official tongue of the Jewish working class, and where religion—and therefore Hebrew—is banned; a Stalin*frei* world where deportations—of Chechens, Crimean Tatars, Lithuanians, or Jews—are unthinkable.

His lips move lightly, like silent trap drums tapping out the symphony that once again blasts in his head. His formidable musculature moves with it, his biceps flex, his fingers extend outward awkwardly, and his groin—the center of athletic prowess—contracts like an inner spring.

Moisey Semyonovich has no plan. Instead, he knows what to expect. When all seems lost, the enemy becomes complacent, and you have a chance. A single chance. Don't miss it.

"You are a military man, Dr. Kogan," says Khromov with a benevolent smile.

Kogan nods.

"You understand that we live in a stern time, when entire nations become unnecessary and therefore must wither."

"You are a strong Marxist, then," interjects Levinson. Now the idiot is talking about himself. He is fully engaged. There is hope.

Khromov nods. "Definitely a Marxist."

"Then how can we help you?" asks Kogan.

"I want you not to be so egotistical," says Khromov. "All of us do. You have committed crimes, so take responsibility."

"And what if they have not committed any crimes, as individuals, that is?" asks Ol'ga Fyodorovna.

"If they have not, then they must realize that sometimes in its history, a great people, the Russian people, must disengage itself from the lesser peoples, which have been sapping its strength. If we are a tree, you are a weed, and we must prune you."

"I promise not to sap your strength, lieutenant," says Kogan.

"Would this cause you to put away your guns, take your wonderful stepson by the hand, and go home to your lovely wife?"

"No," says Khromov. "Afraid not."

"Ah. It has begun then?" asks Levinson.

"Poka net," says Khromov. Not yet.

Khromov looks like a man at peace, almost relaxed, pontificating about his Great People.

They stand six meters apart, enough distance to gather speed, but is it enough to bring down the prey?

A single hit. That's all you get, at best. What can you use?

The bread knife is serrated, but it's at the other end of the table, by Levinson, who glances at it as he spews nonsense.

Fists work quite well, but they require repeated blows, which take time. The hands can strangle, but that, too, takes time.

Moisey Semyonovich needs to inflict instant death, a swap of figures on the chessboard: exchanging him for me. Six meters is a fraction of a second, enough to gather speed, enough to let the body act.

His thoughts: "The carotid artery . . . It's big, it's well-protected. The external jugular, which drains blood from the face, is on the surface . . . It can be found. Perhaps the carotid will be injured, too. We'll see—or not."

It is tempting to leave out the final word of that sequence of thoughts, for Moisey Semyonovich would be deeply ashamed of it. The word is Shema, the opening of a prayer that the fortunate ones are able to utter before their death: "Hear, O Israel, the Lord our God, the Lord is one."

Readers who overanalyze the presence of this solitary word to conclude that Moisey Semyonovich makes his peace with God should be ashamed of their erroneous, smug conjecture.

The truth is much simpler: by setting aside his conscious faculties, Moisey Semyonovich allows his inner animal to make strategic decisions and thus is unable to censor its base urge to acknowledge the Supreme Being.

A shadow is all Mikhail Petrovich Khromov sees before his shoulders, back, and skull spread out against the wall; his arms splay outward, fountain-like; and pressure on his neck starts to constrict air.

Before the pistol discharges and falls out of his hand, before darkness descends, Khromov sees a human ear under his chin. Pressed against the wall, he cannot move. There is an instant when he feels the teeth beneath his chin, and something like a sponge— wet, warm, and sticky—on his neck, but the lack of oxygen overwhelms, and all turns black.

This is the end of their interaction. Neither of the duelists is fully aware of the horrendous melee that follows their exeunt.

To review the full picture of these events, let us return to the beginning of Moisey Semyonovich's leap.

Vasyok is quick, but lacking preparation, he has to raise the gun and aim, which he cannot.

His rifle's bullet would have to fell both men, his stepfather and the Yid who closed his jaws upon Khromov's neck. Vasyok moves to the center of the room and takes aim, thereby opening his jugular, carotid artery, and windpipe as targets for Levinson's bread knife.

A shot rings out, and in the smoke three men slump to the ground in this order:

Rabinovich tumbles first, his brains upon the window and wall, his Godless soul speeding toward the red gates of heaven.

Khromov is technically alive. His heart still pumps, but blood is no longer draining in ways that sustain life. His hand shoots up to cover his wound in the futile hope that hands have the capacity to stop bleeding and make us breathe again. His simple, corrupt soul is packing up to make a swift evacuation.

Vasyok comes down last, his rifle resting in Levinson's firm hand, the ivory handle of the thin serrated knife protruding from the deep nest it has made within his neck, causing his windpipe to whistle softly as his blood gushes to the floor.

"You were as fast as you could be," says Kogan.

"Not fast enough," says Levinson as they rush toward Moisey Semyonovich.

Ol'ga Fyodorovna sits silently in her chair.

"A lovely, lovely man," she says.

"You were close, I surmise," says Kogan.

"I couldn't keep him from dying."

"One never can."

"Remember *The Seagull*, the very end? 'What I wanted to say was, that Constantine has shot himself. . . .' Always they die offstage—suicides, executions, beatings at interrogations, wars, the permafrost. Behind the curtain. Not this time, no more! I looked his death directly in the eye!"

"This is a sad and somber moment, but there is nothing to be done to help the victims," says Kogan. "I want you to come here and witness something extraordinary.

"Note the bite mark," he continues, pointing at an uneven red oval beside the Adam's apple on Lieutenant Khromov's puffy neck. "As surgeons, we are used to seeing human bites on hands and arms, but almost never necks, and never have I seen one like this!

"Until this moment, I did not believe that humans had the ability to bring down prey with our bite. Our teeth are made for chewing. Now, look, our friend has done what wolves and lions do: he hit the neck with murderous force, and he chomped down and held, releasing only as his brain ceased to command him to continue.

"He didn't know it could be done, but he took a chance. Now, note this area, around the bite. It's swelling up. I can find out conclusively later, but for now I believe that the bite has macerated the jugular vein and damaged the carotid artery as well. This bleeding has compromised blood flow to the brain and closed off the windpipe at the same time. It's a masterstroke and a painful way to die. Not that it has happened exactly this way ever before. I have to be right. You see, the swelling and his fitful breathing are happening too fast for any other explanation.

"If I am right, we are about to see something that hasn't been in any medical book that I have seen, something that makes me wish I had a camera."

"Oh, how foul!" says Ol'ga Fyodorovna.

The swelling beneath the tooth marks grows rapidly before the eyes of the plotters, within minutes rising to the size of a cantaloupe. The swelling grows darker as the skin stretches.

"Can't you alleviate this man's suffering instead of delivering an anatomy lecture?"

"Ol'ga Fyodorovna, please believe me, I have no way to help. I could attempt a tracheotomy, but even if I succeed, the patient will likely die of a stroke. And considering the events that led to his injury, I am not certain that his survival is in our best interests. If I were to raise him from the dead, Levinson would insist on killing him again."

Small drops of blood begin to trickle out of the four holes made by incisors, slowly turning into gentle streams. As the skin stretches, the streams grow stronger and the blood broadens its path, spilling out at intervals like waves.

Ol'ga Fyodorovna declines to watch. "This is barbaric," she says, her hands shielding her from this grotesque sight. "An exploding aneurysm is your idea of a spectacle. How could you make yourself so detached from human life?"

"If I can't analyze, I can't help. If I can't help, I can still analyze."

"I see, again, the primacy of reason."

"Proudly so. And what is the nature of your objection to it?"

"Make it objections, plural: aesthetic, ethical, moral, religious. In alphabetical order."

"So it's a clear conscience you want, Ol'ga Fyodorovna?"

"No, I want to be able to look at myself in the mirror."

"You hunger for beauty, then?"

"You guessed incorrectly. Dignity."

In the morning of February 28, when Lewis returns to the dacha, he notes that the place is starting to look like a workers' dormitory in Magnitogorsk.

There are two cots for Kogan and Levinson, a cot for him, and another cot, behind a stretched-out sheet, for Ol'ga Fyodorovna.

During the previous night, Moisey Semyonovich slept on the table, but this morning the table stands bare. Taking off his boots, Lewis notes that the floorboards feel wet from scrubbing. The smell of ammonia makes it difficult to remain inside.

Levinson and Kogan are awake.

"What happened?" Lewis asks.

"The militia paid us a visit," says Levinson, sitting up.

"They were working with the comrades you deposited in the well," says Kogan.

"And . . ."

"They took us by surprise. They had two guns to our serrated bread knife, and bare hands, and teeth," says Kogan.

"I knew Moisey Semyonovich would do something extraordinary," says Levinson. "He had that murderous look."

"And he did," says Kogan. "Never saw a braver man."

"Did he survive?"

Levinson shakes his head.

"He saved us all," says Kogan.

At 8 p.m., as darkness thickens, they gather at the well at Number Four Zapadnaya.

Another pile of bodies, two in burlap sacks, a third laid separately, covered with a red banner.

The burlap sacks go over the edge with no one saying a word, not even Ol'ga Fyodorovna, who bows her head, presumably in prayer.

"Vechnaya slava tebe, boyets Rabinovich," says Levinson as Kima and Kogan lift the flag-draped sack. Eternal glory to you, fighter Rabinovich. He nods.

"Wait," says Ol'ga Fyodorovna. "I want to speak."

Levinson raises his hand. He is willing to wait.

"Ne poet ty Solomon, ne soldat. Ty ubiytsa, Solomon, ty bandit prostoy. Net, ne zrya nad toboy voron kruzhitsya." You're not a poet, Solomon, not a soldier. You are a murderer, Solomon, and a common thug. The raven circles above as you move along.

"Moisey challenged death," she continues, her voice strained. *"V krovi u nas eto—smerti vyzov brosat'."* It's in our blood—to challenge death.

"So off we go, to cover pillboxes with our bodies, charging out of the trenches and into the open fields, rushing into mad duels. Or, worse, we write our challenge in verse and show it to friends."

Steadily, her voice grows firm, grounded, balanced. "Death acts without challenge, too. Challenged, it acts sooner, better, enjoying the slaughter of the unprotected, valorous fools, like my dear Moisey. Again I play a widow's role.

"*Ya dumala, stara uzhe.*" She pauses. "I thought old age had come. I've had my hussars, my little red and white lieutenants. My poets, too. But the contagion struck again, and now the well is full, the raven circles, and we will follow our doom."

She steps aside and silence falls.

"He died for justice," Kogan says. "Surrounded by slaves, Moisey was free."

"*Vechnyy mir prakhu tvoyemy, boyetz Rabinovich,*" says Levinson. This is the second of his standard funeral remarks. Eternal peace to your remains, fighter add-the-last-name.

"A Marxist who invokes the eternal parts roads with Marxism," objects Ol'ga Fyodorovna.

"So be it," says Kogan. "If our non-Jews feel so moved, I'll join them in our Kaddish. Coming from them, it probably means something."

They stumble through the mysterious, prickly words of the prayer for the dead: a Godless Negro, a half-nun, half-harlot, and a wavering Marxist Jew.

"Levinson, are you able to sing '*Di Shvue*' without idiocy? Moisey was a Bundist, after all."

Levinson begins quietly:

"*Brider un shvester fun arbet un noyt,*
ale vos zaynen tsezeyt un tseshpreyt,
tsuzamen, tsuzamen, di fon iz greyt."

(Brothers and sisters in labor and fight,
Those scattered far and wide,
Assemble, assemble—the banner stands poised.)

His voice is goat-like. Kogan's singing abilities are so horrendous that he sings only symbolically, which is to say not at all.

During the second verse, Kogan hears a young woman's voice:

"Zi flatert fun tsorn, fun blut iz zi royt!
A shvue, a shvue af lebn un toyt."

(It flutters with woe, with blood it is red!
We swear. A life-and-death oath we swear.)

"Kenst ot a di lid?" he asks Kima in Yiddish. You know this song?

"Yes," Kima replies in Russian. "This is what my father sang when they took him away."

"Himl un erd veln undz oyshern
Eydet vet zayn di likhtike shtern
A shvue fun blut un a shvue fun trern,
Mir shvern, mir shvern, mir shvern!

Mir shvern a trayhayt on grenetsn tsum bund.
Nor er ken bafrayen di shklafn atsind.
Di fon, di royte, iz hoykh un breyt.
Zi flatert fun tsorn, fun blut iz zi royt!
A shvue, a shvue, af lebn un toyt."

(Our oath is heard by sky and earth,
We swear beneath bright stars,
Our oath of blood, our oath of tears.
We swear, we swear, we swear!

We swear forever to uphold the Bund.
It leads us from slavery's bondage.
The banner is mighty, and red, and held high.
It flutters with woe, with blood it is red!
We swear. A life-and-death oath we swear.)

"Let us review our construct first: a Czar who rules by fear cannot protect himself from those who have none," says Levinson at 10:17 p.m., a few respectful minutes after the body of Moisey Semyonovich is submerged in the well.

> KOGAN: What is this, literary criticism? Should we *convince* him to die? Or demonstrate to him that he is *already dead*?
>
> LEVINSON: This is as real as it gets. If our construct is correct, we shall prevail. If it's erroneous, we'll perish. In either case, why wait?
>
> KIMA: We'll strike tonight.
>
> OL'GA FYODOROVNA: I'm coming with you.
>
> LEVINSON: Aren't you a pacifist of sorts?
>
> OL'GA FYODOROVNA: Your cause is mine.
>
> LEWIS, LEVINSON, KOGAN, OL'GA FYODOROVNA, and KIMA *(in unison)*: We'll strike tonight!

And if this were a play, the curtain would descend, and Act II would conclude.

Act
III

1

LEVINSON: Where will we find him?
OL'GA FYODOROVNA: In the Kremlin.
KIMA: The Kremlin then . . .

She says this with acceptance, devoid of an exclamation mark: *"Kreml' tak Kreml' . . ."*

This acceptance—indifference, is a better word—astonishes Lewis.

Do these madmen believe that they will kill the czar deep inside his fortress? What is the plan? Will there be scaling of the walls?

Country venues make regicide easier, and transit is good. Alexander II was offed in a carriage, Franz Ferdinand in a car, Nicholas II in a provincial house, Lenin—probably something similar.

Kima is not equipped to see the bullet that will kill her. Revenge is all she wants. The rest is details.

Ol'ga Fyodorovna has a cirrocumulus cloud in her head, her thoughts detached and fluffy.

Lewis, too, is irrelevant, but in a fundamentally different way. He breathes logistics, but what logistics can there be in dreams of blood?

Kogan is another story. He is useful. He feels history's pulse as his own. They magnify each other, Levinson and Kogan, as actors do.

The curtain rises to reveal an ensemble of two old men and sundry stragglers.

KOGAN: Ol'ga Fyodorovna, if we really want to find Comrade Stalin, we shouldn't try the Kremlin. I say we try the dacha.

LEWIS: Are you certain, Aleksandr Sergeyevich? Where is it?

KOGAN: He has been indisposed. "Demented" is the pitiless clinical term. Indeed, maniacal. More than before, that is. The classic regimen is limited public appearances. Not much travel. Confinement. Self-imposed, of course. He's still the liege. His isolation stems from paranoia.

LEVINSON: How do you know this?

KOGAN: The doctor grapevine.

LEWIS: Have you been there?

KOGAN: His dacha? No, thank you. But colleagues from Kremlyovka have, over the years. Not recently. His personal physician Vinogradov and I have mutual acquaintances. Doctors gossip. Let me revise that: doctors gossip*ed*.

To tell the rest of the story—i.e., the current place of residence of Dr. Vinogradov—Kogan extends the index and middle fingers of his left hand and crosses them with the index and middle fingers of his right, making a miniature likeness of a prison window.

LEVINSON: Of course, you would be the sort to know the murderers in white coats.

This line is Kogan's cue to bow.

KOGAN: I do my best. ["*Starayemsya*" is the exact word he uses.] I had the privilege to call them friends and colleagues. Dreadfully clueless, hopelessly innocent. Naïve, unfit to plot, and thus distinct from our *komandir*.

LEVINSON: You know where it is? His dacha.

KOGAN: I can deduce. Some years ago, I treated Madame Merzhanov, the wife of Miron Merzhanov, the architect whose specialty was designing Stalin's retreats and sanitaria for NKVD, or MVD, or whatever is the acronym de jour . . . I did my best for her, and she did well, but ended up in prison. And died, as per tradition. The dacha is in Kuntsevo. Accessible by secret road, I understand.

LEVINSON: Kogan, my friend, I hope you are right about the dacha. We will not get two tries.

Turning to costumes, Levinson decides that the women look more believable in the part of young conscripts.

With no obvious regret, Ol'ga Fyodorovna exchanges her haircut for that of a conscript and dons the loathed uniform of one of Lieutenant Sadykov's boys. An identical uniform is laid out in front of Kima.

Again, Levinson puts on the uniform of a lieutenant of state security; Lewis wears one of his own gabardine suits; and Kogan, in expertly applied blackface, wears Kima's blue dress.

KOGAN: Do I look like a minstrel, Mr. Lewis?

LEWIS: A minstrel . . . a little. More like a shtetl harlot.

KOGAN: *A kurve?* I want a red wig now.

Since no one laughs, he lifts his skirt to mid-thigh.

KOGAN: How about tefillin for my legs, like Zuskin?

Still no reaction.

LEVINSON: I thought I had more time to write the play.

He looks absurd. His limbs are far too long to fit inside Sadykov's pants and tunic.

KOGAN *(lowering the hem)*: We'll help you as we go.
LEVINSON: I'll split up what I have.
KOGAN: We'll improvise the rest.
OL'GA FYODOROVNA: I know that Jews believe that with knowledge of God's name, and with a proper incantation, a man can make himself unseen. You think you know the name and incantation?
LEVINSON: They don't exist.
LEWIS: We'll see.
KOGAN: You are insane.
LEVINSON: And you are alive. They can't defend themselves from that which they can't see. I hear that when Stalin travels, he takes an entourage of seven hundred guards, who take positions around his dachas in three concentric circles.
KOGAN: That's preparation for a military assault.
LEVINSON: But we'll evade them, comrades.
KOGAN: By means of what? The Kabbalah?
LEVINSON: We'll blind them with a story. It takes a piece of paper, and here it is. I have handwriting of the sort we need.

Within a minute, the paper starts to tell the story:

Arrest Paul Robeson. Bring for personal interrogation.

The signature is clean and bold: *I. Stalin.*

LEWIS: This is fine work. Have you been planning this?
LEVINSON: I had no time to plan.

The Black Maria stands undisturbed where Lewis left it in the early morning of Wednesday, February 25.

With every snowfall, people have made fresh paths around the ominous truck.

On March 1, at midnight, a slightly stooped old man dressed in an ill-fitting uniform of a lieutenant of state security walks past the *kolkhoz* market gates, gets in the truck, and guns its engine.

Kima, wearing an overcoat of one of Sadykov's boys, waits behind a birch tree at Kogan's gate. After seeing the headlights and hearing the engine, she runs inside to tell the Negroes and Ol'ga Fyodorovna that it is time to go.

At night, with no traffic, a Black Maria traveling at the speed of thirty-five kilometers per hour can cover the distance between Malakhovka and Kuntsevo in a bit under four hours.

Near the cemetery, the Black Maria turns onto the Nizhegorod Shosse. The time is 0:31 a.m.

KOGAN: Is something gnawing on you, Lewis?
LEWIS: Let's imagine for a moment that Stalin is where we
    think he is, that we don't get liquidated before we reach
    him, that we do assassinate him, and even that we survive
    and that we get away. Then what? Remember Lady

Macbeth? She was destroyed by her bloody deed. As was your Boris Godunov.

OL'GA FYODOROVNA: I love Boris Godunov.

LEWIS: *I mal'chiki krovavye v glazakh.* [The blood-bathed boys before my eyes.] Pushkin has Boris admit to hallucinations about the czarevitch he murdered. Regicide causes madness.

LEVINSON: Idiots! Prisons and madhouses are full of people who allowed opera to define their behavior. When you kill, you kill. Life's life, death's death.

KOGAN: Don't blame opera, *komadir*. Read Pushkin's play. The word *komedia* is in the title, and yet it has been missed for a century and change.

Boris Godunov is Pushkin channeling Shakespeare, and operatic foolery, and what have you, in a crazy romp. *Macbeth* made Russian—and made funny, or funnier. Why do we kill? We kill for laughs, and then by laughs we die.

You know, Lewis, I suggest that you work harder to squeeze the inner Shakespeare out of yourself.

LEVINSON: Squeeze him out drop by drop. This is Mother Russia. It's not Shakespearean terrain. We are not liquidating one monarch to install another.

KOGAN: Yes, Mr. Frederich Lewis, you are not in line to become Frederick I, the Emperor of all Russia.

OL'GA FYODOROVNA: That name's been used. The Grand Duke of Baden was Frederick I. I'm not mistaken.

LEVINSON: I saw your Paul Robeson in *Emperor Jones*, by the way. It was a similar story . . .

LEWIS: Fuck you.

LEVINSON: *Fek you, fek you.* If all goes well, we will remain unseen, and unseen we will leave.

KOGAN: And history will get another chance to get it right.

LEWIS: Or fuck it up.

KOGAN: Or fuck it up. As Russian patriots—for this is what we are, make no mistake—we will have done what we can do.

OL'GA FYODOROVNA: Forgive me, but when you negate Shakespeare, are you not also negating the Old Testament notion of retribution and the New Testament notion of salvation?

LEVINSON: Yes and yes.

KOGAN: *Uvy, ya tozhe.* As do I, alas.

LEVINSON: Killing Stalin is no different from killing the night guard Butusov, which is something you know about, Lewis.

KOGAN: The notion that killing monarchs is somehow more vile than killing night guards is as absurd as the notion that killing a usurper is innately noble. And the definitions of "usurper" and "tyrant" and "impostor" are all in the eye of the beholder. They are rooted in the naïve, anti-scientific belief that legitimate rulers draw their power from God.

LEWIS: Which reservoir of your wisdom are you drawing on, Aleksandr Sergeyevich?

KOGAN: I have one well of wisdom, and it's a stretch to call it that.

LEWIS: Touché. I will rephrase: Are you speaking as a doctor or as a killer?

KOGAN: The former, of course. The Shakespearean notion that madness and the subsequent onset of suicidal behavior is the price one inevitably pays for regicide is absurd from the clinical standpoint. It's more simplistic even than Marxism, which similarly has no clinical

applications. You can't treat people based on their relationship to ownership of the means of production. Forgive me this digression. But I can imagine a situation
where regicide can have therapeutic value.

"Speaking of Marx, we need more fuel," says Levinson, whose face
reflects unbridled joy of the sort rarely found on this side of mad-
house walls. "I'll stop somebody and siphon what they have."

In the uniform of the MGB, behind the wheel of a Black
Maria, he is a happy man.

Levinson learned to drive during the war, after the chauffeur
of his troupe's truck died in an air raid, in the same blast that
killed two players: a tragedian from Lvov and an operetta singer
from Tashkent.

In the middle of the Karacharovo Bridge, an unremarkable
railroad overpass, Levinson spots a canvas-covered Willys.

Stopping the Black Maria, he shifts into reverse, gets off the
bridge, and turns off the lights.

Next to a snowdrift, he cannot see onto the bridge or be seen
from it.

"I will go," says Kima, who sits to his right.

"You don't look like a soldier," says Kogan from the cage. "Stay
in the shadows at least."

"She looks more like a soldier than *komandir* looks like a lieutenant," says Lewis.

Indeed, what options do they have? An elderly lieutenant whose
arms are longer than his sleeves? Another soldier who badly hides
her age and gender? The False Paul Robeson and his False Wife,

who is actually an old Jewish doctor in black face paint and a less than tasteful dress? Can an ensemble be less convincing?

Lewis bites his lip, and Kogan smiles, that harlot. Grave danger makes him smile. In 1918, Kogan could laugh while fouling his pants from fear, adrenaline, and recoil from the Maxim.

Ol'ga Fyodorovna chants a poem or a prayer, and Kima is genuinely calm. This isn't a façade: she used up her reserve of feelings beneath the sheepskins the previous night. At least for a while, there will be no more.

Levinson hands Kima a thin piece of tubing. She takes it silently, opens the door, and steps out into the snowy darkness. Walking to the back of the Black Maria, she unsnaps the ten-liter canister.

With the tube in her left hand and the canister in her right, she walks to the middle of the bridge and taps on the window of the canvas-topped Willys.

A man in uniform is asleep in the front seat inside.

The vehicle's engine is running. He is trying to keep warm.

The time is 2:19 a.m.

Seven years earlier, the MGB had an elite force whose business was to fight all anti-Soviet underground forces, both imaginary and real, but mostly the former.

It used terror to combat terror.

The unit, called the Fourth Directorate, was dissolved and renamed in 1946, then the remnants were reorganized out of existence in 1949 and the remnants of the remnants were reassigned to tasks that included security of transportation.

In its sadness, the fate of Klim Grigoryevich Bykov, formerly a major of state security, paralleled the fate of the Fourth Directorate that had employed him.

After getting through the war as a member of the fearsome organization called SMERSH, an astonishing acronym for *smert' shpionam*, death to the spies, he transferred to the Fourth Directorate, only to be busted down to private. At forty-six, he is likely the oldest private in the MVD.

He doesn't know exactly why he is sitting in a cursed Lend-Lease Willys in the middle of Karacharovo Bridge. It has something to do with the lists, the Jews and their treason, and people's anger, and just retribution, and all kinds of things that he has duly noted, but doesn't take to heart.

Why is he here? Does anyone care enough to stop this operation, this deportation of people who matter no more than, say, Crimean Tatars or Volga Germans or Chechens, by blowing up a bridge?

As an insider, Bykov understands that there is no such thing as an internal threat. It is fiction. Useful? Yes. But fiction still. He doesn't really believe that people whose lives he cut short were really wreckers, or spies, or terrorists.

The rumbling of freight trains beneath the bridge produces somnolence, which can be deepened by swigs of Kubanskaya. In SMERSH and the Fourth Directorate you learn to accept that sometimes cadres get overly zealous, that mistakes are made, but you never expect that you will become the target of someone's overreach, even though you know people who have.

He is a good man, and as such, he doesn't deserve to spend his nights in stopped, cold cars atop cold bridges.

Investigators are thorough by nature, and Bykov is capable of producing an account of the string of intrigues and misunderstandings that led him back to the rank of private and the task of sitting atop the Karacharovo Bridge in the middle of the night.

A tap on the window awakens him.

Groggy, he sees the face of a young woman, a girl, really. The girl is wearing an MVD overcoat.

"Since when did we start drafting girls," Bykov mutters.

"*Ey, bratishka,*" says the girl in an absurd deep voice. "*Otley ben-zina chutok. Tak do Lubyanki ne doberemsya.*" Hey, brother, let us syphon off a little gasoline. We don't have enough to get to Lubyanka.

"*A chto u vas na baze ne khvatayet?*" Are you saying you don't have enough at your base?

Bykov has seen many a deception, but nothing this overt, nothing this senseless. Why is this girl in uniform? Where did she get it?

"*Est' to est', bez problem, tol'ko vot daleko zayekhali. Radius, poni-mayesh, bol'shoy, a podzapravit' negde. Tak vot ne dobralis'. V pol-kilometra otsyuda vstali.*" No, they have it, no problem, except that we got too far, a big radius, understand? And no place to top off the tank. Stopped a half a kilometer from here.

Why does she have a gasoline can? Is this a prisoner escape?

This much Bykov knows: when you let people talk, they hang themselves, so keep them talking.

He asks a question: "*A kogo vezete-to? Kogo arestovyvali?*" Whom do you have there? Whom did you go to arrest?

"*Nikogo. Doma ne bylo. Naprasno perlis'. Teper' trekh litrov ne khvatayet.*" Nobody. They weren't at home. Ended up with nothing. Now we are three liters short.

"*A let to tebe skol'ko, paren'?*" How old are you, young man?

"*Devyatnadtzat'.*" Nineteen.

"*Nu ladno, khuy s toboy, otlivay. Tri litra, ne kapli bol'she.*" Fine then, fuck you, go ahead, syphon away. Three liters, not a drop more.

This "boy" will turn around and bend down to get the tube into the can. His motions will betray him.

Bykov is no fool.

He has a plan that serves both his own interests and those of the state that he is stationed on the Karacharovo Bridge in the middle of the night to protect.

They'll benefit equally, Bykov and the state.

They'll share her like brothers.

Kima unscrews the gasoline cap on the Willys, inserts the tube of the syphon, sucks in the fuel till the noxious fluid reaches her lips, then drops the end of the tube down into the can.

The fuel begins to drain.

A train passes beneath the bridge. Its steam has merged with blowing snow, creating shadows of gray that merge with streaks of white. A starry night—in miniature.

It is a freight train. Kima's ear distinguishes passenger from freight.

She senses that the man is now behind her, but that's to be expected. People like watching each other work—and fellow soldiers can be counted on to help. She saw this in camp guards. Crouching above the can, she raises her right hand in acknowledgment.

Were it not for the freight train, she would have offered words of gratitude.

The shadow comes closer. She feels the urge to stand up and does, almost, but it is too late. She is in Bykov's powerful grip, his arms beneath her rib cage. She fights for air as his arms move upward.

"*Baba ty, blyad', a nikakoy ne soldat MGB,*" he shouts into her ear above the sound of the train.

Yes, Bykov cracked this case—you are a woman, not an MGB soldier.

If you were to watch from the side, you would see a woman's hands shoot upward, above her shoulder, into the assailant's looming face.

Her right thumb encircles the globe of his right eye, removing it in an instant. Her left index finger forces its way into the left globe.

The right eye, still tethered to the muscles, slips uselessly out of its socket. The sudden force of Kima's left hand compresses the eyeball and continues, guided by the fibers of the optic nerve, into the skull. The weak spot where the optic nerve exits allows her thin finger to break through.

Sensing this advantage, Kima twists and stabs her finger further inside. Her probing finger finds Bykov's brain stem, and only three seconds after she feels his arms around her this battle is over.

Bykov's body convulses as fluid and brain ooze from his head, producing a viscous stream that drips onto the front of Bykov's overcoat, then down, lower, to the left epaulet of the MVD uniform that not quite a week earlier was worn by a Ukrainian boy who came for Levinson.

Bykov's body quakes on her back. It's a familiar feeling in an ominous way. Is this not what he wanted? There is a term for this in Russian: to take *nakhrapom*.

If you speak no Russian, no problem—say it, with emphasis on *kh*. Feel free to spit. They say to take *nakhrapom* isn't a rape. Not necessarily, because there is no beating, no killing, and there is a presumption on the assailant's part that the victim will silently accept her fate along the way. Men like Bykov happen to believe that women like this sort of thing. At orphanages and camps, an inmate learns that being taken in this manner is no less a part of life than music, food, drink, and air.

She gets up quickly, with a jerk, weightlifter-like. She pulls her fingers out of the empty nests and, boatman-like, carries her burden toward the iron railings of the bridge. More goop mixed in with muscle drips out on her back.

She makes him lean against the railing. Then, lifting his legs, sends him onto the tracks beneath.

The fuel canister is full—the whole ten liters.

Enough to get to Kuntsevo, and partway back.

"Was there a problem?" Levinson asks after she is done pouring the contents of the can into the Black Maria's tank.

Kima is silent.

Looking from the cage, Kogan discerns the viscous goo that moments earlier had been a human eye. He knows such goo. He's seen it in the past and shown it to students, making them vomit. He chooses not to ask.

As the Black Maria passes by the lifeless Willys, Levinson stops, looks, and shakes his head.

"Another guard," he says with disapproval.

The clouds that fill her head enable Ol'ga Fyodorovna to feel the proximity of a sudden, violent end. She looks in Kima's eyes and scans for feeling, even a trace of it, in the cold blue space. Finding none, she utters, *"Dorogusha."*

A dear child.

2

Assassins must make an effort to understand their immediate precursors—not from literature, which as previously established on these pages, is unreliable, but from concrete historical facts.

Kogan is convinced that Lenin's death in 1924 was neither from tertiary syphilis nor from the old wound he had suffered six years earlier. His evidence is thin, fused with belief—but that's the best that can be had.

Kogan thinks the killers were men in white coats—his esteemed colleagues.

His source: a drunken conversation at a colleague's dacha. Perhaps the drunkard told the truth.

It must now be disclosed that Levinson and Kogan also have firsthand knowledge of the execution of Nicholas II and his family.

In 1918, Levinson and Kogan met the perpetrator of regicide proper, Yakov Yurovsky. They were stationed in Yekaterinburg, in the Ural foothills.

Yurovsky seemed to be devoid of Byronism. He was a functionary, and his sidearm was purely for decoration. The only thing worse than following a man of Yurovsky's ilk into battle was having him behind you.

Levinson and his men escorted Yurovsky through Yekaterinburg on horseback, protecting him from some unspecified peril as he self-importantly toured abandoned mines. Levinson and Kogan were on horseback. Yurovsky was in a battered Rolls that kept backfiring on improvised fuel.

In a matter of days, Yurovsky would oversee the execution of Czar Nicholas and his family and the disposal of their bodies in one of those mines. Thankfully, Levinson and Kogan weren't ordered to be a part of the unit that offed the czar, his wife, the czarevitch, the princesses, and their personal physician. (It's doubtful that Kogan would have been able to gather the inner strength to become a surgeon had he been ordered to be a part of that gruesome scene.)

Soon after the murders, Yekaterinburg was captured by the White Army. The Reds scattered, and two of the soldiers who took part in the execution ended up in Levinson's band. They spoke of ricocheting bullets, repeated stab wounds, sulfuric acid, fire, and dumping bodies in abandoned mines. One of them bragged of having shot the czarina and then bayonetting the princesses.

The bragging, if it was bragging, made Levinson ill. After a few days of this, he brandished his pistol and ordered the two men to shut up. Stories of killing young women and children made other fighters question the correctness of their chosen path. Even Levinson and Kogan admitted to nausea and wavering.

Kogan heard an account of Yurovsky's final days in 1938. His source was a colleague, a surgeon at Kremlyovka. Dying at sixty for a man like Yurovsky was a feat. For reasons no one understood, he hadn't been killed in the purges. As strength drained out of his body, Yurovsky was the sort of patient the Kremlyovka staff feared, the sort who keeps a handgun in his bedside table.

Soon after he was admitted, Yurovsky woke up, finding a hand-scribbled note on his pillow.

This wasn't, strictly speaking, a threat. It was an excerpt from Pushkin's *Boris Godunov*, his usurper's soliloquy:

> *. . . Kak yazvoy morovoy,*
> *Dusha sgorit, nal'yetsya serdtse yadom,*
> *Kak molotkom stuchit v ushakh upryokom,*
> *I vse toshnit, I golova kruzhitsya,*
> *I mal'chiki krovavyye v glazakh . . .*
> *I rad bezhat', da nekuda . . . uzhasno!*
> *Da, zhalok tot, v kom sovest' nechista.*

> (. . . Raging pestilence
> Will burn the soul, and poison fill the heart,
> Reproach assault the ears with hammer-blows,
> And spinning head, and rising nausea,
> And blood-bathed boys appear before the eyes . . .
> How glad I'd be to flee—but where? . . . Horrible!
> Oh, pity him whose conscience is unclean!)

Yurovsky thought this note was a threat. (Of course, it was.) And he lost sleep out of fear that a fellow assassin would come to even the score.

And nurses feared being summoned to his bed.

Following the Nizhegorod Street, the Black Maria reaches the Abelman Fortification, then takes Taganskaya Street past the Birds' Market, across Taganskaya Square. It's 3:21 a.m.

Moscow embraces them. This isn't self-deception. They feel its welcome in exactly the same way, with chills that uniformly run down their necks and up again. No metaphor here: a city lives, it feels, it takes your likenesses and your souls. It gives as much as you can take. When you come home, it's to a waltz.

There is a prison here—Matrosskaya Tishina. Look again.

Now a secret: if you succeed, a theater will open at this spot—here—eleven years from now, in 1964. The first performance will be Bertolt Brecht's *The Good Woman of Setzuan*.

Seize the day and see the curtain rise as Moscow's honored guests. And if you fail, the city will die with you, implode, dissolve, become a Troy. These are the stakes.

Kogan and Lewis sit on opposite benches, staring past each other. Lights from oncoming cars (mostly Black Marias) occasionally blink through the small, barred window of their cage.

KOGAN: Lewis, how do you picture Stalin?
LEWIS: *An alter kaker.* [Old shitter.]
KOGAN: The same as me and *der komandir?*
LEWIS: Maybe. Much older, though.

Kogan slams his fist on the window designed to separate the prisoners from the guards.

KOGAN: Solomon, what did you think of Lir?
LEVINSON: The character or the play?
KOGAN: The character.
LEVINSON: I hated him.
KOGAN: Do you think Lir deserves the *tsuris* he gets?
LEVINSON: He does, and how!
KOGAN: It could be the translation. Tanya complained, re-
     member? Lewis, how did it sound to you?
LEWIS: I can't compare. Mikhoels was the only Lir I saw.
LEVINSON: Lir has no right to be a king. He speaks such non-
     sense! I despise him more and more as it progresses. And

in the end, he is completely weak, prostrate. How is that good?

The path of the Black Maria runs through Moscow's heart: Upper Radischev Street, the Street of the International, the bridge over the Yauza River, Yauzsky Boulevard, Pokrovsky Boulevard.

Then, at Chistoprudnyy Boulevard and Sretensky Boulevard, they turn right onto Malaya Lubyanka, and, with surprising lack of trepidation, they pass Lubyanskaya Square, past the MVD headquarters and the Dzerzhinsky monument.

The time is 3:44 a.m. Sunrise is three and a half hours away. The Black Marias are returning from their nocturnal operations, with victims caged.

The city's cobblestones emit their music.

A waltz is customary, but tonight a march is fitting. They'll hear this march but once, and then they'll hear songs that aren't yet written, and may not be. The voices cannot be recognized; not yet. Be valorous, my sons, my daughters, for these gathering trains, these shameful lists and Black Marias proper (i.e., all but one) have made me ill.

They pass by Okhotny Ryad, the Karl Marx monument and the Bolshoi; then past the Kremlin they turn right on Comintern Street and pass Arbatskaya Square.

The Black Maria angles toward the winding streets that surround Arbatskaya: Prechistenskay Pereulok, Kropotkinsky Pereulok, Bolshoy Levshinskiy Pereulok, then Arbat Street. Anyone familiar with the map of Moscow would see that theirs is a circuitous route.

Lewis has seen Stalin's motorcade speed down Arbat, and a colleague, an engineer at Stalin Auto Plant, told him that it was the route to Stalin's dacha. This is all he knows.

Entrusting the Black Maria to luck and intuition, they drift toward the tight and winding curves of nighttime Arbat.

Kima sits silently beside Levinson. She has too many thoughts to sort through in so short a time.

To her, Arbat is home. There is a building nearby. Just to the right. She is afraid to look. On the fourth floor, you'll find apartment eight. Three rooms in all. Nadezhda Petrovna, the widow of a murdered NEPman, lived in one room. She spoke German, English, Czech, and French. She baked Ukrainian bread, and no one made a thicker soup with pork and beets and cabbage. It bent the spoons.

There was a larger room where the commissar lived with his wife, an English teacher. A nanny brought in from the Volga steppes, a German girl, slept behind three bookcases in the corner. The nanny's charge, a girl of four, had a small room, five square meters. There was a rug above her bed: three bear cubs playing on a swing made of a felled tree trunk and a stump. A Shishkin painting, *Morning in the Pine Forest*, depicts a similar scene, but not as well, because it's not a rug. She never saw that painting, just reproductions in the books. It's famous.

Where are those cubs? Did the snakes she drew that night on the pantry walls escape and strangle them? Did all the children who had that happy rug draw snakes on walls when Black Marias came to take away their fathers? Where are those snakes today? They cannot disappear. They slither, and they kill.

Along Smolenskaya Street, they cross the Moskva River.

Outside the city, on Mozhaisk Shosse, the Black Maria is enveloped in darkness.

"They should check our documents about now," says Levinson. The first gate they encounter simply opens before them.

LEWIS: Not even a document check.
OL'GA FYODOROVNA: We are invisible.
KOGAN: "Why, then, is it so bright?"

He whispers a line from Akhmatova.

OL'GA FYODOROVNA: We've slipped from their grasp. We can come up to them and spit in their faces, and should they start to shoot, they'll shoot each other.
LEVINSON: Forget Kabbalah, fools. We are in a Black Maria with prisoners in the back. We can be seen, and stopped, and killed.
KOGAN: Still, mystical constructs like Ol'ga Fyodorovna's Kabbalah hold considerable allure.
LEVINSON: Kogan, if you are able, stem the verbal diarrhea and open the rucksack.

The army rucksack lies at the Negroes' feet, sharing the floor with Kogan's doctor's bag.

LEVINSON: Pull out the bucket.

Kogan does, winking at Lewis as he points at the stenciled word *GOSET* on the bucket's side.

"He took the buckets home to repaint after the 'janitor of human souls' episode," Kogan whispers to Lewis. "By the time he was done, the theater was shut down. Now I have GOSET buckets."

"Your cultural legacy?" whispers Lewis.

"Stop whispering!" says *der komandir*. "There are red banners in it. Probably too many. Take one . . . two . . . three . . ." he counts on his fingers. "Five!"

"Done," says Lewis.

"Fold them and cut a twenty-five-centimeter hole exactly in the middle."

"Mit vos?" asks Kogan. With what?

"Here, use my sword," says Levinson, passing the weapon through the cage bars.

"This isn't really the tool for cutting cloth," says Kogan. "What if we cut out the appliqué with Stalin, Lenin, Marx, and Engels?"

"Why are we doing this?" asks Lewis.

"Costumes," says Kogan. "I want the first three banners here. We'll stuff them in our tunics, behind our backs."

A fleeting glimpse of Kima's bare back makes Lewis think of his life's purpose. What is his real name? Friederich Robertovich? What is his language: English? Russian? Yiddish? *Der Komintern-shvartser*, who knows his Hebrew prayers. A Yid to Kent and Tarzan, Paul Robeson to Butusov, and now Robeson again in this, his final role.

There was a look of wonder on Butusov's face.

With his last breath, the slain night guard forever bound Robeson with Lewis. Does the physiology of death explain Butusov's look of wonder? Perhaps Butusov's insight had come down just as his soul burst into the sky. Lewis believes such things. Assassins often do.

If you have doubts about the existence of so-called souls, if you don't believe that they emanate from higher spheres, you may want to hear about another, terrestrial connection between Lewis and Robeson.

In June of 1949, at the Tchaikovsky Hall, Lewis heard Robeson sing the song of the Vilna partisans, *"Zog nit keyn mol az du geyst dem letstn veg,"* the anthem of Jewish resistance to the Nazis.

Written by a young resistance fighter named Hirsh Glick during the war, it spread from the ghettos to concentration camps both east and west. *"Zog nit keyn mol az du geyst dem letstn veg"* is a subtle opening line for a battle hymn. Don't say you are going in your final way.

The final battle is something Marxists take very seriously. The original French version of the "Internationale" contains the words *"C'est la lutte finale,"* and the same words figure both in Russian and in Yiddish versions. This phrase invited Hirsh Glick to ask: Do you really know this battle is final? Has anyone told you?

A year after the war, Lewis heard several voices sing *"Zog nit keyn mol az du geyst dem letstn veg"* from inside a guarded cattle car at the Sverdlovsk Railroad Station. Lewis joined in the next line:

Khotsh himlen blayene farshteln bloye teg . . .

(Though leaden skies eclipse the day . . .)

What was the story of these prisoners? How did they end up moving from one holocaust to another? Lewis would have loved to swing open the door of that cattle car. Yet he did not, for fantasies of freeing the slaves, albeit enchanting, are self-destructive.

At the Tchaikovsky Hall, Robeson infused the song with the raw pain of a Negro spiritual. In his rendition, the word *oysgebenkte*—final—became four separately emphasized words, *oys-Ge-Benk-Te,* which he rolled out like machine gun fire:

Kumen vet nokh undzer oysgebenkte sho,
S'vet a poyk ton undzer trot: mir zaynen do!

(The hour that we have longed for will come,
Our steps will beat out like drums: here we are!)

Since Lewis was a Negro, no one dared to block his way as he knocked on the door of Robeson's dressing room. Robeson opened the door and, pleasantly surprised to see a Black man, invited him inside.

"Ikh meyn az di blayene teg zaynen shoyn gekumen, Khaver Robeson," whispered Lewis in Yiddish. I think the leaden days are upon us, Comrade Robeson.

Robeson nodded, pointing at the ceiling, for the dressing room was surely monitored.

It is unfortunate that people fated to make history are often unaware of some of its most intriguing episodes. Consider Lewis's brief exchange with Robeson. It would have been so much richer had Lewis known why Robeson chose to sing *Zog nit keyn mol* that night.

He sang it as an act of solidarity with an imprisoned friend, Itzik Feffer, a hack poet whose secret contributions to literature included surveillance reports on Solomon Mikhoels. (Robeson and Feffer met in New York, where the poet-spy accompanied Mikhoels.) Earlier that day, Robeson told his Soviet hosts that he wanted to see Feffer, and the poet was brought to his hotel, as though by room service.

In the room, Feffer used sign language to explain that he was in trouble. Indeed, he was in prison on charges of participating in an international Jewish conspiracy and spying for America. After the visit to Robeson, Feffer was taken back to his cell at Lubyanka.

Four years after his encounter with Lewis, Robeson was tormented by Hoover's FBI and sundry right-wingers. He couldn't work, he couldn't travel, he couldn't claim his Stalin Prize. Does Robeson comprehend the purpose of the cattle cars that choke the railways in February 1953?

If you believe in souls, or if you think of life as evidence-based and bound to earth by science, this story doesn't change. Explain it as you wish: Lewis chooses to act in Robeson's name.

At 4:13 a.m., a cluster of headlights on the horizon makes Levinson slow down. The lights come closer, and he pulls off to the side, toward the woods, leaving his headlights on. A large black limousine, followed by a motorcade of militia and military trucks, speeds down the center of the road toward Moscow.

The driver of the last military truck waves happily to the occupants of the Black Maria with an MGB tag.

The Black Maria comes to a stop. The dacha's gate is closed.

"*Vy chto, karaul, rebyata,*" asks the guard at the gate. What are you, guards?

"I wish," says Levinson. "They feed you well here."

"What do you have?" ("*Kogo vezyote?*")

"Negroes for Iosif Vissarionovich," says Levinson, showing the guard the mandate from Stalin. ("*Negrv dlya Iosif-Vissarionycha.*")

"I hope you understand that my goal is to get away with this," says Kogan as the gate opens. "Yoske should die. Why should we?"

"Now, Aleksandr Sergeyevich, how do you expect to kill Stalin and stay alive?" asks Lewis.

"Things will get chaotic. They'll start blaming each other. They'll start shooting each other. And they will forget to look. If we kill him, we could well survive."

"In this kind of operation, success is determined by the ineptitude of the enemy," agrees Levinson. "Overestimation is a tactical error. I give the enemy his due. No more, no less."

Looking through the narrow, barred windows of the Black Maria, Lewis sees a forest of firs, and outlines of two tanks and a pillbox.

The place looks thoroughly prepared for an invasion or a civil war.

No, Lewis hasn't come here looking for death. He has the skill to sense its presence. He has smelled it many a time since 1919, when his mother hid him and both his sisters in a cellar while gangs of white men roamed the city streets and Omaha's courthouse burned. His father was a club car waiter on a Chicago run.

Lewis is, on balance, a cautious man, determined to take risks but to survive as well. He didn't ask to join this band. The choice was made for him the moment his foot came up against that corpse on Levinson's floor. That was his only chance to run, yet he did not.

At 4:27 a.m., the Black Maria stops by a hulking two-story structure. An actor in a madman's play, Lewis sits and wonders why he is alive this deep into the raid.

Kogan instantly diagnoses what went wrong with the structure.

He can see the rectangular shapes that set back the windows, straight lines that clearly identify homage to the American architect Frank Lloyd Wright's Prairie Style period.

He can see by the seams that the original structure would have been light on the landscape, and—yes—it would have wanted to be white, rising from Russia's glaciar-evened landscape rather than disrupting it. There is a fountain in front, but not like the garish fountains with sculptures that mar Moscow's parks. This is a small affair, devoid of a colossus. In the summer, it would be as light and lovely as a lily pond.

As designed, the Nearby Dacha would have been the kind of place Anton Pavlovich Chekhov would have found even more comfortable than the country houses he immortalized.

Kogan recognizes exactly how this Usonian vision of a white country mansion was desecrated by the addition of an Ussrian second floor. This superimposition makes the place look like a tuberculosis sanitarium. The color of the structure is an even greater abomination: a heinous swamp-water green. Anton Pavlovich Chekhov would have been appalled, and Aleksandr Sergeyevich Kogan feels appalled in his stead.

3

Historians trawl with broken nets. How would they know that, from childhood, specters and visions guided Stalin's life, determining its course?

His visions pulsed with power. He feared them as a child, and in a misguided effort to quell them, he enrolled in a seminary as a youth.

Stalin's father, a drunken cobbler, showed up every now and then to mock him. Often he saw the people he had killed, directly, with his hands, as a bank robber. Those whose deaths he ordered didn't bother him. Some specters threatened him, some mocked him, but he had no cause for fear. What weapons does a specter have?

The old man has no need for sleep. He sits up at his desk, his head upon his hands. He waits for his children, the ones that guide him into his greatest feat, a public execution of killer doctors and all the events that will ensue. Great pent-up power will spill into the streets.

It's 4:32 a.m. He is awake, alert, awaiting the children, yet they stubbornly remain on the walls, bound to paper. Their turn has not yet come. A vision comes instead: a burst of sunlight, changing from yellow to red, then deeper, thicker, richer, like blood that spurts out of throats while hearts still pump.

A panorama broadens on his wall, like a big map. The sun is no longer whole. Streams flow from it. Rivers form. Red waters pulse like veins.

A specter enters next, projecting on a wall, like a film on a screen. He looks familiar: a dead Jew, a blasphemer of his plans, a voice that shouldn't be. What is his name?

"Yefim!" he hears a roar within his skull. And what is this? A sword?

"Go away, Yefim," thinks Stalin, for specters hear thoughts. You speak to them without uttering a word.

Yefim is Zeitlin, a minor commissar, a fighter armed with dreams that cannot cut.

"How many divisions do you have?" the old man mocks. "Dissolve, Yefim, dissolve."

The thought of power over visions amuses him.

Yefim dissolves, as does his sword. Left alone, Stalin waits to hear purring beneath the floor. He waits for the children to step from their pictures on the walls and start their gentle play, like cheerful circus dwarves. They'll gather flowers on the carpet, fly paper planes, and draw. They'll dance as well, but they'll step softly.

He sees them every night, which means they will come again. His head slips down onto the leather surface of his writing desk. That's how it has to be, for slumber presages their arrival. Same ritual. Same children. Month after month.

The Russian historian and playwright Edvard Radzinsky comes closest to offering an accurate account of the events at Stalin's dacha in the early morning of March 1, 1953.

According to Radzinsky, a security man with the last name Khrustalev (first name unknown) instructed the guards who stood at the doors of Stalin's private quarters to go to bed.

Instructions of this sort were unheard of at the Nearby Dacha through its thirty-year history. It was commonplace for the tipsy czar to come within a centimeter of sleepy guards, drill them with his lupine eyes, and taunt them. *"Chto, spat' khochesh?"* Sleepy, huh?

Though Radzinsky's account is accurate, he is missing some crucial details.

"Kogo vezyote, rebyata?" asks Major Khrustalev, coming up to the curb. Whom are you bringing, boys?

"Negrov vezyom," answers a tall man who seems too old to be a lieutenant.

Khrustalev is a muscular man with a round face, blue eyes, and a brooding soul. This does not distinguish him from other men in his position, but this is all that's known. It's late, and Khrustalev isn't in any shape to click his heels and salute.

His gray State Security cap is somewhere in his office, probably on his desk. He threw it there after loading four singing drunks—Politburo members Beria, Khrushchev, Malenkov, and Bulganin—into a Moscow-bound limousine. They had more than two bottles of juice each. Juice, in the lexicon of the Nearby Dacha, is a wicked young Georgian wine. You drink it by the bucket. It benefits the liver. Khrustalev knows that to be the case. That night, two bottles failed to complete the journey from the cellar to the Big Dining Room. As Khrustalev stands alongside the Black Maria, his happy liver is soaked in purloined juice.

Khrustalev has heard from a checkpoint that an MGB vehicle is heading toward the dacha with Negro prisoners and a written mandate from the old man. Of course, it would be prudent to check whether the mandate is genuine, but there is no way to do it short of asking the old man himself. This is dangerous even when the old man is sober. Perhaps it's one of Beria's tricks. There has to be a reason, but it is something from above, and Khrustalev is determined not to get ground up in this.

"Are they under arrest?"

"Comrade Stalin's orders," says Levinson, handing Khrustalev the mandate.

"Arrest Paul Robeson . . . ," the major reads, concluding with "*blya*," a word that connotes a woman of loose morals, but is used in common speech for emphasis, melody, and balance.

"Paul Robeson?" he asks with disbelief.

"And wife," adds Levinson.

"I'll take a look," says Khrustalev.

As Khrustalev creeps up to the back of the Black Maria to sneak a discreet glance, the lieutenant clenches his teeth, the soldiers sit stone-faced, and the Negroes smile politely.

"He looks young, but she is ugly," Khrustalev reports to Levinson. "That nose . . . a *coquette*, too. Where did you find them?"

"Got them off a plane. They say our *chekisty* delivered them across the American border to Canada. They say he had a concert near Buffalo, state of New York."

"Are they arrested?"

"That's what it says."

"Wasn't he a laureate of the Stalin Prize?"

"So was Mikhoels. They think they were rescued, so— quiet . . ."

"Why are we standing here, talking? Let's get them in, comrades. Let Comrade Robeson cheer up Iosif Vissarionovich."

"He would love that. He's been singing for us all the way from the airfield."

Khrustalev walks through the Big Dining Room, singing what appears to be an English translation of a Soviet song:

Fdom bodda undoo bodda,
From oushan un-doo-dunn-blya,
Rayz aap, rayz aap, blya, ze layborink folk,
Ze go-od R-rash-shan folk!

He believes that he sounds a lot like Robeson, and perhaps he does.

Around the corner, outside the Dining Room, Khrustalev's rendition concludes with a non-melodic "U-u-gh . . ." Excruciating pain emanating from the shoulder makes him bend over, albeit not low enough to experience relief.

Levinson has a talent for choking his victims while dislocating their shoulders in a wrestling version of a checkmate. This grip can be executed in a manner that causes death.

Inside the dacha, Kogan's disgust vanishes. He sees a tasteful Frank Lloyd Wright interior, beautiful walnut paneling, comfortable chairs, a well-proportioned table.

That night, the children fail to show up, but specters bother the old man.

Five burst into his room, in robes of harsh red.

"What are you, doctors?" asks Stalin in his skull, but they don't seem to be the same as that preposterous Yefim. They fail to answer.

Perhaps addressing them requires speech. He glances at the clock: 4:34 a.m.

"What are you, doctors?"

"Judges," a tall specter says.

His is armed, it seems. He is holding a curved sword. The old man saw that sword before. Was it not brandished by Yefim?

"Defendant, state your name."

He feels a hand—a corporeal hand—grab hold of his shirt

collar and lift him up. A specter with a hand that grips is something new: a threat.

"Iosif Stalin. Who are you?"

The judges suddenly line up ominously like a firing squad. "Am I awake? Can this be real?" he thinks.

"Mikhoels, Solomon," says the tall judge, the one who propped him up, and held him by the collar.

"Kaplan, Arkashka," another specter says.

"Zeitlin, Yefim," says specter number three.

"Akhmatova, Anna," says the fourth.

"Robeson, Paul," the fifth one says.

What is this? Some alive. Some dead. All known to him but one: Kaplan, or some such. Has the world changed? And this Yefim, again. The old man needs to adjust to the changing boundaries of his new life.

"Paul Robeson?" asks Stalin out loud.

"You lied, and I believed," the specter answers.

"You wanted to believe, and so you did."

"We sinned together."

When did they lose their ability to hear thoughts? When did they learn to speak? Are the children different now, too? Will they still dance and play the way they did last night?

Mikhoels, who is clearly dead, and thus a harmless specter, has to differ from that Robeson fool.

"Mikhoels, do you think I missed the insult in your *Kinig Lir*? You called me a fool for liquidating your old friends. I banished Trotsky. Is he Kent? Cordelia Bukharin? Let's cast Zinoviev, Kamenev, Yagoda. Which one's your Edgar? Which one's Edmund? I am not Lir! I kept my kingdom! I'll make it bigger still, uniting Earth and hell to build a heaven."

"I know why you had me killed. I grew too big for you to handle," the tall one says. "But why kill Zuskin?"

"I read your article about Lir. You said so yourself: Lir and his jester are a single role. You taught me that the king's the fool, and the fool's the king. Agreeing, I decreed that the fool must follow his king to his new kingdom. Not me—the real Sovereign—but you, Mikhoels, the pretender. You left me no choice. You wrote the play. My job was to enact it."

Levinson's stage directions read:

Chief Judge begins a nign.

The melody is as simple as melodies can be. No words, just winding, wailing sounds, which souls carry into the heavens and back.

Ay-yay-yay-yay-yay-yay-yay-yay-yay
om bibibom-bom bibibibibom
ay biri-biri-bim-bom, biri-bim-bom
ay digidamdam-digidamdam, om-bibibibom-bibibibom . . .

"Yefim, I saw you minutes ago. You raised a sword. Was that a warning or a threat?"

"A mortal threat."

"The day I fear the likes of you will be the day I die. I do not fear, so I live."

"You lost your grip tonight," the tall judge says.

"*You* lost your grip, not I. Here's all one needs to know about Jews. You kill each other for a cause, and I control the cause and give you weapons. Then I sit down and watch. One couldn't wish for a better sport. You mocked your God, you mocked each other's deaths and threw the corpses to the wolves. This wasn't symbolism. The wolves are fat. It's real.

"Where is my fault, Yefim? Your people wanted me, and I was there."

The *nign* continues, and its sound makes Kima touch Yefim, her father, like on those happy nights, when she slept in her crib, and he secured the foundation of their bright future. The contact of their souls produces hot tears that come from sadness and from joy.

Ay-ay biri-biri-biri-bim-bom
ay-ay biri-biri-biri-bom
biri-biri-biri-biri-bom . . .

Tears don't cripple her. Her strength increases tenfold. Her hand is steady and her weapon poised.

The sun has yet to rise, and purring has begun.

The children slide off the illustrations and stand along the walls.

"I lived for you," says Stalin to them. This time, he uses his voice.

They look indifferent, detached.

"Our *kinig* is addressing specters on the walls," notes Kogan. "He is as mad as he is lucid."

Levinson's stage directions: *The Chief Judge prepares physical evidence.*

"Let's kill and flee," says Kima.

Orphans have no patience for ritual of any sort.

OL'GA FYODOROVNA: How can we kill a man who may not
    understand why he is being killed?
LEVINSON: Why does it matter?
KOGAN: From the standpoint of ethics, Ol'ga Fyodorovna
    isn't wrong. I am starting to wonder about this myself.
LEVINSON *(reaching inside his rucksack to produce a janitor's bucket)*:
    Ethics? What do you think we are?

LEWIS: Assassins.

OL'GA FYODOROVNA: Not I.

LEVINSON: Not you? Pray tell, what brings you here?

OL'GA FYODOROVNA: Pursuit of dignity.

LEVINSON: You've taken a wrong turn.

KOGAN: Indeed, my dear, assassinations are not especially dignified events. This is my first, of course, so I am only guessing.

LEVINSON: Enough! Please, Kogan, read your lines! I do not care what he understands. I care even less about her dignity and her pursuits!

OL'GA FYODOROVNA: How petty . . .

LEVINSON: Not *those* pursuits. He's dead, besides. Please . . . *sha!* Somebody, read your lines!

KOGAN *(reading)*: For you, Reb Iosif, we stage the first Blood Seder history has ever known. We will pretend that God did not stop Abraham's hand, and human sacrifice flourished.

LEVINSON: We stage this play to make your madness real.

Had Solomon Mikhoels beheld him now, he would have seen his equal. Solomon Levinson is an actor who can direct, a director who can write. No wood. No splinters. Not a railroad spike in sight.

Watch Levinson seize the stage with energy, inspiration, movement. He hasn't felt so young since 1921. On March 1, 1953, Levinson is wiser.

Directions read: *The prisoner is inverted.*

To hoist a man, you need two acrobats. Have them kneel down, then put one hand on each calf, another on the shoulder, and, yanking fast, stand up. The movement is machine-like.

Imagine this: the room is painted black. Chagall designed your set. There is no set, in fact. No seats, no stage. No right, no left, no up, no down. Let Marc design the costumes, too, and stick a cubist beak upon your schnoz. Make all the pieces click, biomechanically, machine-like, a modern unit fused in action.

The czar lurches forward, then to the side, but that is all—for even in his prime, his strength was meager.

Lewis and Kima grab a calf each. Each grabs a shoulder, too. Two acrobats invert the tyrant, as justice triumphs. Vault! The great biomechanical Machine of Truth is blasting off the dust and cobwebs.

Moscow time is 4:42 a.m.

The wheels of just revenge begin to grind.

When you are a little man with a crooked arm, you learn to protect your space. The arm is no problem. It petrifies, turns into granite, hard as a statue, which would be fitting, except the fingers curl. If you can part them with your right hand, a cigarette can be inserted. Or part them further and fold in a pipe. The left arm is decoration. The right arm is what you need when you make speeches.

The elbow moves forward, then back again, but not the arm. It hangs at an obtuse angle. And pain is close, lurking in the left shoulder.

As Stalin's world inverts, he grabs the left arm with the right, to keep it in its rightful place, beside him. He needs no medical advice to know that his shoulder should stay unmoved.

He will be rescued by the guards or, better yet, the children. Inverted but intact, and held together with his own arms.

The children do not move.

"Tear them to pieces!" Stalin cries.

The children weigh allegiances. Specters often do.

LEVINSON: Kogan, your lines . . .

KOGAN *(reading)*: It's said that every generation, and every man, must find his freedom from his Egypt. Our times are cruel. We part one sea after another.

LEVINSON *(holding up a flattened bullet)*: With this I killed a man.

KOGAN: Our freedom is won in battle . . .

LEVINSON: Against the czars.

KOGAN: Against the Fascists.

LEWIS: Against our brothers.

KIMA: Against the tyrants.

KOGAN: Against our God.

He must remember to hold his arm, to ward off pain. Blood rushes to his head. He needs to stand upright, ward off the pain that's setting in the living nerves above that cursed dead arm.

Why do the children keep their frozen postures?

The specter lets the bullet drop into the bucket and, reaching into the rucksack, raises two gutted leather boxes.

KOGAN: Tefillin ripped. Twice desecrated. First by us. The second time by thugs. We gutted God for freedom. They are gutting us for gold, for sport, or for no reason at all.

LEWIS: To kill a man is homicide. To kill a czar is regicide. To kill a demigod is demideicide.

OL'GA FYODOROVNA: What do you call the killing of a madman?

LEVINSON: You have no script!

OL'GA FYODOROVNA: And yet I dare to ask.

LEVINSON: *Meshuge*cide, let's say!

KOGAN *(reading)*: To kill this man is a sin times three.

OL'GA FYODOROVNA: A sin times four, you mean. *Meshuge*cide brings it to four.

LEVINSON: Enough!

KOGAN *(reading)*: A sin times three will equal one redemption.

OL'GA FYODOROVNA: Redemption without God? Incongruent.

LEVINSON: I wrote *Without god.* Lowercase.

OL'GA FYODOROVNA: Such nonsense.

LEVINSON *(raises a jar of syrupy brown liquid)*: This blood is Kogan's. Spilled by thugs, and mixed with snow and lard.

KOGAN: Let's call it by its real name. A brown sauce *mit shkvarkes.*

LEVINSON: Consult your lines, old goat . . . please.

OL'GA FYODOROVNA: If your unleavened bread is called the bread of affliction, this sauce is something else.

KOGAN: Blood of affliction?

LEVINSON: Your lines! Your lines! Keep up the *nign,* Lewis.

KIMA: Let us rejoice at the wonder of our deliverance . . .

KOGAN: From bondage to freedom.

LEWIS: From agony to joy.

KIMA, LEVINSON, KOGAN, and LEWIS *(reading together)*:
From mourning to festivity,
From darkness to light,
From servitude to redemption.

LEVINSON: Without god.

OL'GA FYODOROVNA: No, comrades, with Him. *Tovarisch* Stalin, I come here with an ode of sorts. I come to tell you how rich my life has been because of you. With a firmer hand than any czar, you made the Russian verse a game of life and death. Each time you raised the stakes, I felt a twinge on lips I kissed, on heads that later rolled. The more displeased you were with their songs, the more these men and women pleased me.

LEVINSON: I didn't write this.

KOGAN: Next Year in Jerusalem? Is that the conclusion here?

LEVINSON: This is my play, you fool! I am at home! No! Forever here!

Who are these spirits? What power do they have to get me—
Stalin—under their control?

His right arm slowly lets go, the left one drops, its angle widens, and pain pours in from shoulder nerves.

The world's polarity has changed, and that which was above is
now beneath.

"Judges, read the verdict," commands Levinson.

The judges read:

"The accused, Stalin, I., is sentenced to the highest measure of
punishment: the extraction of all blood, drop by drop."

The czar feels a light pinch in his left leg and, released, warm
fluid comes down upon his belly, his chest, his chin.

He hears a voice: "Why isn't there blood?" It is a judge . . . Mikhoels?

Another judge replies: "This is a catheter, not a drainpipe!"
Zuskin?

"So get a drainpipe!"

"Where?"

"I don't know! In your *farkakte* bag!"

"Am I a plumber?"

"Plumber? Worse! You are a goat, an old goat at that, *an alte
tsig*!"

"This catheter is for *shpritsing*!"

"But our verdict is to drain!"

"I didn't write it. It is your play, your verdict!"

"What do you want to do?"

"In principle, you could inject him."

"*Mit vos?*"

"*Mit* digitalis. Potassium, maybe. Even a burst of air in the veins will stop the heart."

"Then get the digitalis!"

"Let me see . . ."

"A little faster . . . It's almost dawn! The acrobats look tired!"

"I have no syringe."

"A doctor without a syringe?"

"I thought I had it, but I don't."

"What good is your catheter without a syringe?"

"You have a point. Has anyone seen it?"

"We'll cut his throat *mit'n* sword!"

"In the Temple, when it stood, the sacrifices were done with goats being held upside down."

Inverted people spend their fury fast. The children stir. They dance like flames, in rapid, closing, spinning circles that keep the beat of drums that blast on the inside of Stalin's skull. The world is red. It changes to purple, then red again. As their circles spin, the children, one by one, break out to look inside his upside-down eyes. Their faces show no grief, no joy. They don't show anything at all.

"Fine! Fine! We hold him upside down, so—whack! How hard is that?"

How hard is that?

"Whack *zhe*, old goat, whack!"

"No."

"No?!"

Many a man would bargain for that sword. For one swift strike, a lesser man would trade the conviction that murder-punishment is no cleaner than murder-crime. Beliefs, allegiances would fly like worn-out gloves, tossed in the rubbish.

"*Nu-u* . . ."

Forget commandments, oaths.

Kill, Dr. Kogan, kill! You've come this far! Think of your friends, your colleagues. Arkashka Kaplan, for example.

You know the truth. Accept your fate, old goat!

"Your symbolism is backward, *komandir*. If he is to be treated as a sacrificial goat, and if you cut his throat, you might make him kosher. That's a wrong symbol. You'll confuse God. The thing to do is stick him like a pig."

"So, do!"

"Turn out the light."

"Turn out the light!"

The lightbulb dims, yet darkness doesn't fall. The tyrant doesn't pray. His hands grow warm. His body swells and tingles. His breath grows faster, shorter. And he needs air, more, more, more . . .

His thoughts: "The world without Stalin . . . nonsense! This cannot happen, because it cannot happen—ever!"

He watches his spirit break out of the assassins' grip, become upright, and join the *khorovod* of blank-faced children. "I'll dance . . . I'll twirl . . . I cannot leave."

LEVINSON: Turn on the light!

(The light is turned on.)

LEVINSON: You didn't stick him!

KOGAN: No.

OL'GA FYODOROVNA *(crossing herself)*: Thank God. It would have been appalling.

LEVINSON: Fine . . . I have had it, Ol'ga Fyodorovna, dear countess, or whatever you are. Your pursuit of dignity is getting in the way of our pursuit of justice!

OL'GA FYODOROVNA: So kill me, too.

KOGAN: I didn't kill him, *komandir*, but he is a dead man still.

LEVINSON: How can you tell?

KOGAN: I am a doctor.

LEVINSON: But you're the kind that cuts!

KOGAN: Do you see this? *Nit umkern zikh keynmol . . . keynmol . . . keynmol.* He is redder than a crawfish, even his feet. Look on his lips . . . *di lipn . . . zet . . . nu . . . kukt zikh ayn.* He is swelling. And if you call this breathing, my name is Mrs. Robeson. *O, tut a kuk . . .* Look there, look there—we are done. Just put him on the sofa. Or the floor . . . *Azoy . . . Gey, gey!*

As it has been established, shortly before 5 a.m. on March 1, Major Khrustalev tells the guards that the old man gave his blessing for everyone at the dacha to go to bed, and the guards enthusiastically carry out the order.

This is, most likely, correct.

The playwright-historian Radzinsky, who obtained this information by interviewing the last surviving guard, can't possibly account for Major Khrustalev's whereabouts between 4 a.m., when the czar's dinner guests piled into a Moscow-bound limousine, and 5 a.m., when the major dismissed the guards.

Radzinsky is in no position to know that at 4:57 a.m., the plotters, as they make their exit, untie Khrustalev, take a strip of red cloth out of his mouth, and apologize for any pain and discomfort they might have caused.

"Have you heard? The czar is dead," says the tall, elderly lieutenant.

"*Almost* dead," the homely Negress adds. Her voice is deep, her Russian perfect.

"It happened on your watch," a soldier says. "You should be proud." He has a woman's voice.

"You led us to him," the Negress adds. *"A sheynem dank.* Are you, perchance, a Yid?"

"If I were you, I'd send the guards to sleep," Paul Robeson says. "Have some more wine, relax, *gey shlofn.*"

Khrustalev takes Robeson's advice.

The following evening, Stalin is found unconscious, in a puddle of urine on the sofa in his study.

It's no surprise that the story of three *chekisty* delivering Paul Robeson and his wife for an interrogation evaded Radzinsky.

Robeson's visit was an unusual event at the Nearby Dacha, but security guards are not talkative people. Radzinsky had no basis for asking specifically about the Robesons, and no information came his way.

Soon after these events, Major Khrustalev falls ill and dies.

EPILOGUE

On March 1, 1993, a man in a dark-colored Western trench coat walks through the white marble gates of the Malakhovka Jewish cemetery.

Disregarding the Jewish tradition of eschewing flowers at cemeteries, he cradles two bouquets of white lilacs that he purchased from a Chechen woman at a place that is still stubbornly called the *kolkhoz* market.

The elderly pauper at the gate looks up. The world has changed so completely—even the USSR, one of its pillars, dissolved before the pauper's eyes two years ago.

People who search for life's meaning in headstones that connect them with the past look past cemetery paupers. This man seems different.

"Zayt azoy gut, brengt mir tsu Shloyme Levinson un Aleksandr Kogan," he says in Litvak Yiddish.

"Di Royte-armeitses?" asks the pauper, looking up. The Red Army soldiers? This visitor is no Jew. His skin is black.

Years ago, people said that there used to be a Negro in Malakhovka. He was rumored to have first come there in late February of 1953 and returned occasionally for over a decade. He was known to be a close friend of *di Royte-armeitses*. Now they lie beneath identical white marble monuments.

It is said that people looked for the Negro to show up at Levinson's funeral in 1968, and Kogan's a year later. But he wasn't there.

The old men had no families. Only a Russian woman who first came to Malakhovka to work at the bottle redemption station beneath GORPO visited their graves. She went to night school at the pedagogical institute and, later, became a much-admired teacher of Russian literature. She vanished in the 1970s, and the graves are visited no more.

"Kimt mit mir, Reb Neger," says the pauper, motioning for the man to follow. Come with me, Reb Negro.

The two step off the path of the cemetery alley.

"Ot zaynen zey," he says, pointing at the identical headstones adorned with matching bas-reliefs of Red cavalrymen. Here they are.

The horsemen on the graves run toward each other, their swords brandished. The Negro hands the pauper a ten-dollar bill, a fortune.

From a distance, the pauper observes the old Negro cover his face, then straighten as his lips move in what seem like the words of the Hebrew prayer for the dead.

Lewis (for this is, of course, he) isn't bound by Jewish traditions. He doesn't observe the anniversary of every death. Even after returning to America, he chose March 1 as his day of commemoration for all the people who were dear to him in his prior life.

"Forty years," he says out loud.

After abandoning the Black Maria in front of the *kolkhoz* market on the morning of March 1, 1953, Lewis returned to his real passion, engineering. For forty years, most of them back in America, he worked in steel mills, then as an engineer with the American Motors Corporation.

Of course, his sympathies were still firmly with the Left. Sometimes he imagined himself participating in the civil rights movement and protesting against the war in Vietnam. He did all those things, but only in spirit. His body was beyond his control. It didn't protest, didn't march.

After its final, decisive confrontation with evil, it refused to join new struggles. Forty years later, he is still tormented by questions about the night of Stalin's collapse.

"Forty years," echoes another voice.

This is a woman, in her late fifties, heavyset, her hair dyed out-of-the-bottle red.

They embrace, imagining alternative scenarios for their lives, starting with one where she agrees to follow him to Siberia in March of 1953; or where he transfers to Moscow, giving rise to a dynasty of brown children, including a Pushkin or two; or where they meet again before he leaves for America, or she for Israel.

Separating, they look stiffly at each other. Their meeting is not accidental. Lewis tracked her down a year ago in a town near Tel Aviv and offered to pay for her trip to Moscow.

Though prosperity eluded Kima, she declined Lewis's offer of money and bought her own ticket.

"Why did you want to see me?" she asks.

"There is something I must understand before I die," he says. "About that night, about Stalin."

He watches her short neck stiffen.

"Why was Kogan so certain that Stalin wouldn't recover?"

Silence.

"He was a surgeon, not a clown. Levinson was that. No, Kogan wasn't venturing a guess. Did he know something the rest of us did not?"

More silence.

"And what about Stalin turning 'red as a crawfish,' as Kogan put it? I can see why his face was red, but why his feet? A rapid rash is not a symptom of a stroke. Neither is swelling. Yet he was red and swollen."

Another load of silence.

"Why was the syringe missing from Kogan's doctor's bag? He was a thorough man."

"What do you think?" she asks, her voice barely audible.

"I think *der komandir* was wrong to model his blood ritual on the Passover Seder. Should he have chosen Purim? A fitting choice, since Purim plays are the beginning of Yiddish drama . . ."

"Must you?" asks Kima.

"Suppose I'm right, and it's a *purimspiel.* Then who was Mordechai, and who was Esther? Imagine Esther *mit* syringe."

Now Lewis cannot stop.

"I think I know what was in that syringe of Esther's: the fatty, brown brew that bubbled in Levinson's cauldron. Kima, when Levinson turned out the light to make it easier for the suddenly squeamish Kogan to slit Stalin's throat or stick him like a pig, somebody injected that concoction—that brown sauce *mit shkvarkes*—into the catheter, and into Stalin's veins.

"Contaminated, broken-down blood and lard would trigger an allergic reaction that people who don't know better would mistake for a stroke, especially when the patient is found in a coma half a day later. The czar is stung. The rest is simple: sepsis, Cheyne-Stokes respiration, and . . . *kaput.* You killed him, Kima."

"*Dumay chto khochesh,*" she blurts out finally. Think what you want.

She turns around, as though getting ready for a return journey.

"I think I know why Kogan sabotaged the play."

This makes her stop.

"Why do you think?"

She stands by Kogan's tombstone, her fury gone.

LEWIS: I think he did this to let you kill the tyrant who stole your childhood. This was his gift to you: a secret place in history, his treatment for an icy orphan. He gave you life through Stalin's death, and in the process, you saved the lives of millions of Jews whose names were on the lists.

KIMA: What do you want from me?

LEWIS: You stopped the trains. You saved your people. You may have saved all mankind. What more could anyone want? The Book of Esther describes a smaller feat.

KIMA: Ah, Esther! What was her life like after that thing in Shushan?

LEWIS: I never thought of that. I don't know.

KIMA: I breathe, I teach, I write a little. I live a life I never thought I'd have.

LEWIS: One of us died during that raid. And ten on their side—two by your hands.

KIMA: I think of Kogan, and Levinson, and Ol'ga Fyodorovna. She called me *dorogusha* after that night. I buried them one by one, and then I left. I think of fierce Rabinovich, and you, of course.

But no regrets, no blood-bathed boys, no ghostly visitations. This city lives, the Earth is turning, and we are on it still. Five years ago, I found a way to mark this day. I took my grandsons to the beach and watched them play. We are not . . . What's that word?

LEWIS: *Farflokhtn.*

ACKNOWLEDGMENTS

Though I was born six years after Stalin's death, I have multiple connections to this story.

I owe much to my father, Boris Goldberg, a journalist and a poet. In mid-August 1959, in Malakhovka, he took me across the street to meet the man who translated *King Lear* into Yiddish. Shmuel Halkin had returned from the camps a sick man. An entry in my father's diary describes this meeting in considerable detail. Knowing that the author of *Kinig Lir* and I literally, physically intersected on this earth established a powerful link to these fantastic events.

My grandfather—Moisey Semyonovich Rabinovich—provided another link. He told war stories, both real and imagined. In reality, he was an artilleryman in the Civil War and a pharmacist at front-line hospitals during World War II. The fantasies he created for my benefit made him a partisan and a commando. I remember those stories well. In many ways, this novel is an homage to his storytelling. The "fierce Rabinovich" in this book is based on the fictional character he created.

Thanks to my grandfather, I met many men like him, war heroes—old men by the time our paths crossed. Carrying rolled-up copies of *Krasnaya Zvezda*, the Red Army newspaper, in their pockets, they traded war stories in Russian and Yiddish. I listened.

ACKNOWLEDGMENTS

A leap of fiction brings with it the privilege to blend history with fantasy. I am intimately familiar with Levinson's communal flat in the center of Moscow. I spent the first twelve years of my life there. I let Levinson have the room which in reality my parents and I shared. While Levinson didn't live in that apartment, two of the characters—the aforementioned Moisey Semyonovich Rabinovich, who, in fact, was the manager of Drugstore Number Twelve, and Ol'ga Fyodorovna Zabranskaya—indeed lived there.

Ol'ga Fyodorovna was a proper elderly lady who befriended my mother, and I have repaid her kindness by making her a heroine of this story. A few of the trinkets Ol'ga Fyodorovna gave my mother are in my house in Washington.

The Malakhovka dacha where bodies are dumped—Zapadnaya Number Four—belonged to my grandmother.

The idea for this novel came to me when I was around ten.

German Grigoryevich Pervov, the father of my friend Alyoshka Pervov, pointed to an apartment building entryway at Chaplygin Street and said: "This is where in 1944 they arrested a Jewess for killing a Russian girl and putting her blood in the matzos." Then he described watching this woman's arrest. I returned home—a few blocks away—and told my parents, who then told me about anti-Semitic mythology.

This evil myth shook me to the core. Of course, I believe that some hapless woman was led away in handcuffs. I can accept the notion that she had committed murder (such things happen). The exact address is 15 Chaplygin Street. If anyone knows what actually occurred, I urge you to find a way to get in touch with me or a journalist of your choice. I would consider it an honor to unite this woman with her true story. Many of my colleagues would, too. More than anything, that distant event gave me the appreciation of the power of an urban legend.

My aunt Ulyana Iosifovna Dobrushina, who grew up in an illustrious Jewish theater family, told me about her encounters with Solomon Mikhoels, the giant in the background of this novel. She gave me books about the Moscow State Jewish Theater. GOSET was one of the great theaters of Europe, and my aunt was a link to its glory.

I didn't invent Levinson. I took him from the pages of Aleksandr Fadeyev's Soviet classic novella *Razgrom*—translation: *Defeat*—which takes place in the Ural hills during the civil war. In these pages, I give Levinson a different first name and imagine his later life. I imagine him as an inflexible autodidact who stumbles into theater. A sad clown. Conveniently, I let him keep the sword that belonged to his prototype. I didn't invent Commissar Yefim Zeitlin, either. He was a cousin of my grandfather's, and one of the founders of the Comintern for Youth, known under the acronym KIM. Yefim was executed circa 1938. His daughter Kima is entirely fictional. I have no idea whether Yefim was ever a member of the Jewish Bund, or for that matter a Bund sympathizer. He is now.

I could never have made up Kent and Tarzan, the two thugs in this book. Fortunately, I didn't have to. As a young reporter, my father traveled to a penal colony for young criminals and interviewed some of the boys there. Though the book he wrote was never published, a draft survived emigration, and I used it to breathe life into Kent and Tarzan. The name Kent really did exist in the Soviet underworld, as did the verb *skentovatsya*, to bekent (or, better, conkent).

My daughter Katherine Pavlovna Goldberg, now a costume designer for stage and screen, walked me through history of theater and the intricacies (and perils) of method acting. Without her brilliant notes—given to me on a memorable hike in Vermont—this book would have fallen flat. My daughter Sarah Pavlovna Goldberg, a gifted young writer who, on the threshold of going to college, seems to gravitate to comedy, inspired some of the more irreverent lines.

Many of my friends enriched this narrative. Lyudmila Alexeyeva, who as a septa- and octogenarian became the leader of opposition to Putin's regime, helped me re-experience my country, its culture, and its democratic tradition. Lyuda is a teacher, a coauthor, and a friend. She was there, in 1953, struggling with profound doubts. Of course, I was full of admiration for the democratic, "Westernizer" wing of the Russian intelligentsia. I met Lyuda during her immigration period in the United States. Thanks to our collaboration, I gained insight into our common roots.

My Russian friends tend to be in their eighties.

Janusz Bardach, whose prison memoir—*Man Is Wolf to Man*—I had the honor to review in *The New York Times*, helped me a great deal as well. After my review appeared in the *Times*, Janusz and I became friends. Our conversations, which occurred more than daily for years, fuel this narrative. Another witness of that time, Inna Semyonovna Baser, told me what she knew about monstrous events that were brewing in 1953. As a young woman, she knew about the lists of Jews, and she knew about the cattle cars that were coming from outer reaches of the USSR. A gifted editor and a friend, Inna gave me excellent notes.

Jerome Groopman, a brilliant physician-writer, encouraged me to keep this manuscript alive, providing suggestions and helping design the medical component of Stalin's demise. Dudley Hudspeth, a cardio-thoracic surgeon, helped me design the episodes involving acute trauma. The case report of Arkashka Kaplan's surgery was penned by Dudley. Otis Brawley, Steven Hirschfeld, Michael Friedman, Derek Raghavan, Richard Liebeskind, Doron Junger, Svetlana Dolina, Tom Grubisich, Patricia Lochmuller, David Stephen, and Beth Lieberman read this manuscript in various stages and offered encouragement and advice.

ACKNOWLEDGMENTS

I wrote the Yiddish sections of this book myself, and my friend Lee Goldberg helped me correct it, struggling on my behalf with the juicy expressions, including the word in the punch line. In translation of Akhmatova's poetry, I defer to Judith Hemschemeyer. The translation of Pushkin's *Boris Godunov* is by Antony Wood, from *The Uncensored Boris Godunov* by Chester Dunning (Madison: The University of Wisconsin Press, 2006).

My literary agent, Josh Getzler, took me on as a novelist rather than a writer of nonfiction. Despite many failed rounds of submissions of my novels, Josh didn't tell me to go away and delete his contact information from my computer. He persevered, believing that this project would ultimately result in a published novel. His talented junior colleague Danielle Burby helped me pace this narrative, pulling me out of many a proverbial snowdrift.

It's a pleasure to work with James Meader, my editor at Picador. James is one of those rare editors who understand how novels are structured and—more important—why they are written. His notes enabled me to unlock the unrealized potential of the characters I thought I knew well. Isabella Alimonti cheerfully kept the project on track even as the rest of us stumbled in the fog of multitasking.

Finally, this novel belongs as much to Susan Coll, a fellow dark humorist, as it does to me. Soon after our first date, Susan looked over my storeroom of unpublished novels, zeroed in on *The Yid*, and told me how to make this story fly.

ABOUT THE AUTHOR

Paul Goldberg first heard a Moscow version of the myth about Jews using blood for religious rituals when he was ten, in 1969. By the time he immigrated to the United States in 1973, he had collected the Moscow stories that underpin *The Yid*. As a reporter, Goldberg has written two books about the Soviet human rights movement and has coauthored (with Otis Brawley) *How We Do Harm*, an exposé of the U.S. health care system. He is the editor and publisher of *The Cancer Letter*, a publication focused on the business and politics of cancer. He lives in Washington, D.C.